Reno's Funmakers

A Biographical Novel

by

GEORGE MOON

Order this book online at www.trafford.com
or email orders@trafford.com

Most Trafford titles are also available at major online book retailers.

Printed in the United States of America.

ISBN: 978-1-4269-6566-1 (sc)
ISBN: 978-1-4269-6568-5 (hc)
ISBN: 978-1-4269-6567-8 (e)

Library of Congress Control Number: 2011907480

Trafford rev. 07/08/2011

 www.trafford.com

North America & international
toll-free: 1 888 232 4444 (USA & Canada)
phone: 250 383 6864 ♦ fax: 812 355 4082

Introduction

Reno's Funmakers is a story about a theatrical family and their presence during a ten-year period, from 1931 to the early forties. It tells of their way of life at the time of the Great Depression and the Depression's effect on the big top tent shows. Some of the people they knew and met along the way are brought back in a blend of fact and fiction, with segments of their stories as well. It relates the tale of a runaway slave family and the underground Railroad; a "conductor" on the Railroad and his pursuit of Abigail Adams, the deacon's daughter who disliked him; and the young Hollywood hopeful whose experience proved to be much less than expected or desired.

Ed Reno, the son of Edward Munn Reno, dean of American magicians, took his big top theater along the Circuit Chautauqua and the rural Redpath route. Entertaining a week in each town, they offered stage plays, comedy routines, and Ed Reno's magic act.

The Funmakers had a history in show business. It was what they did. It was all they knew. It was a life they loved with all their hearts.

The Great Depression gradually robbed them of their life on the road. Their audiences had less to spend on entertainment. Even if they preferred live shows, reduced incomes forced many to opt for the radio instead. Reno's Funmakers survived until World War II. When the Japanese attacked Pearl Harbor, the big top tent show closed.

The Funmaker family assuaged themselves with the promise to return once the war ended. That hope comforted them for most of their alter life. As with all of our plans, our worst fears and greatest expectations never happen. It is always something in between.

Dedication

There are only two original Reno's Funmakers alive today. One is the writer, and the other is Sylvia Gladys Lipton, whom I've called Dodo since childhood. It is to Dodo, my faux sister, that I dedicate this book. Time has dulled the sharp edge of memories about our life on the road. Fortunately, some events were captured on 8mm film. Tapes taken from that film make up a portion of our family albums. I watched my copy again while researching this book. For the writer, it always brings tears.

"We are such stuff as dreams are made on, and our little life is rounded with a sleep." William Shakespeare

Table of Contents

Prologue

Most of the family memoirs, pictures, and billboards were destroyed in the flood of 1957. Precious memories of lives half spent, gone because of nature's whim. I can vividly recall water going in one basement window and out the other. I was parked in front of my parents' house, and descending streams of water hammered the windshield. Squeak, click, squeak click. The wipers made a rhythmic sound, attempting to keep pace, but to no avail. When I got out of the car, water flowed rapidly and unabated over my shoes and up to my ankles. Eleven inches had fallen overnight. There was no keeping my shoes dry, so I slogged up the sidewalk and the stairs to the front porch. The rain was still coming down in torrents. It was as if Lake Michigan had floated above us and then turned upside down. The look on my parents' faces spoke volumes; they didn't have to say a word.

"We're flooded out," my mother told me. "Your dad tried to pump the basement but finally gave up. Everything down there is lost. Big Dad's magic and all our personal pictures."

Dad sighed. "The furnace is ruined too."

We lived in Kankakee, Illinois, on the 300 block of the east side. There was a slight taper from the main north and south streets down to the river, ten or twelve blocks away. A natural flow took rainwater down to the storm drains, but many were blocked, and the amount of rainfall had overwhelmed them.

Devastation also took place in the village just north of Kankakee. Automobiles were identified by their radio antennas, protruding like river grass through the blackish water. The complete northeast section of homes was submerged, and many people needed to be rescued by boat. Later, property values fell like a rock, and many homeowners never returned to their ravaged residences. Few had flood insurance.

Dad said, "We're going to need a loan to pay for a new furnace. Once it stops raining, I'll look into it."

My father was a person who always took time to figure out the necessary steps to accomplish any task before he started. That process irritated those who didn't know him well, but to the well acquainted, that pause assured them that whatever my father was contemplating would be done right.

As it so happened, the rain finally did stop and the flood was declared a disaster. Dad got a low-interest loan, and a new furnace was installed a month or so later, but it took years to repay.

Ever since coming to Kankakee, Mom and Dad had to work very hard just to make ends meet. Sometimes they couldn't even do that. Almost always, a special occasion, such as Christmas, necessitated a visit to the local loan company. Occasionally, it was needed simply to get by. The life they lived was foreign to the one they had lived earlier. Residing in Kankakee was always supposed to be only a temporary situation, one that would be endured until they returned to a life both of them dearly loved. Prior to moving north, my parents were part of my grandfather's traveling vaudeville show and repertoire theater called Reno's Funmakers—entertaining throughout the south and spending one week in each town presenting plays, comedy skits, music, and magic acts. They followed a route established by advanced booking and similar to the Redpath Lyceum and Circuit Chautauqua. They would engage a town, arrive, set up the big top, and stay for the week. The entertainment was wholesome, morally respectable, and diverting. It became a week in which people could put aside their troubles for a while. The sight of the big gray tent never failed to excite both young and old.

During the 1930s times were tough, and for many that week was a hiatus from the drudgery of eking out a living. The Great Depression brought an end to most shows of this type, but it took World War II to shut down Reno's Funmakers and force it to come in off the road. Once the war ended, everyone expected to reunite and continue the life each favored more than anything else. Now that America was in the war, most believed it wouldn't last very long, and life on the Circuit Chautauqua would soon resume.

Edward Reno Jr. grew up in Kankakee with his three sisters, Emily, Auline, and Ruth. His father, Edward Munn Burdick, took the name Reno as a stage name, kept it all his life, and was buried under the same name. He was known as Reno the Great. More famous than his son, Reno the Great took an interest in magic at the age of twelve, when he became a drum beater for a local magician named Professor Collier. Young Edward was paid ten cents a day to beat the drum to attract crowds to Professor Collier's tent at a county fair near Baldwinsville, NY.

The Burdick family dated their history in America back to 1655. Edward Munn's father, Captain Isaac Burdick, belonged to the New York militia. His grandfather before him, Ebenezer Burdick II fought in the Revolutionary War, serving under General Green, and battled also in the War of 1812. Isaac's family was proud and planned for Edward Munn to join their successful construction company, but young Edward dreamed of being in show business. His choice was a disappointment that caused bitter resentment, to the point that Isaac did not speak to his son for many years.

With a world-famous magician as a father, it was natural for his children to follow in his footsteps. During the summer they traveled the Redpath Lyceum circuit, performing in the Hagenbeck and Wallace circus as trapeze and tightrope or wire walkers. Second only to Ringling Brothers and Barnum & Bailey, Hagenbeck and Wallace traveled across America entertaining young and old alike. During the Depression, the famous clown Emmett Kelly started with Hagenbeck and Wallace as "Weary Willie." Another story told by my family concerned Red Skelton. Joe Skelton was a noted performer as a clown. His son Red also performed with the circus as a youth before entering vaudeville. My father showed young Red how to put on his first makeup. Red did pretty well after that lesson, and the rest is history.

For years after, whenever we watched the Red Skelton Show on television, my grandmother would tell me, "Your father taught him how to put on his first stage makeup."

With Hagenbeck and Wallace's trapeze act, Ed Reno Jr. served as a catcher. However, he always concentrated more on his magic act. When the show passed through Hurdland, Missouri, he met a beautiful young woman named Gladys Payne. She joined the troupe and performed on the high wire and trapeze. She was most noted for her daredevil act, hanging by her teeth from an airplane that passed over the big top. They were married in Chicago during the winter of 1913.

As it turned out, 1913 was a historic year, especially remembered by those living in Peru, Indiana, the winter home of Hagenbeck and Wallace. It was the year of the Great Wabash River Flood. Peru suffered heavy losses from the flooding. Over two hundred people drowned that night in the south end of the city. Never before in the history of Indiana had there been such destruction of life and property from high waters. It was also one of several tragedies endured by the ill-fated circus. The flood caused the loss of eight elephants, twenty-one lions and tigers, and eight performing horses. Today, the building that formerly served as winter quarters is now home to the Circus Hall of Fame.

In 1918, perhaps the worst circus train wreck in history occurred. Known as the Hammond Circus Train Wreck, it also involved Hagenbeck and Wallace. At about four o'clock in the morning, a railroad engineer fell asleep and ran his locomotive into the rear of the Hagenbeck and Wallace express, which was stopped for inspection. The sleeping engineer had missed two automatic warning signals, plus the red marker taillights posted by the brakeman of the twenty-six-car circus train. When the locomotive plowed into the caboose and four rear wooden sleeper cars, eighty-six people were killed instantly. Then the wreckage caught fire. Of the 400 people on board, another 127 were injured.

Even with such disasters, the circus continued operations, emblematic of the maxim, "The show must go on." As the result of the Great Depression, the show did close in 1938.

As a youth, Ed was very athletic. He loved boxing and wrestling, and was undefeated. Because of his large torso and strong arms, overpowering an opponent came relatively easy. He could maneuver the opponent into a leg or arm hold before the other man could react. Because of his strength, almost all wrestling holds were submission holds, and contrary to most matches taking an hour, his were over quickly. Boxing matches lasted only until a clean shot landed. He could end it with either hand. Many felt he should become a professional, since a few boxers who claimed to be pros were bested by him. That was unheard of. Still, he was expected to follow in the family business, and if it had been left entirely up to him, he would have done just that. Magic was his first love.

My grandmother, Gladys Sylvia Payne, was a beautiful woman. I always felt she resembled the movie actress Claudette Colbert. Her naturally curly hair, which she kept cropped short, added to the resemblance. I called her Nannie, because at two years old, I couldn't pronounce either Grandma or Granny. It's been said that after my mother gave birth to me, we garnered all the attention. Everybody wanted to see the new baby. Rumor had it that the "green-eyed monster" cast his shadow on Nannie, and eight months later the opportunity arose for her to adopt a baby girl in Athens, Georgia. So Sylvia Gladys Reno, freckled like the egg of a white-breasted nuthatch, joined the show.

That wrinkled red baby with fuzzy carmine hair and a wee character of independence and bravery became like a sister to me, not just an aunt eight months my junior. Accordingly, we were raised as brother and sister with a tie that exists today. Inseparable as children, as adults our lives have taken us miles apart; she with her husband and family, and me with mine. And as we have become older, those beautiful freckles of hers have faded with time.

Along with her various trapeze skills, my grandmother played the piano and accordion quite well. While living in Kankakee, Illinois during the war, I spent a great deal of time under her watchful eye. The fact that she wouldn't hesitate to cut a switch from the lilac bush to keep both Dodo (my nickname for Sylvia Gladys) and me under control didn't alter in the least the love we had for her.

Looking back, I'm amused to recall her concern over our underwear. It was very important to her that they were clean. I saw no reason for any uneasiness in that area, since we had to take a bath every Saturday night. She told us, "It's important, because what if you got hit by a car and had to go to the hospital?" Kids with dirty underwear would be too embarrassing for her.

There aren't many around today who remember the Circuit Chautauqua, but there was a time when just to mention the name brought thrills and excitement. It all began in 1874 in western New York

State on Lake Chautauqua. The Circuit was founded by a businessman, Lewis Miller, and a Methodist minister, John Heyl Vincent, whose program was originally created to train Sunday school teachers. It became so popular that in less than ten years, independent Chautauquas began to pop up around the country. Their goal was to offer informative and inspirational stimulation to rural and small-town America.

Today, the traveling tent show is gone, along with vaudeville and burlesque. With each passing year, the memory fades further. The flame of its history will continue to burn as long as our memory serves as a bellows. Perhaps the humble words I've written down can reach out and hold these memories just a little longer.

Due to the respect and esteem we hold for our parents, it's quite difficult to visualize them when they were young. How they thought and actually conducted themselves. How they fell in love, had sex, and raised a family. What their worries and concerns were. For most of us, parents are saints and did nothing that could be construed as naughty or wrong. Accordingly, when writing about their lives, our imaginations go on lockdown when certain behaviors are considered. We relate their lives as best we can, knowing that if we were writing about merely imagined characters, the mental padlock would be tossed aside. Therefore, with all that being said, a small segment is taken out of their lives and the story now begins.

Sylvia Reno

VERSATILE AEROLIST
CHALLENGE

Chapter One

The year is 1931. The stock market crash on October 29, 1929, changed the sentiment and expectations of the future for most Americans. It began a period of unemployment, low profits, high poverty, and stagnant trade, affecting the entire world for the next decade. Besides heavy industry, one of the worst damaged sectors in America was agriculture. Farm prices fell 60 percent. Thus, commodities were sold at a loss, if sold at all. Many families lost their homestead and land due to unpaid taxes.

Coupled with the 1930s drought, the agricultural heartland seemed to suffer the most. Farmers in the Great Plains states had to deal with what was called the Dust Bowl. A constant wind brought clouds of swirling dust across the land, darkening the sky for days. The summer heat was intense, oppressive, and unending. Rainfall was nonexistent. Cattle died from inhaling so much dust, their lungs clogged. As if all that wasn't enough, grasshoppers swarmed and ate what crops remained. Though nearly 20 percent of all workers were unemployed, farmers, for the most part, were self-employed. With their hopes and dreams lost forever, many began the exodus to California, looking for work. Others rode the rails and lived in Hoovervilles, willing to labor just for food. The mood was dour and sad. Reno's Funmakers offered a respite, if only for a few hours.

Local officials assigned a pasture southeast of town for erecting the big top. The grass was tall, but once activity began, it was trampled down enough for patrons to have no trouble negotiating their way to their destination. A small creek winding around the edge of the pasture helped to beautify the area, and off in the distance a horse could be seen grazing. A stand of trees on the southwest side partially enclosed the field, giving the setting a comfortable feeling. The open end faced east, with the town a little to the north. Reno's Funmakers had arrived the evening before, just before dark. Like a slow-moving train, the cars, trucks, and trailers found the prearranged location and parked in an orderly fashion, to spend the night and brace for the morning's activities. The cookhouse tent was set up first. Ed Reno recognized what was most important to his crew and roustabouts. Nothing like a full belly to relax the workers before the tent went up.

The trip from Athens had taken most of the day. It had rained the day before, and roads were still wet and muddy. Several times trucks would get stuck, mired in mud, and had to be pushed, pulled, and, in some cases, dug out. The auto du jour was Ford Model Ts, with one or two Model As; and due to road conditions, the caravan traveled at only twenty miles per hour. Many roads were still dirt. The better ones were gravel. While the Depression had taken its toll on the auto manufacturers, government highway projects had improved state roads.

The following day began with a sliver of whitish yellow appearing in the east at the junction of land and sky. It slowly spread upward, brightening the horizon. The lightened sky promised sunrise anytime now. Sparrows began to shake their feathers, and before long a bird chorus was struck. Their gentle wake-up symphony filled the air. Folks in the area could make out songs of certain birds. Were they listening now, they could hear the familiar sounds of tanagers, mourning doves, bobwhites, sedge wrens, and blue jays, just to name a few. An occupant they would not hear rested high in a Georgia pine. A great horned owl overlooked the goings-on. As the morning dawned, his activity was completed. His consisted of night operations. His roost could be identified by the buildup of whitewash and regurgitated pieces of bone, the undigested remains of prey, beneath the tree where he made his home. Strong talons, a bill hooked like a hawk's, eyes with one hundred times our light-gathering ability, and keen hearing allowed him to hunt in total darkness. His prey never heard him coming. While the forest contained oak, sweet gum, elm, maple, and magnolia, owls preferred the pines.

The heavy knock on Ed's door signified an emergency of some sort.

"Ed, it's me, Jess Backster. You got to come quick. Whitey's mean as all get out and beating up folks down at the tavern."

Ed looked at Gladys and shook his head. "I had a bad feeling about that son of a bitch when I hired him."

A worried Gladys said, "Please be careful. Let the law handle it."

As Ed went down the steps, he thought of how bad news traveled fast. If Whitey did something seriously harmful, it surely would hurt the reputation of the show.

Ed could tell something was wrong the moment he opened the door and walked into the tavern. It's the feeling one gets when a room is full of tension. It's like you've just interrupted something. Ed knew the feeling all too well. He looked around the tavern and spotted Whitey at a table by himself. As always, Boyd was nearby, but only cautiously close.

"Okay, boys, the fun's over," Ed said in a raised voice. "Let's everybody get back. We've got a busy morning ahead of us." That was welcome news to most everyone, and Reno's group began moving toward the exit.

"You ain't the boss of me. I quit," Whitey shouted as he rose to his feet, taking a fighting pose.

"No matter," Ed answered. "You're causing a disturbance and wrecking this man's business. That's got to stop."

The bartender leaned over to Ed and whispered, "I've already called the sheriff and he should be here pretty soon."

Ed looked at Whitey. "Let's just simmer down. No sense making more trouble."

The red-faced giant lunged forward and aimed a vicious punch at his ex-boss's head.

Ed hunched his left shoulder, making the blow glance off target, and followed with a short right counterpunch that landed flush on Whitey's cheek. The cracking sound was shockingly loud, and the next thing everyone heard was Whitey landing on the floor with his right leg twitching.

The sheriff arrived five minutes later, with Whitey still out. After the bartender explained what happened, the sheriff assured Ed he would keep Whitey behind bars until the show moved on.

"How did he do that?" asked a bystander, who was trying to recover from the emotional shock of witnessing such swift violence. "That feller is twiced his size." Another gave his opinion that the speed of the smaller man allowed the rapid and unforeseen counterpunch. No consensus was reached, however, as to the result of such a swift blow. There was general agreement that their own champion, a swarthy brute from the hills, could, "Take the little feller." Little did they know that that opinion had been reached by three score or more, with the result of them waking up bewildered and not knowing exactly what happened.

After the tavern cleared, the sheriff called out, "Somebody give me a hand with this guy. I can't carry him by myself." A couple of locals moved forward to help, along with Boyd Roberts, who did not return with the crew. He chose to remain with his hero and be there when he came to. It was good riddance to both of them, was Ed's thought, but Reno's Funmakers hadn't seen the last of either man.

Whitey had been born in the mountains of West Virginia. He apparently wanted to be an albino. Mother Nature had other ideas, so a settlement was reached. His hair, a shocking white, gave him his nickname. One of nine children and big for his age, he learned early on that by intimidation and coercion, most of his simple pleasures could be attained. It began at the supper table, where siblings were aware firsthand of his meanness, and out of fear gave part of their food to him as payment against physical retribution. At age twelve, Whitey ended his formal education, when he beat the teacher half to death for ordering him to stop pestering the girl seated in front of him. Because the teacher was a rather large man and the children in the class remained silent, the sheriff let him go. Over the next few years, Whitey's work consisted of general farm labor, until that day the circus came to town. Fascinated by all the trucks and wagons, some with elephants and caged animals, and with the gigantic canvas tent, he knew then and there the life he wanted to live.

"I'm stronger than any two men and can do the work of three," he lied, once he found the owner. The first part was obviously true, judging just by the size of him. The lie was to be learned later. Earlier in the day, the owner had discovered that two laborers had failed to appear for the morning exodus. Probably sleeping off last night's frivolity, he had thought.

"You might be needed," he told Whitey. "Go find a fella named Clyde Holderman and tell him I sent ya."

"Is your name Holderman?" Whitey asked a man. It had taken him about thirty minutes to find Clyde Holderman, because the animal cages were too fascinating. He'd only seen pictures of most of the animals, so to actually see them for real was an awesome experience.

"Who's asking?" Clyde asked as he turned away from a group of canvas men and faced the giant standing in front of him.

"Boss man told me to talk to you about work."

"Yeah, I am shorthanded right now," Clyde responded. A noise made him look over at some workers trying to unload a roll of canvas side wall from a flatbed truck. "If you want to work, go help those men unload."

Things couldn't have worked out better for Whitey. "You guys need a little help?" he asked, walking over to the truck.

"Too damn heavy for just two men," they replied.

Whitey said, "Step aside, boys." He hoisted the canvas roll up on his back and asked, "Where do you want it?"

It didn't take long before word reached all the crew about a strong man who could pick up a canvas roll by himself.

He had been fired from three previous jobs, the last one at gunpoint. Today he could have sued for wrongful discharge and received a sizable settlement, but back then, going against your word and breaking trust were considered more important. It didn't take very long before Whitey lost this job as well, but he hung around town long enough to be hired as a replacement when Ed Reno needed two helpers. One had married a young local widow and stayed to work her small farm, and the other had been hospitalized with appendicitis.

Like many roustabouts, Whitfield "Whitey" Carney moved from one "Toby" show to another for various reasons, ranging from larceny, drunkenness, and fighting. Abuse of the bottle was common but not easily tolerated, because without exception, fighting came next.

Traveling shows on the Circuit Chautauqua worked hard to maintain the image of high morals and respectability. Most of the time, the fighting took place in town after the work was completed and the men were paid. It was a ritual to visit the local inn and let off steam. Even after the men received harsh warnings, once the alcohol began to flow, the mind tended to become murky, with resolve in short supply.

With the last show concluded and the big top prepared to be taken down in the morning, several workers and roustabouts decided to visit the town tavern for a few laughs and cold beer. The rules for such activity were cast in stone. Do nothing to embarrass them or draw dishonor on the show. Rules such as these gave traveling shows a good reputation, and Ed Reno, for one, demanded close adherence to the discipline. With Whitey, the distance between self-control and irrational behavior was as thin as a shadow. He did his thinking with his mouth, and when he drank, restraint disappeared completely. Predictably, once the gang settled in at the local watering hole, it was Whitey who became boisterous and argumentative. To make matters worse, a couple of his toadies always seemed to encourage him. In particular was a sycophant named Boyd Roberts, who had latched onto Whitey early on. Up until Whitey joined the show, Boyd was the butt of most jokes. And you would need to look far and wide to find someone more worthy to be the recipient of such jokes. He had the most annoying way of repeating himself, as well as comments made by others. If someone said, "It looks like rain today," Boyd's response would be, "Looks like rain today, looks like rain today." Over time, his idiosyncrasy irritated callous canvas men, and they referred to him as Boyd Boyd.

Meanwhile, back in the lockup, Whitey was slowly regaining consciousness. His speech was jumbled, and pronouncing words was difficult due to the worst headache he'd ever experienced. Boyd was there, having asked the sheriff to let him be with Whitey when he came to.

"What happened?" Whitey asked. "How did I end up here?"

"Ed Reno hit you with a table leg, with a table leg," Boyd responded. He knew the astonishing truth, but felt unsure about revealing it to his hero. No telling how Whitey would react if he knew the truth. He would take it out on whoever stood the closest, and Boyd was locked in the same cell.

"Let me out of here!" Whitey shouted. And he continued shouting until the sheriff came back and told him to pipe down.

"You aren't getting out until tomorrow, so make the best of it," the sheriff said.

"He hit me with a table leg," Whitey bellowed.

"That isn't the way I heard it," the sheriff replied, and walked back to his office.

Chapter Two

The author owes his existence to an event that occurred during the summer of 1931, when a tall young man appeared at the big top, looking for work. His looks were classic for the era. Black wavy hair and well-trimmed mustache gave the look of John Boles, popular movie idol of the time. Women on stage were frozen where they stood, wondering who he was and why he was there.

"Are you Mr. Reno?" he asked one man.

"Yes, what can I do for you?" Ed Reno said.

"I'm looking for work."

"Who isn't in these times?" Ed asked. "What's your line? What can you do?"

"I'm a singing evangelist. Been working on my own for a while, but can't make enough to survive. I thought maybe I could join up with the show."

"A singing evangelist!" Ed exclaimed. "I think I've heard it all this week. I'm sorry, son, but as you pointed out times are tough, and we just make it with the people we already have. If you're hungry, you can go to the cook tent and eat your fill."

At that moment, as the brooding evangelist walked to the cook tent, Gladys Reno approached and asked her husband what the discussion was all about. Like the other women on the show, she was attracted to a good-looking man, and this one piqued her curiosity. After a short huddle with Ed, she stated that the man could probably work for a while, just for meals and a place to sleep. They could feature him singing a gospel song when the performance was over. Though disinclined to hire the man, Ed always found it hard to refuse Gladys, and he agreed to present the offer. He slowly walked over to the cook tent.

"If you're willing to work for room and board, we'll give you a try," Ed said. In the back of his mind, he wasn't quite sure how this newcomer would help the show. Plus, an explanation would be due to the rest of the troupe. Where the evangelist would bunk also needed to be determined.

"I was hoping to get some pay, even if it wasn't much," the somewhat dejected man replied. "I trust somehow I can prove my worth."

"You can bunk with Frank Keagan over there," Ed said, pointing to a trailer by the makeup tent. "You sat next to Frank when you were in the cook tent. Frank's my advance man. He books the show in advance here on the Redpath circuit." Ed scratched his chin and asked, "What do they call you?"

"Most folks call me Dutch. My mother's nickname was Dutch, and I guess I was a momma's boy, so that's where the name came from."

"Sounds like a gangster, but if that's what it is, we'll call you Dutch," Ed said.

And so, George Carson Moon joined the show.

Meanwhile, back at the trailer of Gladys and Ed, a conversation was taking place between Gladys and her young daughter, Pauline.

"I've talked your father into hiring a quite handsome young man. He's an evangelist or something or other and sings. Your father can have him sing a gospel song to close the show." Gladys beamed. "All the ladies couldn't keep their eyes off of him."

"Is he married?" Pauline asked.

"I don't think so, but honey, he's much too old for you," Gladys said. "You're only sixteen and shouldn't be thinking that sort of thing. Not yet anyway."

"When will we see him?" the girl asked.

"Probably at rehearsals."

Though only sixteen, Pauline looked older than her age. She was booked as the *Leading Lady of the South* and had the main role in most of the plays. She also entertained by tap dancing, with an occasional song or two.

All the women took extra care as they prepared for rehearsal that day. More hair was washed and set than ever before. Not to be outdone, Gladys and Pauline took so much time, they arrived nearly an hour late, much to Ed's chagrin.

"Let's get right at it today," he said sharply. "I want to introduce a new cast member. This is George Moon. He goes by the nickname of Dutch to his friends. Hope you become his friend and can call him that. Today I want to rehearse *The Trail of the Lonesome Pine*, a good one to open here on Monday."

Turning to the young evangelist, Ed said, "Dutch, just sorta observe the play. I want you to sing 'In the Garden' at the end of the show. Guess you won't need much rehearsing."

Dutch was an instant hit with the women. By the time rehearsal was over, the whole troupe had had a chance to meet him, and everyone was enamored.

Later that night, for the last act, Ed performed his magic and illusions show while the orchestra played "Stars and Stripes Forever." When the applause died down, Ed thanked the audience and announced, "Tomorrow the play will be *Rags the News Boy*, but at this time it's fitting to close with a hymn. The singing evangelist, Dutch Moon, will sing 'In the Garden.'"

Dutch walked to center stage, a tall, handsome man, dressed in a tuxedo and stood in front of the audience. To a soft instrumental background, the "speech of angels" was heard.

I come to the garden alone,
While the dew is still on the roses,
And the voice I hear falling on my ear
The Son of God discloses.
And he walks with me, and he talks with me
And He tells me I am his own;
And the joy we share as we tarry there,
None other has ever known
He speaks, and the sound of His voice
Is so sweet the birds hush their singing,
And the melody that He gave to me
Within my heart is ringing.
And He walks with me, and He talks with me

And He tells me I am His own;
And the joy we share as we tarry there,
None other has ever known.
And the joy we share as we tarry there,
None other has ever known.

A hush fell over the crowd. These were country people, many were mountain folks. Their religion was uppermost in their thoughts, especially since the Great Depression had deprived them of even meager incomes. Most were poor, living on farms and depending on the crops they raised for sustenance. After a moment of silence, Ed reappeared, reminded the audience about the next day's show, and said, "That concludes tonight's performance."

The crowd dispersed in an orderly manner, almost like in a state of shock.

"I think that was the purdiest hymn I ever heard outside of church," a tall mountaineer said to his wife.

"We're comin' back tomorrow," she responded.

"But it cost twenty-five cents for each of us," he said.

"I don't care. I got a little saved up and I want to see the next play," she said.

"You only want to see that singer again."

"What if I do? He's even purdier than the hymn," she replied with determination. The mountain man knew his wife too well. Once she made up her mind, he couldn't win.

On the second night, every seat was filled, and some people were even standing. Enterprising Ed Reno, for the first time, sold standing room only for five cents.

I wouldn't call him smug, but that word is pretty close to the way Ed felt when he said to Gladys, "They really liked our show last night. Just look at the crowd."

Gladys was definitely smug when she replied, "Yes, but the hymn singer had a lot to do with it."

The next morning Ed and Dutch had occasion to stroll over to the cook tent together.

"I've been meaning to talk to you," Ed said. "Now don't let this go to your head, but things are looking better, and we might be able to get together and talk about a little salary. It isn't going to be much, just a bit of cash over room and board."

Dutch could not conceal his delight, and said, "That would be wonderful. Anything is great and will help a lot."

"Let's talk about it at supper in my trailer tonight," Ed replied.

Dutch couldn't be happier. At last he would be with Pauline in a social setting, something he had thought about ever since he first met her. He had made up his mind from her first smile that someday she would be his wife. Ever since he'd gone to Butler College in Indianapolis, Dutch had been known as a ladies' man. His striking good looks guaranteed a following of eligible beauties. For some reason he could never get serious about any of them, but now he was finally smitten. He couldn't wait for dinnertime.

The dinner took forever to come around. Finally, the clock struck six. Dutch stepped down from Frank Keagan's trailer and began walking to Ed and Gladys's. Off in the distance one could hear a dog barking and muffled voices from the cookhouse, but Dutch was oblivious to just about everything.

"Don't know why you women go to so such trouble," Ed said to his wife with a sigh. "He probably isn't used to a lot of fancy stuff."

"We just want to make a good impression," Gladys replied. "And besides, Pauline insisted on a special meal."

"It wasn't just me, Mother," Pauline countered. "You said it should be a festive dinner."

"I think you're both crazy," Ed said. "He'll probably leave once a better offer comes along."

Just then a faint knock sounded at the door.

Chapter Three

Erecting the big top was no small chore. Canvas men would lay out the main cloth and run up the center poles. Side poles helped form the outer walls, and guide ropes held them in place. The guide ropes were secured by iron stakes driven in the earth around the tent's periphery. The stakes were about three feet long and driven in with sledge hammers. Usually a two-man crew performed that task, similar to spike drivers on the railroad. Taking turns, each would raise the sledge over his head and bring it down with enough force to drive the stake far into the ground. A rhythm naturally came about, which tended to make the work seem easier.

One day Ed was unhappy about the pace of getting the big top up. As the story goes, he challenged the canvas men, saying, "I can drive those stakes faster than you guys using only one hand. Now let's speed it up." Strong men take pride in their muscular assets, and the canvas men took Ed up on the challenge. The next time the big tent went up, Ed would drive the stakes by himself. Well, not only did Ed drive the stakes by himself (about fifty in all), he did it using a sixteen pound sledge and with only one hand. It did take several minutes longer; but nobody said a word about that. A lot of bets were made that day, and they were mostly collected by old-timers.

The times were difficult, and providing income had been a challenge for the last two years. The main focus for Ed Reno was to devise methods that would provide enough income for survival. The next booking was a week away. Such intervals were used to make repairs to the big top and rehearse new plays. With Frank Keagan called away due to illness in his family, Ed planned to drive ahead and look for another engagement.

Dawn was beginning to present a new day, and Ed was awake and out and about. He always found it difficult to sleep when anything was planned the following day. This day was no exception. Early morning was a quiet time on the lot, perfect for organizing his thoughts. He also knew Dutch was sound asleep and would be for some time longer.

Checking his watch, he found it to be half past five. As daylight approached, the spotlights that illuminated the big top were turned off. Tiny flying creatures gave up their orbits around the lights and disappeared somewhere across the field. Off in the distance a rooster crowed. The morning sky had an ominous red and orange cast; clouds were turning purple. Ed recalled the old adage: Red sky at night is a sailor's delight. Red sky in morning, a sailor takes warning. Summer storms were frightening since they could cause violent damage to the tent. Center poles had to be laid down and the canvas secured to avoid being torn to pieces. The crew was well experienced, having practiced the drill before moving to the next town. Ed would keep the weather in mind when he and Dutch took off that morning. The trip also offered another opportunity to drive the new 1932 Plymouth coupe, a four-cylinder beauty that could reach sixty-five miles per hour when roads permitted. It was an extravagance used by the booking agent to kind of "put on the dog" when he entered a new town.

"Hey, Dutch," Ed called when he reached the trailer where Dutch was staying. "You about ready to get up? I'm thinking of driving over to Lonesome Pine to see if we can get a booking on the return trip." Ed smiled, knowing Dutch could sleep till noon if nothing was pressing.

"Give me ten minutes," Dutch replied, trying to stifle a yawn.

"You'll need breakfast first. The cookhouse will be up and running in an hour."

Ed walked back to his trailer where Gladys was frying fatback bacon. She wasn't overly fond of breakfast in the cookhouse. If she ate in the trailer, she didn't need to dress before breakfast. Ed didn't care one way or the other, but made it a point to visit the cookhouse frequently. He could learn a lot from the roustabouts, plus give orders for the day when it was still bright and early. Today he would polish the platter with Gladys and tell her his plans.

"They got any good stores there?" she asked.

"Don't think so, but you're welcome to come and ride in the rumble seat," Ed answered.

He knew she wouldn't ride there because the wind would mess her hair.

"We'll go there ourselves later on," she said.

Breakfast in the cookhouse was more than just an opportunity to break bread. It also served as the main meeting place for the entire troupe. All the latest scuttlebutt was heard and discussed, along with who was most in need of money or consolation. A repertory company was like a close-knit family, and quite generous when it came to helping one of their own.

A new member was added that morning. David Shirkie, nephew to Ed and Pauline's favorite cousin, had come to spend the summer. David would be put to work right away. He brought his own movie-star looks and tons of musical talent. Dreams of Hollywood and movies came up short for him, but after years of being a nightclub entertainer, his career ended in California with his own TV show.

After breakfast was over, the trip to Lonesome Pine began. This was the first time Dutch had ridden in the new Plymouth. He would have preferred a convertible, but he was satisfied with his influence, suggesting Ed buy this hot little number. Ed, however, being very conservative, would have bought something in black rather than tan, and definitely not a coupe.

Roads and highways improved vastly during the Great Depression. President Roosevelt initiated the WPA, a federal agency created by executive order that provided employment for many in the South through public works projects. Major expenditures went to the construction of highways and roads. The program continued until 1943, when the government felt the Depression had ended and its emphasis had shifted to the war effort.

"How far is it to Lonesome Pine?" Dutch asked.

"About thirty-five or forty miles I think," answered Ed. "Not much in between that would be good for us. This little baby can really skip along, can't it? They said it can do sixty-five on the highway. I ain't going to try it on these roads."

Dutch was more comfortable knowing a speed test wasn't being planned. While Ed was conservative when it came to money, he also was a free spirit at times. He might stop along a mountain stream just to soak in it and cool off. That part of his personality made him fun to travel with. Anything might happen on the spur of a moment. Spontaneity figured prominently in his character, yet he was solid in judgment and precise in important matters that pertained to business and family. A loving human being who eschewed outward expression. A generous soul that counted every penny.

"What's so good about Lonesome Pine?" Dutch asked.

"I've been told it's a favorite of the gold miners. They like to travel there and do their buying and banking."

Just then the car bounced over something on the road.

"What the hell was that?" Ed asked as he hit the brakes. "Looked like something lying across the road." He turned the car around and shouted, "Holy Christ, it's a snake. Biggest one I ever saw. Let's catch it and show the girls when we get back."

Not a very good idea, Dutch thought, who had a fear of the slinky creatures. Feigning bravery, and hoping the snake was gone when they got there, he said, "Yeah, we can put it in the trunk." Ed dashed to the spot and grabbed hold of the reptile just as it slithered between two rocks. Dutch exited the car and cautiously approached Ed, who shouted, "Goddamn it, Dutch! Grab on to this thing. It'll take us both."

Ed was wrong. Even with the two of them hanging on, the snake continued on its way and disappeared.

"Ain't nobody going to believe us," Ed lamented. "Sure wish we would have caught him. He looked ten feet long."

In all likelihood it would have measured eight or nine feet long. A snake that size had to have been an East Indigo, common to the area. Bluish-black in color with a red-orange throat, they often live in tortoise burrows and are basically nonaggressive. It also is known to eat small turtles, rats, frogs, cottonmouths, and rattlesnakes. Apparently it is immune to their poison. All in all, it's a good thing Ed didn't "bring it back alive," The East Indigo serves an important role in the South's environment and needs to be protected.

The rest of the trip was uneventful. As the two itinerant adventurers drove into the city limits, Dutch asked, "Where do you think we can find somebody to talk to?"

"More than likely at the courthouse, and it looks like that's it over there," Ed stated, and pulled up in front of the building.

Opening the door, they found themselves in the midst of local banter.

"I hear they're having a revolution over in China. Their leader is making rich people do manual labor just so they can experience what it's all about."

"We need to do that over here," someone commented.

"What good would that do?"

"Well, we could put Chester White's fat ass behind a team of mules and make him plow twenty acres."

The thought made everybody laugh until they got tears in their eyes.

"Make sure it's your twenty acres and not mine," one man said. "I wouldn't want that dumb son of a bitch ruining my land."

The laughter intensified.

"Yeah, if Chester ever had to haul ass, he'd have to make two trips."

Ed approached and asked, "Where can we find the mayor?"

At his question, the humor abruptly ended.

"He's in his office," the clerk said, pointing to a door down the hall.

Chester White, as Ed had suspected, was the mayor. He realized immediately what the joviality was about. The portly mayor stood about five foot six, and he had soft pink skin covered with baby powder. It was apparent the mayor and physical labor had never been introduced. His shirt, wet under the arms, gave evidence of heavy perspiration, even though it wasn't a particularly hot afternoon. Weighing over two hundred pounds was more likely the cause.

"What can I do for you gentlemen?" the mayor asked.

Ed and Dutch had just stepped into the mayor's office and closed the door, when the courthouse door opened with a rush and a teenage girl hurried in.

"Hi Tootsie," everyone in the front room said in a chorus. Her father had given her the nickname, and it was used by most everybody in town.

"Is my daddy here?" Teresa White asked.

"He's here, but he's got company," a clerk named Rodney replied. "Some folks from a vaudeville show. Sit for a spell and I'll get you a cold soda."

Visibly upset, she took a seat and thanked Rodney for the drink. As the daughter of the town mayor, Teresa White had more advantages than any girl in town. Being beautiful and talented only enhanced her popularity. Her hair was blond with a slight auburn tint, and a country-club tan made her slim body fascinating. Yes, Tootsie White occupied the dreams of nearly every boy in school, in spite of the fact that for years she had gone steady with Walter Collins. Walter was popular too, although not to the extent of his high-school sweetheart. He and Tootsie first met in Sunday school at Asbury Methodist Church. From the beginning, they were a pair that belonged together—she with her sparkling beauty and he with his ruggedly handsome good looks. It was taken for granted that they were made for each other and would be married in the near future.

George and Mary Collins were honest farm folks, and Walter was their only child. He stood well over six feet, with a frame hardened by physical labor. Sports came easily to him, making him a star athlete. By the end of his junior year, he was selected as all-state quarterback in football. The summer between his junior and senior years, tragedy struck. George had felt poorly for a couple weeks. A nagging pain in his belly finally forced him to the hospital. After two weeks of tests, the doctors concluded he had pancreatic cancer. They buried George exactly one month later. Tootsie's and Walter's lives were changed forever.

Ed introduced himself to the mayor. "My name is Edward Reno, and this here is Dutch Moon. We represent Reno's Funmakers, a traveling repertory theater and magic show. You may have heard of my father, Edward Reno the Magician."

"As a matter of fact, I have heard of him," Chester White replied. "Read about him just the other day in the newspaper. Never met or seen him, though."

Ed went on, "Well, my magic act in our show uses many of Edward the Great's illusions. The audience is always amazed by them."

"Do you have a girlie show?" asked the mayor.

"No, the other part of the show is Vaudeville Theater, where we act out different plays each night. Our plays avoid profanity and express high moral endings. With music and comic sketches, we offer an evening of fine entertainment."

Disappointed to hear that there wasn't a girlie show, the mayor asked how he could be of help.

"Well, we need a good field to put up the big top with a water well close by," Ed said.

"We got just the place," White said. "There's a small fee to use it, though."

Actually, the mayor was referring to his own property south of town. Never one to miss an opportunity to pick up extra cash, Chester White saw this as a natural.

"How much would it cost?" Ed asked. "You are well aware of the times we presently live in and the cost to run a show such as Reno's Funmakers. Very little is left after expenses."

The mayor rubbed his chin, as though giving the issue serious thought. "I probably can get it for you for … let's say $100 for the week."

"That's too rich for our blood your honor," Ed said. "We only charge 25¢ admission. Kids pay a dime. Thanks for your time. We'll look at another town nearby."

"Hold on now," White said. "I might get it for $50."

"It's still too high," Ed said.

"Can you afford $25?" the mayor asked dryly.

Ed said calmly, "I believe we can handle that. We play Milford next, but can catch you the last week in August on the way back to Athens."

"Then it's a deal. Be looking for you in August," the mayor said, extending his hand. After a moment's pause, he asked, "Can you pay in advance?"

Once Ed and Dutch left, Teresa burst into her father's office. Her cheeks flushed, she said with excitement, "Daddy, there's something I just have to tell you and it can't wait until supper. I'm not going to college this fall. That can wait until after Delores Persack and I go to Hollywood."

"Hollywood?" the startled mayor replied. "But you were going to go to college with Walter Collins and get married after."

"Things have changed. With Walters's father gone, he says he has to take care of his mother and help on the farm. I sure as hell ain't going to end up a farmer's wife," Teresa said tersely.

"I thought you loved Walter."

"I'd love being in the movies better. Seems like I've been with Walter forever. Delores says I've never been out with anybody else, so how do I really know if I love him?"

"Have you told all this to Walter? I mean about going to Hollywood," asked her father.

"I told him yesterday."

"And how did he take it?"

"Oh, you know Walter. He just said whatever I want is okay with him. Now don't worry about me and Delores, 'cause her aunt and uncle run a boarding house and said we can stay there once we arrive."

Chester White didn't like it at all, but ever since she was three years old, he couldn't deny Tootsie anything she wanted. There was truth in the aphorism, "There's many a slip between the cup and the lip," as we shall observe later.

As Ed and Dutch drove back that evening, the weather turned nasty and dangerous. A thick fog had settled in, and the road ahead was as faint as the moon at noon. Headlights seemed to make vision worse, and Dutch had opened his door to lean out and watch the edge of the road. The trip back took over three hours and frazzled their nerves. Ed's eyes burned from the constant strain of looking through a windshield and seeing nothing. Even the hood ornament disappeared at times. His mouth, parched and dry, made swallowing nearly impossible. Dutch, looking down from the open car door, navigated by calling out left or right. Both men knew a mistake could mean going off the road, and in the mountains, that could result in serious injury or death.

"Dutch, light me a cigarette," said Ed. "I can't take my eyes off the road. Have you ever seen fog this bad?"

"I've never seen anything like this before," Dutch replied. He lit up a Lucky Strike and handed it to his future father-in-law. "All I can do is pray like hell we make it back in one piece."

Just then the Plymouth entered a stretch where the fog was breaking up. Both men breathed a sigh of relief and started laughing, not an uncommon reaction in such circumstances. The remainder of the trip was without incident. As they turned onto the field, the big tent, illuminated by spotlights, came in view, and the chug-chug of the electricity generator was music to their ears. After any trying experience, home becomes a mental oasis and refuge against harm. In the minds of our traveling pair, seeing the big top proved exactly that. The remainder of the week was uneventful.

Chapter Four

Ed was always the last to leave the big top. It was his practice to make a survey of both the tent and surrounding property before going back to his trailer and count the receipts with Gladys. One beautiful midsummer day, brilliant sunshine was followed by light rain. Ominous dark clouds blocked the last of the sun's illumination, but occasional brightness could be glimpsed in the distance, as lightning shot earthward, followed by the rumble of thunder. (They say you can determine how far away a storm is by counting the seconds between the time you see a lightning flash and hear the thunder.)

The wind picked up, and Ed had to shut his eyes to mere slits against what felt like grains of sand hitting hard against his face. Mounting concern about a storm erased any thought of ending his day. He knew it wouldn't be the first time a big top was destroyed by high winds. If conditions didn't improve, he'd have to rouse a crew to take down the center poles and lay the canvas flat.

Whitey and Boyd were tarrying in the wooded area near the big top, waiting for the final show to end. Whitey wanted to avenge the embarrassing defeat he had suffered in the town bar. He didn't remember seeing a table leg, but for the sake of his pride, he told himself that was the case. Boyd swore it was true, and that was enough for the bully from the West Virginia hills. Getting even never left his thoughts. In fact, the hard steel of a revolver inside his coat pocket meant that he intended to get more than a little even.

Ed kept going through the shutdown procedure, but at a much faster clip than normal, in order to hurry back to the welcome warmth and comfort of the main trailer. As the misty rain persisted, the skies continued to grow darker and darker. The stars were obliterated and robbed of their visible light creating darkness similar to when the lights are extinguished in Wonder Cave. Ed would be on alert all night, should the tempest become more dangerous.

Call it fate or whatever, but there was another person on the premises that night. Ezell Williams, the county sheriff, had been investigating a disturbance nearby, and he decided to stop by to catch the last show, especially Ed Reno's magic act. Unfortunately—or fortunately, in this case—he arrived too late for the show. As he turned his car around, he noticed someone walking with a flashlight. Recognizing Ed, he went over to say hello.

"Here he comes now," whispered Boyd as he slinked along behind Whitey.

Whitey had never shot a human before. He usually dispatched people with his fists and physical prowess. He wasn't the only one angry that night. High in a Georgia pine, the great horned owl was furious. Uninvited guests were hiding nearby, ruining chances for his evening meal. His dinner had been frightened away by the presence of Whitey and Boyd. The great bird took flight and headed straight toward Whitey, who was engrossed with revenge and oblivious to his surroundings.

"Hey, Ed, sure is crappy weather, isn't it?" Ezell called out.

"Is that you, Sheriff Williams?" Ed lifted his hand to his forehead to block the rain from his eyes.

"I missed your last show 'cause some asshole was beating up his wife and I had to arrest him," the sheriff said. "I was meaning to ask you how some of the magic tricks was done."

"Why, Sheriff, it's done with magic."

The sheriff smiled. "I thought that's what you'd say."

Whitey took aim directly at Ed Reno. He had hit other targets from this distance and was sure he could put a bullet right between Ed's eyes. As he slowly pulled the trigger, from out of the darkness came the whomp-whomp-whomp sound of large wings flapping, and then the great horned owl struck the side of Whitey's face. It was a startling smash from out of nowhere, making his shot miss badly.

"What the hell was that?" Ed asked

"Get down!" the sheriff ordered. "That was a shot from those woods."

By this time Boyd was dashing away from the scene, never to be heard from again. Whitey, however, stubbornly refused to run and tried to take another shot. He missed again, and this time the flash from his gun was seen by Sheriff Williams. The sheriff emptied his service revolver in the direction of the flash. Six shots rang out, four of which hit Whitey. No more would anyone be bullied by the giant, because that day the bewildered coward died.

Reno's Funmakers completed the season by giving performances in Georgia, South and North Carolina, Virginia, and West Virginia. On their return to Athens, Georgia, they gave a performance in Lonesome Pine the first part of September. Attendance was good enough to make it a regular stop. Mayor Chester White took an active role in promoting the magic act and the nightly stock theater, with an eye on increasing the next year's lot fee.

The show closed for the winter, and the cast dispersed until the following spring. Some went home looking for work. That was a difficult undertaking, considering the times. Others took up residence at winter quarters. They would be needed to make repairs to the big top tent and perform general maintenance on all equipment and vehicles. The work provided steady income throughout the winter.

Dutch was invited to spend the winter with the Renos in Athens. He accepted without hesitation. He was given a room in their home and free board. It allowed him to be near Pauline, although he knew she would be well chaperoned. It also provided time for him to build his own trailer. He had purchased, sight unseen, a frame and chassis for a pittance, and would soon have those around him dumbfounded by his building skills. He incorporated his own designs, such as increasing the amount of storage cabinets, an idea Pauline suggested, since she obviously considered both of them would be living in it soon. He wired it so power could be provided by a kerosene-run generator (known as a light plant), which he located outside to reduce noise. When the show began in the spring, many felt Dutch's trailer was one of the best in the group.

In spite of the ongoing, deep depression, the year was filled with many special events. Cab Calloway, the celebrated band leader, actor, singer, and songwriter, put people in a happier mood. Noted for his zoot suits and flamboyant style, Cab Calloway was moonwalking fifty years before Michael Jackson became famous for it. His hit record, "Minnie the Moocher," sold a million copies, a first for jazz and the Brunswick label. Hi De Hi, Hi De Ho.

"The Star Spangled Banner" officially became the national anthem. That reminds me of a joke, in which an army sentry shouts, to a soldier standing in the shadows, "Halt, who goes there?"

"American," the soldier replied.

"Recite the national anthem."

"Hell, I always get confused with the words," the soldier says.

"Pass, American."

Alka Seltzer was introduced. I can't think of a better time. In New York City, the first theater was built for rear movie projection. That one caught on. Also, the Empire State Building opened for business.

Kate Smith sang on the radio, and Al Capone was convicted of tax evasion and sentenced to eleven years in prison.

John McGraw was about to retire from baseball. McGraw managed the New York Giants for thirty years, winning 2,669 games in the senior circuit, making him the greatest player to ever become manager. As a player, his hot temper and tactics on the field were responsible for the decision to increase the number of umpires. Initially there was only one umpire, and when John played, it was difficult for the umpire to catch every trip, block, and impeding of the opposing runners. Never one to be without an opinion, John emphatically predicted, "Night baseball will never catch on."

Chapter Five

The Great Depression continued. In 1932, the Dow Jones Industrial Average hit a low of forty-one. President Hoover cut his own salary 15 percent. In Washington D.C., during the spring and summer, over 43,000 World War I veterans and their families set up shacks and other dwellings on Anacostia Flats, demanding immediate redemption of bonuses granted them eight years earlier. Most had been unemployed since the beginning of the Depression. They were referred to as the Bonus Army. The problem, however, was that the certificates matured twenty years after the date of issuance, or in 1945. President Hoover finally authorized General Douglas MacArthur to remove the Bonus Army by force. Removal was swift and harsh. The US infantry and cavalry, supported by six tanks, drove the veterans out, along with their wives and children, using fixed bayonets and adamsite gas (an arsenic derivative that caused vomiting, headache, and weakness). Their shacks and belongings were burned, which incited a riot. Two veterans were killed. The number of wives and children killed was not officially determined. Later, in 1936 and over Franklin Roosevelt's veto, Congress gave the veterans their bonus ten years early.

Elsewhere, Amelia Earhart flew solo across the Atlantic, and German physicist Albert Einstein was granted a visa to the US. Perhaps the most emotional domestic event was the kidnapping of twenty-month-old Charles Lindbergh Jr. After Charles Lindbergh Sr. turned over $50,000 as ransom, his son was found dead. America mourned its hero's tragic loss. An event of little note also occurred in 1932: Adolf Hitler received German citizenship. Finally, New York Governor Franklin Delano Roosevelt was nominated for president at the Democratic Party convention in Chicago.

The Great Depression presented a particular challenge to every citizen. Unemployment exceeded 20 percent, with soup kitchens and bread lines in the cities. (Al Capone opened the first soup kitchen in Chicago.) America had become a country where large numbers of its people were starving. Schools closed due to lack of funding; three million children left school to find work. Many people became hoboes, traveling the country in groups, hunting for food or jobs. For those in rural America, times had never been very good, but now they faced the loss of their farms and homes. Occasionally, when farms were put up for auction, they were sold in what was known as penny auctions. Buyers would bid just a few cents on foreclosed farms, only to sell it back to the original owner for next to nothing. Most people, however, were not so enterprising. They needed escape from the harsh reality playing out around them. For them, any diversion was a blessing, and Reno's Funmakers provided just that with a few hours of entertainment.

As the traveling show prepared for another season on the road, the cast was smaller than the year before. Some had found other means of making a living, foregoing the work they held most dear. Others managed to latch onto one of the few remaining tent shows. Undaunted, Ed Reno knew entertainers would come aboard during the summer while the show was on the circuit. In fact, many family members joined, or at least visited, the repertory show mainly to renew ties and secure three square meals. Most were talented and musically inclined. They would take part in stage plays or perform with the orchestra. Pauline, a talented singer, dancer, and actor, had written new plays that would be performed that year. Since they would revisit towns where they had performed before, it was important to be fresh and new. Her favorite cousin, David Shirkie, (he later took the name Dave Reno) was part of the cast that season. His mother lived in Chicago, and she promised to take Pauline to see A Century of Progress when the World's Fair opened in 1933. It proved to be a wonderful experience that Pauline never forgot.

Reno's Funmakers opened the spring season by returning to Elberton, Georgia, a traditional kickoff point for the past three years.

From there they traveled to Hartwell and Lavonia. To people in show business, home is where you hang your hat, but it's comfortable to begin in familiar territory. The cast had been working on a couple new plays, and a friendly audience is usually more forgiving. Frank Keagan had been on the road for weeks assuring the show's return to previous stops, as well as visiting potential new billings for the remainder of the year. In view of the hard times, it looked like a reasonable year, but far from a good one. Everybody in the business felt the pinch from the Depression, and Ed was no exception. After paying taxes on the winter home in Athens, he had little left to finance the operations ahead. It was definitely belt-tightening time. That would mean, among other things, Pauline would not receive a diamond ring for her birthday, a ritual since she had turned thirteen.

Up until then, borrowing from a bank had been avoided. Ed wasn't sure any bank even would make a loan if he needed one. Word was, banks were not making any loans at all. These things he kept to himself. "Never let them think you're broke, and smile even if you're hurting," was his credo. Words he had lived by his whole life, and he wasn't going to change now.

The big top was erected faster than usual in Elberton. Stage hands and roustabouts displayed an uncustomary amount of enthusiasm. During hard times, having a job meant more than ever. Nothing was taken for granted, and everyone concentrated on doing their jobs right and quickly.

Dutch pulled his house trailer for the first real test without mishap. His design proved superior to many others. He found that very satisfying, since he planned for it to be home on the road for him and Pauline once they were married. That will still be a long way off.

When opening night came, Ed was in for a big surprise. Ernest Caldwell normally played piano in the orchestra— or rather the band, since it was composed of trumpet, fiddle, piano, guitar, and drums. The size of the band would increase, depending on the number of family visitors. The piano was the most important instrument. It was the best accompaniment for Dutch's gospel songs, and it intensified parts of the stage play, such as when the villain enters or when the helpless heroine is pleading for something. Ed also preferred a piano when performing his magic act. Tonight there was a problem. Caldwell was found incapacitated. Always a friend of the grape, he kept a bottle by his bed for "medicinal purposes." That night he apparently overdosed, succumbing to the evil influence of drink. While attempts were made to sober him up, Caldwell thought it was all very funny and became the jolliest person in the room.

"How could he do this on opening night?" someone asked. "Ed's going to be plenty pissed."

"Hey, don't tell Ed," Caldwell said, his words slurred as he failed an effort to stand. "I'm okay." And, before commenting any further, he passed out.

Ed was beside himself. Of all the things that could happen, this was one he hadn't thought of.

"Let me get you a cup of coffee," Gladys said to him. "This ain't the end of the world."

"Might as well be," Ed replied. "It's going to screw up Pauline's new play and make the magic act seem dull and unexciting."

Dutch sat listening to them and finally spoke. "I think I know the routine pretty well. I can play the piano for you."

Gladys, Ed, and Pauline stared at him to see if he was joking.

"Now's not the time to kid," Ed said.

"I'm not kidding! I think I can do it."

"You never told us you played the piano. We thought you just sang."

"He can act too," Pauline said.

"We know that, Pauline," Ed said, a smile beginning to break out. "What we didn't know is that he played the piano."

"You already had a piano player, so there was no reason to mention it," Dutch explained.

That night the show came off without a hitch. There seemed to be no end to Dutch's talents. Besides being handsome, he sang beautifully, was a convincing actor, had built his own trailer home, and now played the piano. Ed felt very fortunate to have him as part of the troupe and, soon, as a son-in-law.

Chapter Six

The bus arrived in Los Angeles after the long journey across the country. Though for the most part their sightseeing had been done from the windows, Teresa and Delores agreed with each other that such a trip made them more knowledgeable about America and definitely more grown up. They were met by Delores's aunt Tilda. After affectionate greetings, the aunt said, "You poor dears, you must be worn out from such a long ride. Let's get you home so you can relax and rest up."

One of the first things Teresa did after getting settled at the boarding house was to try to find an agent. She and Delores agreed that approach was best. Since they didn't know a soul in town, the thing to do was go to the phone book.

"Bingo," Delores shouted, as they found an agent specializing in aspiring actors, young and unknown.

His name was Buddy Baker. A few years earlier he, too, had had aspirations for the silver screen, but had only been hired for bit parts and stand-ins. Hardly enough to support him, let alone a wife and child. To make matters worse, a nasty divorce ended any chance for him to "trip the light fantastic." After several menial jobs, he landed one working for the Talbot Agency. At one time the Talbot Agency had been recognized as one of the leaders in the industry, representing such notables as Louise Branch, Bob Robinson, and Tom Taylor. However, the advent of "talkies" had ended the careers of these and many other silent stars. It became increasingly difficult for Talbot to sign contemporary actors. Attrition and the Great Depression forced him to furlough his associates, until only Buddy Baker remained. At seventy-years-old, Talbot had to have a helper. Buddy's wages were the lowest, therefore, he remained.

Even with the paltry pay, it was better than many jobs Buddy had held over the last few years. On New Year's Day, Anderson Talbot was found lifeless in his bed, dead from an apparent heart attack. At the funeral, tactless Buddy asked the family what they intended to do with the agency. They showed no interest in keeping it running and were willing to sign a quit claim deed. Buddy kept the name Talbot— and the same amount of business. So when the phone rang one day, it came as a shock. He let it ring several times, thinking it was probably a bill collector. Eventually his curiosity got the better of him and he answered, simply saying hello. He didn't announce the business name in the event it was a bill collector. In that case, he would simply tell the caller he had the wrong number.

"Mr. Talbot please," said a girl's voice.

"May I ask the nature of the call?" responded Buddy.

"We want to see about getting an agent to represent us," she replied.

Trying to hide his excitement, Buddy lowered his voice and said slowly, "I believe that can be arranged." All he could think about was that at last, some paying customers. "We might be able to see you on Tuesday next week, say at ten o'clock?"

"That would be fine."

Teresa couldn't sleep. All she thought about was that at last, her career was underway. Delores managed to contain her own enthusiasm. Not as pretty or as talented as Teresa, she had set her sights on more modest goals. Her desire for screen acting had never been as strong as Teresa's, and she kept it well under control. She did want to live in Los Angeles, but wasn't that concerned about a vocation. She had accompanied Teresa mainly because they were best friends.

In better days, the neighborhood where the Talbot Agency was considered had been quite active for various businesses and actors' representation. Silent film stars could be seen almost any time of the day. Now, new buildings uptown housed most of the talent agencies. Eye-popping rent, however, still forced many to settle for more modest digs. Such was the case of the Talbot Agency and Buddy Baker. The brick building that housed his office revealed telltale signs of aging, and several windows exposed fan blades, vitally important during the summer heat. Talbot's office was on the second floor. A hand-printed out-of-order sign was taped to the elevator door.

"I guess we take the stairs," Delores said. "Thank heavens it's just on the second floor."

The top three floors had been converted into small apartments. A broken elevator made coming home drudgery to those tenants.

Standing in front of a door with Talbot Agency painted on its window, the girls swallowed hard and then walked in.

"Mr. Talbot?" Teresa said to the man sitting at the desk.

"Talbot is no longer with us," Buddy replied. "He passed away last year. My name is Buddy Baker, and I run the agency now. What can I do for you?"

"We have a ten o'clock appointment."

"Oh yes, please have a seat." Buddy pointed to a couple chairs situated by his desk. "Now, what is it I can do for you girls?" he asked as his eyes focused on Teresa, the more attractive of the two. He had already mentally answered half of his question when it came to the other girl.

"I guess the best way to say it is that we both want to be in the movies," Teresa replied.

Attempting to assume the sincere attitude of a veteran talent agent, Buddy said formally, "You must realize, my dear, hundreds of young girls have had similar desires, and very few were successful."

The look on Delores's face told it all. She knew her chances were not only slim, but impossible. Perhaps not so with Teresa. She had always had the lead in school plays, was the first one selected as a cheerleader, and had been sought after by all the boys, in spite of going steady with the most popular one, Walter Collins. As Delores looked around the room, she saw no evidence that a woman worked there. Windows in need of a good washing revealed only a filmy, indistinct view of the landscape outside. While Buddy rambled on, Delores's attention drifted, and she focused on the dust particles floating in the weak sunbeams shining in the room. To her it was obvious. The Talbot Agency was no dynamo of business.

"Starting out from scratch," Buddy was saying, "and totally unknown makes it even more difficult, more problematic, but not impossible."

"This is my life's dream," Teresa said. "I know I have enough talent to make it."

"Our fee is usually 10 percent of earnings, but it's going to take extra cash to get you known here in Hollywood. How are you fixed for the added expense of dinners in some of the more popular places and a major photo shoot?"

"I have my college savings, and my father would send me more if I asked."

"If you're serious about this, then you're going to need it," Buddy said frankly. "First of all, you've got to get noticed. The places we'll need to go to are on the Sunset Strip and they aren't cheap. I'm recognized at most places where the powerful producers hang out and that will help. I'm referring to the Cocoanut Grove and Plantation Club."

Buddy narrowed his eyes, now knowing he was dealing with a wheat—someone totally unfamiliar with big city ways. He also wondered just how far she might go. No matter. As long as she was paying, he didn't want to lose a free ride. It had been quite some time since he had frequented the Strip, primarily because he didn't have the money.

Nightclubs along Sunset Strip operated in spite of Prohibition. Alcohol was served under code names. In addition, it was okay to bring your own. Dancing always included famous orchestras that made the evening come alive. Usually the orchestras were made up of black musicians; the patrons were white. Other entertainment consisted of singers, comedians, and chorus lines of beautiful girls. Better nightclubs featured a woman photographer who took pictures of guests at the tables (for a price), and a cigarette girl, dressed in a short skirt, parading her wares. The most popular places, such as the Ambassador Hotel's Cocoanut Grove, were the hot spots for the rich and famous in Hollywood. The power crowd of backers, producers, directors, and movie stars were in frequent attendance. Celebrities of every stripe could be seen every day. The Sunset Strip was definitely the place to be noticed.

Buddy asked, "Do you have an evening gown? If not, better get one, something with an open back. White is the best color, but as long as the color is light, like a pastel, it should be all right. After you get it, call me and I'll make a reservation."

There was no mention of anything for Delores. Apparently, she thought, the Talbot Agency had no interest in her. It didn't bother her one iota. On the way home, Teresa asked her to help find the proper evening dress. Delores promptly put the question to her aunt.

"I think the best place to look for what you're talking about is Crystal's Boutique on Sunset Boulevard," Aunt Tilda suggested. "They have replicas of gowns by Adrian, the most popular among the movie stars, and you can't tell the difference between their dresses and the originals. It won't set you back a small fortune either."

She turned to her niece. "Delores, you haven't said much about it. Are you also looking for a gown?"

"No interest anymore, Aunt Tilda. I'm facing facts. I would never make it in Hollywood."

Tilda smiled at the wisdom displayed by the young woman and said, "You know, our business has grown in the past couple years in spite of the Depression. We planned on advertising for a receptionist, but your uncle didn't want to have to interview a hundred applicants. Morris would be thrilled if you took the job. Free rent, home cooking, and a better salary you could not get anywhere else."

"I'd love to have the job," Delores replied. "That would be more than I could ever hope for."

Her smile told it all. Finally, Delores was really enthusiastic about Hollywood. She saw it as the chance of a lifetime, away from the rut back in Lonesome Pine, with an opportunity to live in California and even save money. Wow!

Teresa bought an evening gown, cloak, matching gloves, and shoes for $25.00. The gown's color was sort of a robin's egg blue, but lighter. It was the most beautiful dress she had ever seen, and she wanted to call Buddy Baker "quick as a click." Delores suggested it was better to wait at least one day.

When they got home, Teresa couldn't wait to try her new things, and she loitered in front of the mirror making facial expressions. That night, sleep did not come easy. Images of being in the movies dominated her thoughts until morning.

"Talbot Agency." Buddy answered the phone quickly. He'd been expecting her call.

"Mr. Baker?"

"Call me Buddy," was his reply.

"Er … Buddy, I have the gown we talked about."

"Well then, I guess I need to call the Ambassador Hotel and make reservations for dinner at the Cocoanut Grove. I'll call you back to tell you when I'll pick you up. Be ready for a little drinking and dancing. Your career is now beginning."

The excitement was too much for Teresa. She was so dizzy, she had to go lie down and put a wet rag to her forehead. Aunt Tilda began to worry that Teresa might be in for a very big disappointment and would not handle it well. Just then the phone rang. It was Buddy saying he would pick her up at 8:00 o'clock.

On the way to the Ambassador Hotel, Buddy asked, "How much money did you bring?"

"About $150."

"Better give it to me now. I'll need to cover some people and pay for the dinner."

Teresa handed him the money, wondering how much "getting recognized" was going to cost. She might need to call her father when the savings ran out.

"Reservation for Baker," Buddy announced to the maître d'hôtel.

"Yes, sir. Right this way, please," replied the head waiter after checking his list.

Teresa was in awe. She had only read about places of glamour and glitz in magazines; now she was actually in one. Another lifetime dream come true.

After ordering wine, Buddy excused himself, saying, "I need to see some people at the bar and find out who all is here tonight. Be back in a minute of two. Just sip the wine and don't gawk."

The people in the barroom all seemed to know one another. That was commonplace at bars in general. Even in rural areas, the same people congregated at the same places, spending hours that would be better spent elsewhere. Members of the same society, so to speak. Mostly unattached, they came together to commiserate over the vicissitudes and conditions of life that had befallen them. Though not exactly friends, after a couple drinks they would console each other, blaming their misfortunes on everything but themselves. Buddy Baker was a member of this club with paid-up dues. Tonight, however, thanks to the trusting young hopeful sitting back at the table, he had a free ride and, who knows, maybe more.

"Hey Buddy, who's the muffin?" someone asked.

"Kind of easy on the peepers," said another. "Is that your new flame?"

"Mitt, me boys, this one's a pip and cute as a bug's ear," Buddy replied. "I just came in here to see if any of the Who's Who is here tonight."

"The hell you did. We know you're back here just to show off. Anyway, a couple names are in here tonight."

After he'd found out what he needed to know, Buddy turned back to the table. "Thanks for the lowdown, boys. I'd better shake a leg and get back. Don't want to gum up the works."

After he left, they all had a good laugh, agreeing that the girl Buddy was with "sure ain't no gold-digger." Then they complained about how a dumbass like Buddy could be so lucky. It set the stage for another round of drinks and another round of similar stories.

"Hey barkeep, set us up again."

"We're in luck," Buddy told Teresa when he returned to the table. "The place is loaded with the right people tonight. Holy shit, did you drink all the wine?"

"I got nervous. I didn't know what else to do, so I kept drinking. It surprised me, too, when I saw the bottle was empty."

"How are you feeling?"

"Oh, I feel fine."

Buddy ordered another bottle of wine and a martini with a twist. Leaning over, he whispered to Teresa, "Act natural, but glance to your right and look at the table near the wall. It's Frank Capra and Barbara Stanwyck. Rumor has it Capra is hopelessly in love with her, but she's married to some guy that's mean to her. Don't know exactly how she feels about Capra, but they're seen together a lot. He is the hottest director around today."

"Are you going to talk to him?" Teresa asked.

"Ah … I don't think that would be wise right now," Buddy replied. "Besides, you still need to be better known. You need to have photos taken. I'll set it up for you."

Buddy failed to notice other prominent couples there that night. John Wayne and Jean Arthur were having dinner. Loretta Young and her husband Grant Withers were celebrating something, and Jean

Harlow was seated near the stage with two men who were strangers at the Grove.

"You still feel okay?" Buddy asked Teresa. "Maybe we better eat something."

"Make it something light. I'm too excited to eat."

Buddy ordered chicken marsala for both of them and another martini for him. Teresa continued to work on the wine. She was feeling a little queasy, as things were beginning to have a woolly appearance. The last time she'd felt like this was the night of senior prom, when she got well-oiled and passed out. A little food was probably an excellent idea.

"Better go easy on the wine," Buddy warned her. "I don't want you to get sick on me."

"Don't worry about me, I can handle it," she lied.

The dinner came off well. Buddy ate like a stevedore and downed his martini as if it were water. Teresa barely ate, only picking at her meal. Thankfully, the sick feeling passed for a while. She also thought she saw Jean Harlow by the stage, and Buddy confirmed it.

"Let me get the check," he said. "You don't want to overdo it on the first night. Listen, it's a beautiful evening to take a ride. It'll help digest the meal and give us a chance to plan the next move."

Teresa now had confidence in Buddy. Her movie career might be just around the corner.

"Stick with me, honey," he said as they drove away. "It won't take too long before the studios start calling."

It really was a beautiful evening. With the windows rolled down and refreshing air hitting her face, her worries and cares seemed to melt away. They drove for about a half hour, their conversation mainly small talk. Teresa had no idea where they were, when the car turned down a darkened road and stopped. After a period of silence that seemed to last forever, Buddy reached over and pulled her to him. The kiss was strange to her. The only other man she had ever kissed passionately was Walter. Buddy's kiss was very different, and although she questioned her feelings, she responded.

Later, her thoughts clouded from alcohol and the excitement of her first exposure to the "in crowd," Teresa only gave mild resistance when she felt Buddy's hand between her legs. That night, something Walter

Collins would cherish and give his life to defend was surrendered to the shallowest form of humanity by the name of Bartolo Moretti, known in Hollywood as Buddy Baker.

For the next few weeks, they had dinner at various hot spots, and their nights invariably ended up the same way. Finally, Teresa asked about the photo session he had promised earlier.

Buddy replied, "I'm just waiting until your father sends enough money."

"I have nearly $300 left," she said.

"That ought to do it. I know a good photographer and I'll make the arrangements. Hope you understand that some shots will be cheesecake, but that's what gets their attention best of all."

Later that week they arrived at the photographer's studio. It was located in the basement of a rundown building, and Teresa said "Looks kind of crummy to me. Are you sure this guy is any good?"

"Can't judge a book by its cover. The man is a genius. We've done business before."

He told his clients it cost $100. He'd give $50 to the photographer and keep fifty for himself.

Like many in the trade, Bruce Wheeler needed outside income to make ends meet. Photography, his first love, couldn't cut it on a full-time basis. Business had been better before the Depression, but now people either wouldn't spend the money or simply didn't have it. He had made friends with Buddy Baker one night in some gin mill, and it sure had paid off. This latest job couldn't come at a better time. He didn't mind splitting the fee with Buddy, when he considered the long, smooth green fifty for himself.

Buddy introduced them. "Bruce Wheeler, I'd like you to meet Teresa White. She's the young lady we spoke about. She's going to need some promotional photos."

"I think I know what she will need. When do you want to start?"

"Today. Right now, if it's possible."

"Yeah, I can do it now. Just give me a couple minutes to get set up."

Buddy turned to Teresa. "This is going to take a couple hours. What say I leave you here and come back for you later?"

Teresa hesitantly agreed. After Buddy left Bruce had a hard time keeping his eyes off her. Buddy had told him she was a hot number and clearly a wheat, but he hadn't expected this good a looker. Buddy's regulars were mostly sluts, and definitely not much to look at.

"Have you had photo shoots before?"

"No, this is my first time," she said.

"Just try to relax, it doesn't hurt at all," Bruce called as he set up the lighting. "If you look behind the screen, you'll find a gown. You can change into it back there."

Teresa put on the gown, but when she stepped out from behind the screen, Bruce shouted, "Hell no, that will never do. You can see your underwear through the dress. Take them off so we can begin."

Teresa stepped back behind the screen. Her heart was pounding like a bass drum doing double time.

"It's an awfully sheer dress, don't you think?" she said in a weak voice.

"That's the idea, sweetheart," he replied. "Don't get nervous and freak out on me. As I understand it, you want to get noticed and be in the movies. Well, I guarantee business will pick up once these pictures are circulated. Here, drink this. It will help settle your nerves."

Bruce had poured two glasses of vodka. He told her to come sit at a table and handed a glass to her. She took a sip, grimaced, and with a contorted face said, "What is this? It tastes terrible."

"It's Bruce's magic elixir and inhibition remover. Drink it down fast and you'll see what I mean."

"I can't drink it fast."

"Then drink it slow. The result will be the same."

When she had finished the glass, getting up was easier said than done. Once that was accomplished, she seemed to float through the gown photo shoot.

"That wraps up this part," Bruce said as he poured two more glasses. "Come sit back at the table and take a break before we continue."

Teresa felt like she was in a trance as she sat down again. The vodka went down easier this time, but she knew she still needed to sip it slowly. Her voice seemed to come out of a cave, sort of echoing after she spoke.

"What's next?" she asked.

"See those pillows in front of that couch over there? That's where we'll shoot the nudes."

His words registered slowly. It sounded like he'd said "shoot nudes." Teresa hadn't planned on that.

"I'm not doing any nude pictures."

"Sure you are, honey," Buddy said, taking hold of her arm and half walking, half dragging her over to the couch.

"I said, I'm not doing nudes," Teresa repeated angrily.

They scuffled, with her trying to keep the sheer gown on and him trying to take it off. Bruce was too strong for her resistance, and the struggle intensified the urge he had felt the first time he saw her. Teresa couldn't prevent the assault. To her the rest wasn't real, only a bad dream as the camera flashed and Bruce positioned her on the floor. At last he tossed her a towel and said he was done. All she thought about was calling the police as soon as Buddy returned.

"You're welcome to stay here 'til Buddy gets back," Bruce said. "I got another appointment and need to leave. The studio is rented for four hours, so time wise it should be okay."

"Is there a phone here?" she asked.

"Nope, sorry about that."

Later, when Buddy returned, he asked, "How did it go? Has Bruce left already?"

"He raped me. I want to call the police."

"Now hold on. A scandal isn't the kind of publicity you need," Buddy cautioned. "I can't handle that kind of spotlight either. What's done is done. We need to think this over."

"Take me home."

Buddy didn't call for over a week. Finally, when he did, she wouldn't come to the phone. Teresa was catatonic and still in shock. Her life was miserable. Delores and Aunt Tilda knew something terrible had happened, but felt it was wrong to pry. All Teresa did was lie in bed. It took several days before she could even cry. Sometimes a good cry is a catharses and therapeutic. Teresa began to see herself in reality, and realized she needed to make different plans. A career in the movies was out. She could no longer live under the Stevens' largesse. Going back to Lonesome Pine was impossible. Her embarrassment overshadowed ever facing her people at home.

The thing to do now was get a job, find a place to live, and begin a new life. Remembering a help wanted sign at a local eatery, she thought that would be a good place to start. She applied for the job, although she had no previous restaurant experience. In fact, Teresa didn't have any work experience at all. She was hired with the promise that she could train on the job. The days were long, but the nights were even longer. Her appearance took on a hard look that belied her youth. Days turned into weeks, and weeks became months. At first, the patrons enjoyed having a pretty young girl serve them. As time passed, she transformed into a callous waitress. The pretty young girl was gone. She began to suffer deep depressions that lasted for days. Delores cautioned her about the seriousness of her state of mind, and told her to see a doctor. She said she would, but didn't. After a hard day at work, she would come home defeated and go to bed early, perchance not to dream.

There is something forgiving about morning. After a night of worry and stress, a new day can provide great relief to those who are downtrodden. It promises a better time and a new beginning for the discouraged, oppressed, and misused. For Teresa White, a new day only meant continuing the drudgery her life had become.

One morning she sat at her kitchen table, despondent and listless in her robe. That first cup of coffee wasn't helping much. Her sleepless nights only emphasized her unhappiness and regrettable life, leaving her numb the next day. This day was no exception. She didn't hear the first faint knock at the door. The next one was louder. She opened the door and stared in amazement at the man standing there.

"Walter, what are you doing here?"

"Can I come in?"

Teresa flushed. The tips of her ears turned hot, and with a heart pounding so hard, her temples hurt. "Don't look at me," she said. "I haven't even showered or brushed my teeth." She made an effort to reshape her hair, but then gave up and dropped her hands. She had reached the lowest point in her life and didn't care anymore.

Like a lot of women, for Teresa cosmetics were a lifesaver that prevented a sallow appearance. But even with a weekly check from her father, purchasing them was too much of an extravagance. Her waitress job at the diner barely paid enough to eke out a living and put a roof over her head.

As Walter stood before her, she saw a man deeply tanned from working outside and the characteristic white forehead, where his skin was protected by his cap. She used to hate that about him, but somehow, at this moment, it didn't seem bad at all. In fact, the evidence of his work made him appear more handsome than she remembered.

He explained why he was there. "Your friend Delores told her mother that you gave up being in the movies. I had to see for myself."

"Come in, Walter," she said, backing away from the door. "Can I get you a cup of coffee? I just made it fresh. Come sit at the table."

They sat there looking at each other without saying a word. Walter, in his easy manner, smiled as he stirred in milk and sugar. Teresa's eyes began to overfill. She squeezed them shut, but tears ran down both her cheeks. Wiping them with the back of her hand, she said in a voice quivering with emotion, "Oh, Walter, how could I have ever done what I did? I've disgraced my family, and most of all, you."

Walter could never stand seeing her cry, so she wasn't surprised when his eyes began to fill as well.

"Well," he said, "I guess you had a dream and you had to follow it. It was the most important thing you wanted to do. Everybody has to follow their dream at one time or another." He reached across the table and put his big hand on top of hers.

"You will never forgive me when you hear what I've done," she said with blunt honesty.

"A long time ago we promised our love forever, and I know you meant it. That kind of love never says good-bye. You're my sunshine in the morning and my stars at night. Don't you know you have touched me ever since grade school and that my life ends without you? You amaze me, girl. When you left, my life wasn't worth a nickel. Teresa, you belong with me and we belong together. I've come to take you home."

That morning, Teresa's tears flowed until none were left. She realized she had traded away a diamond and got a lump of coal in return. She had worked hard to build a wall against Walter's memory in order to pursue her dream. Like running to catch the rainbow, it could never really happen.

While Walter took great pride in the way he lived, his work, and his farm, his heart had remained pure through it all. His image in the mirror appeared smaller than it actually was. Some said that to continue working the farm as though Teresa had never left, he must have had a heart of granite. What they couldn't know about his granite heart was that her memory was deeply etched on it. Each day was filled with indescribable pain and longing. His thoughts were unending about her fascinating bouquet, the little curl of hair at the back of her neck, and the spark that leaped from her skin to his whenever they touched.

Three months later they were married.

Teresa "Tootsie" White wasn't the first girl with visions of stardom who succumbed to the vicissitudes of Hollywood. Tinsel Town is a magnet for women whose dreams, hope, and determination are dashed against the rocks of an inimical shore. Desire and hope isn't enough to protect the fragile psyche in Hollywood's dog-eat-dog world. The women would sometimes find themselves addicted to prescription drugs in the effort to stabilize their subliminal selves. Others become so despondent, they commit the supreme sacrifice.

The tragedy of Peg Entwistle comes to mind. Born in Wales, she left Britain to pursue an acting career in America. In 1931 she had performed in eight consecutive Broadway shows that failed. While the public liked her, the critical press disapproved. She made a couple films in Hollywood before her career came to a standstill. She spent her time going to auditions and waiting for work. The candle was burning to the end of its wick.

A woman walking near the Hollywoodland sign noticed a female's shoe and jacket, and then found a purse containing a suicide note. On September 16, 1932, Peg Entwistle jumped from the *H* of the famous sign, landing one hundred feet below. In later years the *LAND* portion of the sign was removed. In order to get a better perspective of its size, just consider that the letters are thirty feet wide and forty-five feet tall.

Robert Burns had it right when he wrote, "The best laid schemes of mice and men often go awry." We enter through the mysterious door of life with misconceptions of what lies ahead. Reality is always buffered by our fantasized anticipations. It's been said that, "Our greatest expectations and worse fears never materialize. It's always something in between." We all can relate to that.

Chapter Seven

Attendance and gate receipts were noticeably down at the halfway point of the season. For the first time, cash on hand barely met expenses. When times were good, the notion items sold during intermission provided substantial revenue. This was not the case anymore. Candy and popcorn sales were practically nonexistent, even with the surprise bonus of a diamond ring in one of the boxes. People just didn't have enough to spend on superfluities. These days required innovation in order for a person to keep his head above water and stay alive. Reno's Funmakers, as well as the whole traveling entertainment industry, faced a battle to survive. Ed increased the number of grandstand bleachers to accommodate more 10¢ admissions. He also gave discount coupons at select stores in town. With a coupon, a 25¢ main seating ticket could be purchased for 15¢. One night was set aside for amateur night, when local talent competed for prizes. That always proved to be a big hit. Locals performed everything from bird calls to playing a carpenter's saw, and the performances energized the crowd. Some acts brought raucous laughter, but occasionally the audience was stunned by a singer's beautiful voice. They'd had no idea that much talent belonged to one of their own. Attendance improved, and with it came a slight increase in overall revenue. If the house was full each evening, cash receipts would make them profitable the rest of the summer.

Ed tried to cover all the bases. He even reluctantly met with the owner of a similar traveling vaudeville show to explore the possibilities of merging their shows and sharing expenses.

* * * * *

To.
My Darling
With
Eternal Love
Pauline

At last the wedding day came. On August 26, 1933, in a simple ceremony performed by a justice of the peace, George "Dutch" Moon and Pauline Ruth Reno became man and wife. While their engagement had fostered a good relationship between Dutch and Pauline's parents, their growing desire for each other had become an unfulfilled frustration. Some time of unwatched togetherness is the right dose to heal the hunger of two people in love. No longer did they need to act as though their relationship was staid and unemotional. No longer would they be chaperoned. Their honeymoon was to be two days at the local hotel before the show moved to the next town. On their wedding night, after Dutch closed the door to their room, and deafened by the sound of their pounding hearts, they fulfilled all their desires, and their dreams came true.

The Democratic Party candidate, Franklin Delano Roosevelt, had won the 1932 election in a landslide, becoming our thirty-second president. He offered change to a weary and disheartened electorate. His promise to return America to prosperity convinced nearly everyone.

Once he was sworn in in March 1933, the national spirit was revived by his sanguinity. Roosevelt worked diligently to create change. He promised the people a greater share in the distribution of wealth. Fearful for their future, the population fell in behind him. Change was good, whether it succeeded or not.

Farm prices had fallen 60 percent, and industrial production by over half. Relief was urgently needed by the thirteen million unemployed Americans and the over two million homeless Americans. By surrounding himself with Eastern elites, his advisors consisted principally of academics with a socialist bent. Those who were more conservative in policy were suspicious and awaited the results of any action.

The first hundred days after Roosevelt's inauguration saw major legislation and a volume of executive orders that became known as the New Deal. In order to stimulate the economy, Roosevelt took the path of immense federal spending.

The Works Progress Administration, WPA, was created and soon employed two million heads of families. His Civilian Conservation Corps hired 250,000 unemployed, unmarried young men to work on rural and local projects.

Another piece of legislation directly affecting business was the National Industrial Recovery Act of 1933, or the NIRA. It was designed to end competition by forcing industries to set minimal prices, restricted production, encouraged unions, and suspended anti-trust laws. (In a unanimous decision, the Supreme Court later ruled the NIRA unconstitutional.)

The new Agricultural Adjustment Administration (AAA) tried to force higher prices for commodities by paying farmers to take land out of production and cut their livestock herds. Food and livestock were also purchased by the government, and then destroyed and slaughtered. Some deemed it a questionable action when millions in the country were starving.

Shortly after Roosevelt took office, the banks in thirty-two of the forty-eight states closed their doors because panic-struck customers had been withdrawing their money. Their trepidation prompted Roosevelt to declare a banking holiday. The Emergency Banking Act was passed and the Federal Deposit Insurance Corporation (FDIC) was created. Many banks never reopened. To counter deflation, by executive order, privately owned gold became the property of the government. The value of the dollar dropped to 60¢.

Roosevelt created the largest government-owned industrial enterprise ever in the United States—the Tennessee Valley Authority. The TVA built dams and power stations, controlled floods, and modernized agriculture and home conditions in the poverty-stricken Tennessee Valley.

During the campaign, Roosevelt had promised to cut the federal budget. The billions being spent on New Deal activities were considered part of special emergency relief and were credited to a separate budget account. Accordingly, to fulfill his promise to the country he cut 40 percent of veterans' benefits and military spending. In doing so, he removed 500,000 veterans and their widows from the pension rolls, and slashed benefits for the rest. Further, he reduced spending on research and education.

Repeal of Prohibition brought in new tax dollars, and Hoover's 1¢ per gallon tax on gasoline also increased revenue.

The economy improved, and the federal jobs created by the New Deal gradually reduced unemployment from 25 percent to 22 percent.

Emergency relief spending doubled the national debt, which reached 40 percent of the gross national product. As the GNP increased each year, spending remained at 40 percent, thus increasing the national debt even more. Because jobs for the unemployed were basically with the government, unemployment numbers continued to be very high levels.

Americans broadly supported Roosevelt's actions, and he slowly created a large coalition of supporters that kept him in office for eleven years. He died before his third term ended.

* * * * *

As the Great Depression continued taking its toll on the citizens, radio became the most popular escape from the daily grind. It also became the political tool of FDR. His fireside chats allowed him to encourage listeners and explain the new programs being created. Americans trusted radio to bring them news and entertainment. Despite the poor economy, 60 percent of homes owned at least one radio. And for those who couldn't afford the cost of a movie, radio was their only source of entertainment. Hit songs of the day were heard on the radio, performed by the artists who made them. Listeners were involved in the lives of the owners of the Jot 'em Down store in Pine Ridge, Arkansas. The shenanigans of Lum and Abner made everyone's days a little brighter, as the duo stumbled on different schemes to make money. Their ideas nearly always failed, resulting in their being fleeced by their nemesis, Squire Skimp.

Once Lum came up with the idea of having tickets at the meat counter, to make things more orderly so the clerk would know who was next in line. The following day when Mousey Grey came in to buy hamburger, he stood in front of the meat case for a while before calling to Lum, who was seemingly ignoring him.

"I'd like to buy a pound of hamburger," Mousey said.

In a cool manner, Lum asked, "Do you have a ticket?"

"I'm the only one in the store," Mousey replied.

"Then you won't have to wait too long," Lum said dryly.

The characters of Pine Ridge were affectionately presented as simple small-town folk. They met at the Jot 'em Down store just about every day, to sit around the pickle barrel and discuss the goings-on. While reminiscing about their town in its early days, Grandpappy Spears recalled when they only had one phone in town. It belonged to the mayor and its phone number was one. As the town grew, more phones were installed, and they had numbers of two, three, four, and so forth. Finally, when enough people moved in, the phone number reached eleven.

"Yeah, I sure remember that," Lum said blandly. "I had to write that one down."

Housewives listened regularly to a kindly, trusting widow, who owned and operated a lumberyard in Rushville Center. She was always ready to offer practical advice to local townsfolk, whose troubled souls were in need. Ma Perkins was heard by millions every day. People felt a part of Ma and her three children's lives. Fans were unaware that the role of Ma was played by twenty-three-year-old actress Virginia Payne. Miss Payne had to wear a wig and heavy makeup to appear older during public events.

The popularity of radio expanded during the Great Depression. Many people who couldn't afford a "talking box" found relatives or others that had one. They became regular visitors in order to get the news and listen to favorite programs, like *Amos 'n' Andy*, *The Lone Ranger*, *The Shadow*, *Let's Pretend*, *Lux Radio Theater*, *Easy Aces*, and Jack Benny. The list goes on and on. Radio became the place to be for contemporary talent. Except perhaps for Greta Garbo, who turned down $25, 000 to make a single appearance. Guess she just wanted to be alone. Considering the average annual income for those with jobs was $1,601.00, the amount offered Garbo bordered on the obscene.

* * * * *

Ed Reno was fascinated with radio and took up the hobby of making crystal sets. Using materials found around the house, he constructed little devices that picked up the signal of popular broadcasts. Once he got them to work, he gave them away. To Ed, the fun was in the making, not the keeping.

Chapter Eight

Dutch and Pauline kept a honey pot, or commode, in the bedroom for emergency purposes. It so happened that one night it was full. Not full, as one might declare when it needed to be emptied, but full to the brim. The hour was late. The last performance was finished and the various duties to close down the show had been completed. Once they returned to their trailer, Pauline needed to use the aforementioned chamber pot. Unfortunately, it needed to be emptied first. The job, naturally, fell upon Dutch.

"Don't you want a flashlight?" Pauline asked.

"No, sweetheart, I don't want anyone to see me," Dutch replied.

"But it's pitch black outside. You can't see a thing. Where are you going to empty it?"

"Don't worry. I'll just throw it in the open field."

The night had never been darker as Dutch descended the steps, balancing the commode so as not to prematurely spill any of its contents. Clouds completely blotted out any illumination given by the moon and stars. He could see nothing but blackness. Crickets gave their chirping songs to guide potential mates to their location. But Dutch, sans flashlight, was guided by only intuition and a faint memory from when it had been daylight. He recalled the open field to the left and lightly trod in that direction. His job required great care, because a stumble or wobble could disrupt the necessary smooth motion needed to complete the task. After he'd walked what seemed a proper distance, Dutch felt confident he could safely discharge the pot's contents. Planting his left foot in front of him, he carefully swung the pot behind him and then threw it forward with a mighty thrust. The total blackness did not disclose the fact that at the end of that colossal fling stood the side of a barn, about two inches away. What went out with the toss came back as a shower.

Moments later Pauline heard her beloved whisper, "Honey, can I have a towel?" Fortunately, no one heard the commotion around their trailer home that night. And for one of the few times in her life, Pauline didn't tell her dad.

The scuttlebutt in the cook tent was about Wiley Post's solo flight around the world. The work crew couldn't even imagine such a daring feat, especially in an airplane. Ed and Gladys had met Wiley when they all performed during their barnstorming days. Gladys had a wing-walking act, in which she hung from the airplane by her teeth. Wiley was a parachutist with Burrell Tibbs Flying Circus. Like most in show business, the three had become instant friends. Wiley was astonished by Ed's magic, and constantly tried to figure out how certain illusions were accomplished. It became a standard scene, with Wiley asking, "How did you do that?" and Ed answering, "Wiley, it's just magic." Like most of America, the Renos were extremely proud of Wiley's achievements. Tragedy struck two years later, when Wiley and his friend, humorist Will Rogers, were both killed in a plane crash.

The year progressed, and Reno's Funmakers was nearing the season's end when David Shirkie, Ed's nephew, came to discuss his future.

"Uncle Ed, if you don't mind too much, I think it's time for me to go back to Chicago. Mom tells me that my girlfriend, Christina … You remember her, Christina Stavros? Well, Mom tells me that she stopped by to see how I was getting along and told her that her father bought a nightclub and wanted to have live entertainment. Chris thought about me and said there would be a job playing the piano. Dutch has taught me a lot, and he thinks I could make it on my own."

Dave went on, "You guys wanted to see the World's Fair, and I could scout it out for you. I know Chicago pretty well, and if you don't stay in Kankakee with Granddad, you can stay with me and Mom. Besides, I'm not that important to the show, and I know I'm here as a favor to Mom."

"Dave, everybody is important to the show," Ed answered frankly. "You of all people should know that. If Dutch thinks you can make it on your own playing the piano, then I'm sure you can. Remember, we are family. Everybody on the show is family. That's always been the way.

"Have you told Pauline? You two have been buddies ever since you learned how to talk." Ed well knew that whenever their conversation wasn't serious, the two spoke to each other with funny noises. Pauline called him Dritt, and he referred to her as Dreeough.

"Yes, we talked about it," Dave said. "We can always write and talk on the telephone. We don't visit that much since she and Dutch married. Dutch thinks we're both crazy."

Farewells are always sad occasions. Especially so when a family member departs. Dave Reno's return to Chicago brought both smiles and sadness.

A job did await his return, but it was not without problems. Dave was a magnet for women. Entertaining in Dmitri Stavros's club added celebrity status to his appeal. Christina, a beautiful woman in her own right, hadn't given any thought that jealousy might enter the picture. Their relationship became strained. Dave knew Dmitri was one step removed from the Chicago underworld and began to develop ulcers. This job definitely wasn't going to work. After a long talk with Dmitri, Dave headed west to California, sans Christina. Dmitri had become very fond of Dave, but he was not Greek. He wanted his daughter to marry Greek and maintain tradition. Dmitri knew Christina would be brokenhearted when Dave left, but it was for the best; and he helped by recommending Dave to a confederate out west. Over time, Dave Reno gained success as a songwriter, singer, and musician. For over a decade he had his own television show in San Diego. More than likely, Christina married a Greek man, making her father very happy. *Opa!*

One of the most popular stars during the Depression was Jim Londos. Born Christos Theofilou, he became known as the Golden Greek. After coming to America, he worked at an assortment of jobs, including catcher in a carnival acrobatic act, before turning to wrestling. It was wrestling that won him acclaim and fame. Well-known for his good looks and muscled physique, Londos was matched against the ugliest and meanest opponents. He soon became a favorite here in the US and a national hero in Greece, where he once drew a crowd of 100,000 fans.

One of his opponents was George Zaharias (Theodore Vetoyanis), the Greek Hyena, a fellow American Greek and later husband to perhaps the greatest woman athlete ever.

Mildred Ella Didrikson was truly an astonishing person. Known as the Babe, she won two gold medals in track and field at the 1932 Olympics. Musically talented, she recorded several songs for Mercury Records. A champion swimmer, diver, and bowler, she was best known as a golfer. Babe won eighty-two professional golf tournaments and made the cut against men in others. As opposed to other female golfers, Babe drove the golf ball like a man. In fact, the best male pro golfers said she ranked in the top ten in driving distance against men. As an example of her overall athletic ability, in a 1934 exhibition game, she pitched a hitless inning for the Philadelphia Athletics against the Brooklyn Dodgers.

Not everyone at Reno's Funmakers readily believed her achievements. Advance agent Frank Keagan was leery of her and became embroiled in arguments whenever Babe Didrikson was mentioned. He ended any discussion with, "I'd bet a million dollars that if you took her clothes off, you'd find a willie." There were a few sportswriters who shared that conviction.

Chapter Nine

The 1933 World's Fair was called The Century of Progress. Since it coincided with the celebration of Chicago's centennial, events were particularly festive. In spite of the Depression, the fair was a financial success, primarily because it had been financed by a $10 million bond issued the day before the stock market crashed. Additional financing was provided by the sale of memberships. Memberships allowed for the purchase of a certain number of tickets. The entire debt was paid off by the time the fair closed in 1934. In two years nearly forty-nine million visitors attended, forty million of which were paid admissions. For the first time in American history, an international fair paid for itself.

The fair's theme was "Science Finds, Industry Applies, and Man Conforms," and featured a Sky Ride, perpendicular to the shore of Lake Michigan, on which passengers could ride from one end of the fair to the other. Fair buildings were painted in various colors to create the appearance of a rainbow city.

Exhibits offered a menu that ranged from manufacturing to nightclub entertainment. On display were the automobiles of the future, Frank Buck's African Animal Zoo, and Ripley's Believe It or Not, just to name a few.

The midway contained several nightclubs with exotic themes. In the Old Morocco, Judy Garland and the Andrew Sisters performed. Another nightclub featured Sally Rand and her famous fan dance.

Sally was born Helen Harriet Beck and began acting on stage as Billie Beck. After she appeared in silent films, Cecil B. DeMille gave her the name Sally Rand. While designated by the motion pictures advertisers as one of their "Baby Stars" on the threshold of movie stardom, she became more noted for her ostrich feather fan dance.

The Reno's Funmakers group met with her backstage. At one time all of them had been burlesque actors and dancers. The fraternity of theatrical performers was always welcome backstage, whenever the occasion permitted. They understood the joys and sorrows of their chosen careers as no others could.

"You guys should go to Hollywood," Sally said. "There's no better time than now for getting in movies."

"Well, I don't think the chances are that good for me and Gladys," Ed said, "but I agree Pauline and Dutch can make it."

"I could never leave Mom and Dad," said Pauline.

"You got to grow up sometime, honey," Sally said bluntly.

Ed added, "There are a lot of people on the show to be considered. Shutting it down would seriously interfere with their livelihood. And disposing of the big top and trucks would be a major undertaking as well."

"I didn't say it was easy," Sally said. "I just said now is the time if you ever do it."

"It's certainly something to think about. How are things going for you?" Ed asked.

"I'm going to make more in two days here than what I made all year."

"Heard you had a little problem," Ed commented dryly.

"Oh shit, would you believe it. I got arrested for public indecency with all my clothes on. The outfit I wore gave the illusion of being naked. You know about illusions, Ed. Well, when I explained it to the judge, he let me go. Did I mention I gave him some free tickets?"

Everybody had a good laugh. "It sure is nice to see everybody again," Sally said. "Seems like we get so busy with our own problems that we forget how fortunate we really are to have such good friends." She smiled as she wiped away a few tears.

"Better stop with the tears or you'll have us all crying," Gladys said, wiping her eyes with a tissue.

The visit ended with promises to stay in touch and many hugs. Shakespeare wrote, "Parting is such sweet sorrow." Nothing was more apropos at that moment.

Ed wanted to see the first All Star baseball game held at Comiskcy Park, but good tickers couldn't be found. Instead, he visited Frank Buck's Jungleland. He had admired the famous "animal collector" after reading *Bring 'Em Back Alive* and seeing the movie of the same name. Frank now was on a roll, although the market crash in 1929 had left him penniless. Attendance for his Jungleland at the World's Fair exceeded two million people.

"I know your father," Frank said to Ed. "I think everybody all over the world knows him. People talked about the great magician wherever I went. Even on safari, the equipment bearers and guides knew who he was. I understand you continue in his footsteps."

"We have a traveling repertory show called Reno's Funmakers," Ed answered, "and yes, I have a magic act. It's impossible to walk in his footsteps, he has accomplished so much. Did you know he started when he was nine years old? Today's youngsters are still babies at that age."

"I know what you mean, Ed. We tend to protect them too much. These times, however, are making them grow up a lot faster. A lot of kids that see my show are homeless runways. God only knows what's going to come of them if this Depression hangs on. Has it affected your show much?"

"It hurts like hell," Ed said frankly. "It seems like nobody has the extra money to see the show, and we only charge 25¢ for the main seats and a dime for the cheap seats. Of course, we mainly play the South, and they're being hit the hardest."

"Is there anything I can do to help?" Frank asked.

"Not that I know of. Thanks for the offer anyway. Show people always are ready to help each other, but today we're all in the same boat."

"Ed, you've got to keep at it, though. This business is too important to just let it die out."

"That's the way I look at it as well. We can't hire as many people as we did a few years ago. Revenues are down too much." Ed gave a deep sigh.

"I think we've hung enough crepe for a while. Let's talk about things that are brighter. Are you enjoying the World's Fair? What have you seen so far?"

"Well, for one thing, we had a nice visit with Sally Rand. Your show is the only other I've been to, and the family is catching about everything around." Ed laughed.

"Good old Sally and her famous fan dance. You know, I met her when I was making movies in California. She helped me a lot and told me she was scared to death of animals. I kept teasing her about bringing a gorilla on the set just to see her. She could be sort of like Fay Wray."

"I bet that really sunk the duck," Ed said jokingly.

"Say," said Frank, "what are you guys doing for dinner? The treat's on me."

"I really appreciate the offer, but I promised my father we would drive down to Kankakee today," Ed said, sincerely disappointed. "That takes about three hours and I hate driving at night."

"I understand. Tell Reno the Great we had this conversation, and please let him know how much I admire him. We all like to get stroked once in a while."

Ed wanted to tell Frank about the big snake he and Dutch had tried to catch, but considering that one got away, he thought better of it.

The conversation on the ride to Kankakee was filled with comments about the fair. Pauline was still amazed by the giant in Ripley's exhibit. He had taken off his ring, and she could wear it as a bracelet. There was a lot of talk about Aunt Jemima's Kitchen, where you got all the pancakes you could eat for 10¢. The beauty and splendor of it all would never be forgotten, and they were exceedingly happy they'd been there and seen it.

By taking Route 54, they were able to go from central Chicago directly to Kankakee. The highway had improved to the point where they motored at the maximum speed of thirty miles per hour most of the way. The only things that slowed them down were passing through small communities and one stop for gasoline. The price of gas was 10¢ a gallon. In addition to the fair, the conversation focused on Reno the Great Magician and his recent marriage. Grandmother Emma had died in 1927.

Granddad married Helen Curtis two years later, but she passed away the same year from breast cancer. Now, at age seventy-three, he had married Minnie Oliver, a widow with several grown children. That marriage did not sit well with the passengers in the car.

"I still don't know why Granddad married her," Gladys said. "Wasn't she his housekeeper or something?"

"I guess so," said Ed. "Auline told me she was a neighbor and helped with keeping the house clean. He was concerned about his health and didn't want to live alone. The onset of Parkinson's forced him to slow down. Minnie can take care of him if he gets worse."

Gladys sighed. "Well, Auline's probably right, but it just doesn't seem proper."

"Don't say anything when we get there. We don't want to upset him."

Edward M Reno

FOUNTAIN PARK

Chautauqua!

Remington, Indiana

Aug. 6th to 20th, 1939, Inclusive

45th Anniversary

FIRST WEEK'S FEATURES

SUNDAY

SUNDAY SCHOOL-Free admission, 9:15 A. M.
SERMON LECTURE-W. O. Schanlaub, 10:30 A. M.
LECTURE-Dr. John Holland, 3:30 P. M.
CONCERT-Morocco Band, 4:45 P. M.
JACK'S XYLOPHONE BAND
        Afternoon and Evening, 2:30 and 8:00 P. M.

Childrens Story Hour, 9:15 Each Week Day
Drawing and Art Classes, 10:15 A. M. Each Week Day
Lecture by Rev. W. H. McLain on "Relation of Art and Religion"
        2:30 P. M. Each Week Day

BESSIE LARCHER DUO, Tuesday Afternoon and Evening

OXFORD CHOIR, Wednesday Afternoon and Evening

EDWARD RENO, MAGICIAN, Thursday Afternoon and Evening

THE COFFING SISTERS, Friday Afternoon and Evening

ATHLETIC CONTESTS, Directed by Prof. Albert Verrill, Saturday Afternoon

H. A. HENDERSON, TRAVELOGUE, With Pictures, Saturday Evening

This program is for your education and enjoyment. You will be pleased with the natural beauty of FOUNTAIN PARK

H. L. Williams, Pres., Remington, Ind.   Lee Evans, Sec., Remington, Ind.

"Now do you think I'm a dumbass who would mention that to him?"

"There sure is a lot of black flat land in Illinois," Pauline said in an attempt to change the conversation. "We don't have this in Georgia."

"You're right, hon," Gladys said. "We have too much red clay."

"Sylvie," Ed said. Sylvie was Gladys's nickname and mostly used by Ed. "You don't hold your tongue when you get pissed off. I just meant to remind you his marriage is a ticklish subject."

"If he didn't want anybody to talk about it, then the old bastard shouldn't have married her in the first place," Gladys said, and got in the last word.

Dutch, sitting in the back with Pauline, had his eyes shut, feigning sleep. He didn't want to be part of that conversation.

Route 54 made a sharp bend around Mound Grove cemetery on its way to Indiana Avenue. It was called Cemetery Curve by the locals because of the accidents when motorists took it too fast. The danger was hidden by newly planted elm trees, giving it a serene appearance. Even with knowledge of the pending peril, people would invariably test their speed, resulting in several accidents each year.

The minute the door opened, they were greeted with the familiar odor of cigar smoke. Edward Munn loved a good cigar after supper. His routine consisted of him getting up from the table, complimenting Minnie on the meal, walking to the parlor, sitting in his favorite rocker, and lighting up. Today was no exception, especially since he didn't know the exact time of arrival of his son and granddaughter. Minnie answered the door and ushered them into the parlor. After the customary hugs and kisses, they all took seats and got comfortable. Edward Munn always presented a striking appearance, since he was rarely seen without being dressed in suit, vest, and tie. His ample wavy white hair, combed straight back, added to the poise of this handsome and dignified man. Though no longer traveling, he still performed magic, entertaining at schools and at other special occasions. Unquestionably, Reno the Great continued to be the most famous celebrity in town. Several times during the week, visitors would pay their respects—a mandatory stop whenever they were in Chicago or anywhere thereabout. The visitors consisted mostly of show business personalities and other magicians, like Harry Blackstone and Howard Thurston. (Thurston passed away unexpectedly in 1936 due to a stroke and pneumonia. Pneumonia is referred to as "the old man's friend," but Thurston was only in his forties.)

The locals got their opportunity to pay court to the conjuror each day during his constitutional walk to the courthouse, where he would sit on his favorite bench. Along the way he would perform prestidigitation for those he met, especially youngsters who were totally captivated. He continued that practice well into his eightys.

A few animals used in his magic show were sentimentally retained and caged in the backyard as sort of an ersatz zoo. My great-grandfather was either proud of them or thought guests were interested, because visitors were given a tour, even if they had been there the week before. Rather than hurt his feelings, everyone maintained congeniality and observed the rabbits, guinea pigs, and doves as though for the first time.

In 1939 the International Brotherhood of Magicians held an encomium in the Gold Room of the Kankakee Hotel to honor his lifetime accomplishments. The convention lasted two days, and consisted of seminars, demonstrations, and activities of interest to the magicians in attendance. At its conclusion, the convention named Edward Munn Reno the Dean of International Magicians—a rare and most deserved honor for the pioneer showman of magic.

"We still have supper on the table," Minnie announced. "The mister already ate 'cause he didn't know when you all would get here. I'll just heat up a couple things and it ought to be done in about fifteen minutes, so you have time to wash up."

It was music to their ears, for nothing had been eaten since Aunt Jemima's pancakes that morning. As the ladies headed to the bathroom, Edward Munn said, "Eddie, wait here for a second, I want to ask you something." Ed Jr. took a chair next to his father.

"How are you doing? How much has the Depression hurt the show?" Edward asked in a sincere and serious tone.

"To be honest, it hurts like hell," Ed replied. "Receipts are terrible, nobody has any money with the economy the way it is. And to make matters worse, I'll probably lose the winter quarters in Athens."

"Don't you have a couple colored folks living there when the show is on the road?" the father asked.

"Yes, Hattie Robinson and her husband Frank. They work as housekeeper and maintenance. I couldn't afford to pay them very much, but they have room and board, plus free run of the place during the summer. You couldn't find anyone more trustworthy. Hattie does all sorts of things and cooks for us when we're back for the winter. Frank helps with repairs, getting the big top and trucks ready for the next season."

"What about the rest of the theatrical troupe?"

"They go their different ways and keep in touch for when we hit the road again."

Like many father and son relationships, periods of silence were part of the conversation. Neither party could truly open up and be himself. It's different for a man when talking with his mother. Mother and father both love their child the same, but the father is more of an authority figure, while a mother is more nurturing and forgiving. Many times, the mother serves as intermediary between a son and his father. This love-tension relationship between father and son, in all likelihood, began with Adam and his two boys, Cain and Abel. A son is always on a quest for praise from his father. For the most part, that quest is only occasionally fulfilled. Disappointments are shared with the mother, who continuously provides comfort and reassurance.

"Conditions are hard," Edward Sr. said. "I've never seen it this bad. Farmers around here may be hurting the most. Prices are too low to break even, let alone make a buck. They're afraid of losing the family farm to the bank. Roosevelt is trying lots of different things. So far, nothing helps very much. I've been told Al Capone, of all people, opened the first soup kitchen in Chicago. We don't have soup kitchens here, but the churches are working overtime. Minnie said little kids have come to the door and asked for food. It breaks your heart."

"On the trip up here we saw hundreds of people riding freight cars. I guess to look for work. It seems like a lot of them are just moving to be moving. Staying put gives them nothing. They live in tents and anything else that makes a shelter."

His father leaned forward and said in a low voice, "Did you know I married Minnie?"

"Yes, Dad, Auline told me. It came as a surprise, though."

"She's here all day anyway, cleaning house and doing laundry, so being married won't make much difference." Edward looked at his son. "You can't fool me. Your sister Auline is upset because Minnie comes in for a share of inheritance."

"Oh, Dad, I think she is only concerned for your happiness," Ed said.

"If she's so concerned about my happiness, then she can get off her butt and come see me once in a while."

"She was here last week, Dad."

"Well, she didn't stay long." Changing the subject, Edward said, "Anyway, if ever you feel like the show can't continue, you come to Kankakee. I own a couple houses and you're welcome to live in one. In fact, I'll give you one."

"Thanks for the offer, Dad, but I'm not ready to give up just yet. I've got an idea or two that will help me keep going. Got to try them first."

"So what are your plans now?"

"We plan to go and visit Sylvie's family before heading back south to Athens. First, I plan to sample some of Minnie's cooking," Ed Junior said, laughing, while hissing through his front teeth – his own fetching way of chuckling.

After the meal, everyone was in good humor and gathered in the parlor. The conversation centered on family and reminiscing over halcyon days in the past. As the evening progressed and the hour grew late, talk began to be interrupted by stifled yawns. There's no better way to end the day than to have a good meal and be surrounded by loved ones. The mood is comfortably sanguine, serving as the harbinger for a night of deep sleep and rejuvenation.

The next morning at breakfast, Dutch complimented Minnie, saying, "I don't know when I've had a better meal. You're an excellent cook."

"Oh, pshaw," Minnie said, embarrassed by the flattery. "There are two things my mother always told me—hunger is the best seasoning, and it's the company, not the cooking, that makes the best meal."

Dutch smiled. "That may be true, but I know a good meal when I have one, and it has to do with the cook."

"Well, forbid me from contradicting," Minnie replied.

Later they made the obligatory tour around town to see what changes had taken place since their last visit. Such tours mainly involved the Kankakee River and associated parks.

"Where should we go first, Dad?" Ed asked.

"Let's drive down to Electric Park. This will be the last time you see it," his father answered.

"Why's that?"

"They're shutting it down. Going to build a country club and golf course. A lot of the land was given by Frank Waterman, the fountain pen magnate. The park's gotten kind of run down the last couple years. I still think people are going to miss it."

As they approached the park, the outline of a roller coaster came into view. They could see also the dance pavilion and several picnic areas, which gave the scene a festive atmosphere. Other buildings included a live theater and food kiosks. Farther south was the swimming beach on the shore of the Kankakee River, great for boating and fishing. It was also a popular tourist attraction, and people could get there by taking a trolley car that traveled directly from the Illinois Central depot.

"Not much happening this time of year," Edward Munn said, "but in the summer the place is loaded. I've performed here several times myself to full houses. Times change, especially with this Depression going on."

They continued driving south until they stopped at the Kankakee River.

"That river is a story in itself," Edward said. "At one time it ran for two hundred miles and served as significant portage for French trappers to the Great Lakes and the Mississippi River. Actually, the Potawatomie Indians occupied the area first, hunting, fishing, and trapping beaver and the like. Back then the river meandered through the largest marsh and wetlands in the United States. As time went by, an effort was made to drain some of the swamp to cultivate farmland. Several large ditches were dug in order to bleed off the water. This, in turn, increased the size of the Kankakee, so it had to be dredged to help prevent flooding. We still get floods but, not to the extent we would have gotten without dredging. Today the river is about a hundred miles long and, as I mentioned, it serves for good fishing and outdoor recreation."

"Granddad, what happened to the Indians?" asked Pauline.

"Well, after the Civil War they were moved to reservations. Eddie, drive over to the dam."

The Kankakee River dam and powerhouse were located at the junction of River Street and Washington Avenue. It provided hydroelectric power to the state hospital and other residents on the southwest side of town. The dam was seventeen feet high and four hundred feet across. In late summer, when the river was low, the dam was boarded up to raise the water level. At such times, it became a great place for area fishermen, who could walk across below the dam and catch large fish by hand.

"That's impressive," Dutch said as he walked to the fence and watched a fisherman reel in a big catfish. He shouted, "Nice fish," but couldn't be heard over the roar of cascading water.

They watched the falls for a while and then decided to go to Old Fair Park. The Kankakee County Fair was held there annually. The accommodations were perfect, since they featured a large parcel of land and animal barns for livestock. There was also a half-mile track for both horse and automobile races. Not much was going on that day, except a few youngsters playing baseball on one of the diamonds. At one time Casey Stengel played there and managed the Kankakee baseball team.

"Is anybody getting hungry?" Edward asked.

Gladys replied, "I thought you'd never ask. I'm so hungry my stomach thinks my throat's been cut."

Edward grinned. He had always liked Gladys, because she never pulled any punches. You knew where you stood with her; there were never any doubts. She reminded him of his wife Emma. Life had stopped its upward progress when Emma died. Now it had just leveled off, taking each day as it came.

"Let's head home," he said. "Minnie is preparing the meal early today so she can visit one of her daughters."

As they drove back to the house, Edward stated, "I rode in one of those electric cars the other day. Can't remember what company made it. My neighbor has it in his garage and took it out for a spin. I kind of liked it. There wasn't any vibration or engine noise or smell of gasoline. He told me it would go for about ten miles and then the batteries needed to be recharged. I guess nobody makes electric cars anymore. Not very practical with the roads the way they are and gas at 10¢ a gallon."

"I think over in England they still make them," Ed said, "but you're right, Dad, not over here. Someday there may be use for electric vehicles other than cars. If they had a future, you can bet old Henry Ford would be making them."

"This is sure a nice car you got, son. What kind is it?"

"Naturally it's a Ford. A 1930 Model A sedan. I bought it used from a fellow who gave it up to feed his family. I probably paid more than I needed to, but my conscience is clear."

"The Depression is a terrible thing," Ed's father said hoarsely. "Folks are making so many sacrifices just to exist. Roosevelt tells us the only thing we have to fear is fear itself, but he's never been without. Let him lose his home and watch the wife and kids starve to death, and he'll see fear ain't got a damn thing to do with it."

"I think he was referring to people making a run of the bank, Dad," Ed said calmly.

"You know that I've been a Democrat my whole life. But it's been three years now and things aren't any better, maybe even worse. The people that's advising him scare me to death. They don't seem to have a clue as to what's going on or how to fix it."

"We can only hope things are better next year," Ed said.

Minnie was true to her word, and dinner was prepared almost as they walked in.

"Glad you're back," she said. "I'm going to visit my daughter Bernice for a while. She's been a little under the weather lately and could use a mother's visit, if you know what I mean."

That night, on the radio Gabriel Heater announced the arrest of Bruno Hauptmann for the kidnapping and murder of Charles A. Lindbergh's baby. Gabriel Heatter was better known for commenting on uplifting true stories. He was a man for the times, when Americans were in need of a morale boost. Tonight, however, the mood was somber. Heatter would later cover the trial and execution of the convicted killer. Gabriel Heatter became so popular that no one would believe it until they heard it from him. During World War II, his catchphrase became "There's good news tonight." I, too, have fond memories of staying with my grandparents and listening to Gabriel Heatter before going to bed.

Chapter Ten

Gladys's family came from Hurdland, Missouri. She had two sisters. Leota stayed in Hurdland, while Noemah moved to California. Her two brothers, George and Claude, resided in Minnesota. Gladys's visit was timed so she could attend their family reunion. Normally, Ed wouldn't get too excited about taking part, but this time, it fit into his plans. There was a bank in Kirksville that had previously made him a loan. The bank president, John Cornelious, was a great fan of vaudeville and passionate about magic. With the right collateral, Ed might be able to secure a loan to finance the 1935 season. Nothing ventured, nothing gained.

Leota Mills lived on a farm with her husband Joe. It was a typical little farm for the area, where the inhabitants raised their own food. The terrain was a combination of small hills and a goodly amount of flat, arable land. One knoll in particular was excellent for sledding in winter. You could start from the top and glide for nearly a quarter mile before coming to a stop. The trip back up was made effortless by an adjacent road. Looking from her kitchen window, Leota could see the peaceful landscape and a distant forest. In between stood the chicken house and other small outbuildings. The main barn, located to the side of her cottage, was unseen from her window. A free-flowing creek wound its way through a portion of plowable land, which meant Joe had to take his team of horses over to the road and across a bridge in order to work the other side. Joe's brother, Frank, owned a tractor but lived several miles away. However, there were certain terrains that required Joe to plow with his team of Prince and Pet.

Electric power had not yet reached the area. Therefore, farms were illuminated at night by kerosene lamps and, of course, candles. Until electricity became available, rural folks adhered to Ben Franklin's maxim of "early to bed and early to rise." It might have made them healthy and wise, but hardly wealthy. The Great Depression took care of that.

Mostly dirt roads lay between the Mills' farm and the town of Hurdland. It became the responsibility of each farm to grade the roads after heavy rainfalls, to flatten furrows. Funny how farm life appears idyllic to the outside observer, when in fact it mostly consists of very hard work.

Ed and Gladys had forgotten the exact route to the farm, so they drove straight to Hurdland and telephoned Leota from Gousset's country feed store and gas station. It wasn't long before Joe Mills arrived in a Model T Ford and suggested they follow him back.

When distant families reunite, it becomes a joyous occasion. Personal troubles and worries seem to fade away, to be replaced by the delight of togetherness--a tranquil period when the actual and truly important parts of life take charge. However, worries and woe never disappear completely. They just take a break for a while.

Leota and Joe were complete opposites. Leota was unpretentious, a dynamo of energy with a manic zest and a salty tongue. Joe, on the other hand, was tall, thin, and comfortable in his own skin. His calm composure seemed to inspire visitors to relax. He favored sitting in a rocker, smoking his pipe and staring straight ahead, his gaze giving the appearance that he was in deep thought. Blessed with a wry sense of humor, he made the perfect counterbalance for the extroverted Leota.

At first, plans called for holding the dinner in the house. That would require dividing into two groups, one in the kitchen and the other in the living room. But Mother Nature smiled on them and created a beautiful warm and sunny day. They ate outside. Everyone pitched in and helped Leota prepare the meal. Soon fried chicken, mashed potatoes and gravy, green beans, corn, and carrots were on the makeshift picnic table. All the vegetables were homegrown. Homemade bread and butter arrived next. For dessert, there was chocolate cake and ice cream. Joe purchased the ice in Hurdland and would start the cranking after the meal was finished. The men would take turns on the crank until the ice cream was made.

"Somebody go in the cave and get the milk," Leota shouted.

The "cave" was her storm cellar. This one was built underground just off the side porch. Storm cellars were commonly used for protection from tornadoes and high wind storms, but they also served as a place to store the glass jars of preserved food. Below ground, the temperature remained fairly constant year round. It provided a cool place in the summer to store milk while waiting for the cream to rise to the surface.

Once everyone was seated, Leota said tersely, "Dutch, you're a damn preacher, so why don't you say the blessing?"

Dutch smiled. "Shall we bow our heads and assume the attitude of prayer? Dear Heavenly Father, we come to you today to give thanks for this meal and our many blessings. We thank you for our family and the sunshine here outside, but most of all, we thank you for the sunshine you place in our hearts. Lord, we ask your blessing on the gentle hands that prepared this meal, and keep us all in the center of thy will, not only today, but forevermore. Through Jesus' precious name we pray, amen."

Everyone said amen, and then Leota said, "You're full of bullshit, Dutch, but that was a nice blessing." The meal commenced with Joe saying, "Please pass the chicken."

George and Claude Payne operated a paper mill in Minneapolis, Minnesota. After a few years of hard work, it began to be profitable, only to become a victim of the Depression. Hard times painted everyone in the room with one brushstroke. Each was hanging on as best he could, but the grip was getting weaker.

"We had to lay off all the workers," Claude said as they moved inside. "We do the best we can by ourselves, but it takes a week to do what we did in a day before."

"Selling out isn't an option," George said bluntly. "Not in these times: you could never find a buyer. How's Reno's Funmakers getting on?"

"The same as you guys," Ed confessed. "I've lost half the people, and the rest are mainly there for room and board. I have to put off maintenance on the equipment. We fix things now after they break down, and you know that's not the best way. All I can do now is hope things are better next season. At this very moment, I don't have enough to pay the taxes in Athens or start off on the road next summer. I've held off trying for a loan. Banks don't give a shit, so they're not freeing up any money. My hopes rest over here, or in Kirksville, that is. If I can't do something there, I'm out of ideas."

The kitchen cleanup was over, and Leota bounced in with a tray. "Cheer up, you bunch of sad sacks, I've got the coffee. You know what they say. 'Coffee should be black as hell, strong as death, and sweet as love.' How do you want yours, Claude?"

Claude answered with a grin, "Just the way I like my women, blond and sweet."

Leota stared at him, her eyes squinted, and said, "Hell will freeze over before you ever get one."

The mood lightened considerably. The room became full as everybody took part with the affable group. Much of the conversation included humorous anecdotes about themselves or their offspring. Self-deprecation, or joking about yourself, always tends to ingratiate a storyteller with his listeners. Plus, a good dinner reconciles everybody. In turn, each one had a story to tell. Pauline desperately wanted to tell about Dutch and the chamber pot but was stopped short by the look in his eyes.

The evening drew near, and they reluctantly realized they'd have to end the festivities. Claude said jokingly, "Well, if the ice cream is all gone, I think I'll leave."

"You ate enough to feed Coxey's army," June said.

"Just trying to be sociable."

"Like hell you were," she retorted. "Just think, I've got to sleep with him tonight."

"If he starts farting, make him sleep outside," Leota said.

With that, the party broke up.

Chapter Eleven

The following day Ed and Dutch made the trip to Kirksville. Gladys and Pauline stayed at home with Leota. As they were finishing with the breakfast dishes, Pauline said, "I'm still hungry, even with all I ate yesterday. I've got a serious craving for pickles, of all things." The sisters caught each other's eye.

Kirksville was only twenty miles from Hurdland, and the roads were good once they hit the highway. The bank of Kirksville, chartered in 1914, operated on good principles when it came to lending. By maintaining a strong cash reserve, it was able to still serve the community while withstanding the major effects of the Depression. Also, a strong Christian ethic on the part of the customers guaranteed people would borrow for needed items, rather than something they merely wanted. Bank president John Cornelius, shrewder than most, had one weakness—his love of vaudeville and conjuration. He had been smitten with the big top ever since he first went to a circus. The moment he stepped inside the tent, he knew what he wanted to do with his life. The pungent smell of canvas and hay, the towering center poles and high wire, plus three breathtaking rings of live excitement clinched the deal. He would join the circus. Over time, however, it was an unfulfilled desire when he faced the reality and responsibility of his father's bank. Slowly, through the years, the dream faded away. It became an unfulfilled wish, stored in his memory, which, like partly burnt ashes, rekindled with the slightest spark.

Rising from behind his desk, John extended his hand to Ed, saying, "My friend Ed Reno, it's been a while. Please take a seat and tell me why I have the pleasure of your company today. What's happening with Reno's Funmakers? Still going strong, I trust."

Ed introduced his son-in-law and then said, "We're still operating, but the tough times have taken hold. I'll come right down to it, John. We need a loan to cover taxes and start next year's season. I honestly believe I've made enough changes to be profitable in spite of everything. People want to see the show, but can't spare a dime. I've reduced my costs to where I can make it if only I had money to begin the year."

The bank president responded frankly, "Were it entirely up to me, there'd be no problem, but we have a board that has to approve any loan. I guess that's the reason we're still operating at a profit. Do you have any additional collateral besides your word and equipment?"

Ed reached for a small velvet bag with a pull string and emptied its contents on top of the desk. "These are the family jewels acquired during much better times. They originally cost a great deal. I'm hoping they retain enough value to get the loan."

"Exactly how much were you looking for?"

"Whatever amount my collateral covers," Ed replied.

At that point Ed's heartbeat slowed down, his tension lessened, and his stress began to subside. There was nothing more he could do. The decision would determine the future of the family and those connected with the show. Their conversation focused on show business and went on for over an hour. John told how he'd seen Blackstone's magic act and how impressive he was. To John's delight, Ed explained a little about how some of the illusions were done, carefully omitting principal parts. John was in seventh heaven when his secretary announced his next customer.

"Ed, you know I could talk forever about my favorite subject. Not many folks around here understand. Give me the phone number where you can be reached. The board meets tomorrow. I guess I've got to get back to work."

When Ed and Dutch returned to Leota's, Gladys and Leota had settled all questions. They were confident Pauline was expecting. All they could get out of Pauline was, "It's possible." Leota was elated. She immediately got on the party line telephone, listened for several minutes, then passed on the news. Leota wasn't the only one who would listen in for a while on the party line before announcing her presence. Sometimes a person would even interrupt an ongoing conversation to express his or her opinion on the matter. In cases of emergencies, however, the line was quickly relinquished. Best be careful of what you say on a party line, or the gossip mill will be operating full blast.

Later, Joe took Ed and Dutch rabbit hunting. Now Ed loved to fish, but he wasn't keen about killing animals. Dutch, on the other hand, had never gone hunting before, or even shot a 16 gauge shotgun, for that matter. Joe felt a 12 gauge wouldn't leave much of the rabbit after being hit. He explained the mechanics of firing the shotgun, and off they went. Frank, Joe's brother, also joined the party. He hunted with a pole about six or seven feet long.

Across the undulating fields, the expedition paraded with three coon hounds cavorting in front. It made quite a sight to Gladys and Leota, watching through the kitchen window. The first hour was invigorating, breathing in cold fresh air and with an optimistic autumn sun refusing to surrender to the coming winter. Frank kept them in stitches with non-stop banter and off-color jokes he couldn't tell with the women present.

"Over to your left, Dutch," Joe whispered. "Take careful aim and squeeze the trigger real slow."

Dutch, following instructions, put his cheek against the stock and pulled the trigger. There was a thunderlike report and small cloud of smoke as the shotgun kicked back and gave Dutch a black eye. The discharge made a crater five feet in front of the rabbit, who leaped in the air and dashed to a thicket in a nearby ditch. Joe couldn't keep himself from smiling and Dutch, though in pain, laughed as well.

At that point Frank climbed on the thicket and, using his pole, jabbed downward, killing two rabbits. Later, they became supper at Frank's house. The group continued hunting until dusk before deciding to call it a day.

Upon returning home, Leota shouted to Ed, "Mr. Cornelius called and said to tell you that your money is ready."

Three days later the 1930 Model A Ford was heading south, traveling to Athens, Georgia, its passengers happy as clams are in high water. Optimism abounded.

There was nothing like another chance to succeed and the eternal promise of future days.

Chapter Twelve

Gladys was anticipating another winter in her beautiful home. Ed was planning next summer. Dutch was considering a better mobile home design. And Pauline couldn't wait to see Hattie.

As they motored along the winding road, they could see the house. Its four white pillars gave it distinction and a reminiscence of bygone years. For Gladys, it evoked living in another world, the opposite to the one that required living in a trailer and moving from town to town. Ed appreciated the property for other reasons. The land and outbuildings provided storage for the tent and a place to repair and service the vehicles. The fear of losing it all was never totally erased from his mind. He kept telling himself that positive thoughts gave positive results. Also, in his possession was enough cash to bring about another season. Things had to improve by next year.

Hattie and Frank were standing on the front steps as the car pulled up. Their smiling faces said more than words could tell. Frank began carrying the suitcases inside, and Hattie gave everyone bear hugs, saving Pauline for last. The first chance Hattie got to talk to Ed alone, she said quietly, "Mr. Ed, that tax man has been around asking about you all."

"Don't you worry any, Hattie. I'm going to see him tomorrow."

Hattie was a big woman, not so tall as she was wide. Frank, her husband, referred to her as "plump as a dumpling." In spite of her corpulence, she was the undisputed champion for winning the hearts of those who knew her. Her pleasant face, black as ebony, would brighten any room she entered, as well as all its inhabitants. Hattie's delightful individuality was only outdone by her prowess as a chef. She could literally make a silk purse out of the proverbial sow's ear. Everyone loved her.

Before marrying Frank, Hattie's name was Littlefield. More than likely, as was the custom, her family came by that name when it was passed on by a plantation owner. Hattie's grandparents, Marie and Wilbur Littlefield, had been slaves. Slavery is the terrible blemish that stains the history of America and will never be forgotten.

In antebellum Georgia, a slave's life was harsh, even at its best. Most lived in wooden shacks with dirt floors. The less fortunate were forced to reside in hovels made with boards nailed together, its cracks stuffed with rags. Their beds consisted of straw or grass and one blanket. A single room often housed up to twelve people, including men, women, and children. Their diet was mostly cornmeal, and they received about eight pounds of pork or fish each month. For clothing, men received annually two linen shirts, two pairs of trousers, and one pair of shoes and socks. For this they were expected to work hard six days a week from daybreak to late afternoon. Slaves lived under the constant threat of being sold. When a baby reached one year old, the mother sometimes was put up for sale. Even babies were marketed. A child of seven or eight was expected to work on the plantation.

Governing rules for slaves prohibited them from going outside after dark, to gather in groups of three or more, to leave the property without a written pass, to own a weapon, and to learn to read or write.

Severe discipline was imposed to make slaves too frightened to revolt. However, some did rebel, and each time, more stringent laws were put in effect. The names of Gabriel Prosser and Nathaniel Turner come to mind. Back in 1800, Prosser, a literate enslaved blacksmith, planned a large slave rebellion in Richmond, Virginia. Slaveholders, however, learned about it beforehand and ended it before it began. Gabriel Prosser, along with members of the revolt, was ceremoniously hanged. Because Prosser could read and write, more laws were passed restricting the education of blacks.

Nat Turner was perhaps more successful, but his rebellion ended with the same results. Turner had natural intelligence and learned things quickly. Deeply religious, he learned to read the Bible and experienced visions. In one of his visions, he was convinced God gave him the task of slaying his enemies. He told a few trusted slaves about the vision and asked that they join him. In 1831 there were two solar eclipses, one in February, the other one later in August. He took the one in August as the signal to begin the rebellion. He and other slaves traveled from house to house killing any white people they met. Before the militia could respond, more than fifty men, women, and children were slain. The rebellion was put down in two days, but it took until the last of October to capture Nat Turner. He was found hiding in a hole covered with boards. For his actions, Turner was convicted, sentenced to death, and hanged. Several more blacks were executed for their part in Turner's slave rebellion. More than two hundred others were either beaten or killed by mobs.

Across southern states, even more laws were passed prohibiting the education of blacks.

Chapter Thirteen

It was in this atmosphere that Hattie's grandparents lived. While their particular master treated them well, the prospect of being sold was always in their thoughts. So much so that one night after working in the fields, Wilbur said to Marie, "I hear talk about running away. People are saying Master Littlefield don't got no more money and he's fixing to sell off some of us."

"Oh, Wilbur, I'd just die," Marie cried.

"I'm gonna keep my ears open, 'cause we ain't gonna be split up."

The seed of a plan was planted and getting ready to sprout. Wilbur began to look actively for a way to escape. Avoiding attention, he only spoke with allies, making sure they always appeared jovial. Laughing, while discussing the most serious event in their lives—escape. At last the day of departure was agreed upon. It had to be a Saturday night, because on Sunday, their day off, their absence would be less noticeable. At 11:00 p.m. on the appointed day, six shadows crept behind the houses, making their way from tree to tree, until a dash to the woods allowed them to disappear. In the breakaway, two older men, Patrick and Ben, had joined Wilbur, Marie, and their children, Leroy and Celia. After reaching the woods, their plan called for traveling north until they were out of Georgia. They knew the journey would be long and arduous, but they entrusted it to the Lord. Fortunately, the sky was overcast and the moon hidden, allowing them to walk the road and run for cover if lantern lights appeared. Even with the children they should cover at least twenty miles before daylight.

As morning broke, Wilbur found a place to hide until nightfall. There was a hollow depression on the side of a creek bed large enough to keep everyone out of sight. Patrick and Ben had other ideas, though.

"We ain't stopping," Patrick said. "Me an' Ben can put another twenty miles between us and Littlefield before they start looking."

"But it's too dangerous to be running in the daytime," Wilbur said.

"I'm too jumpy to stay put. Gotta keep rolling. We be wishing you an the missus good luck an' hope to see y'all in Beulah Land."

Quicker than a sneeze, they were gone.

On the southern plantations, "Beulah Land" was a term slaves used to refer to heaven and freedom. It later became a well-known gospel hymn with the chorus:

O Beulah land, sweet Beulah land!
As on thy highest mount I stand.
I look away across the sea
Where mansions are prepared for me.
And view the shining glory shore
My heaven, my home forever more.

That evening Marie and Wilbur resumed their pilgrimage north to freedom. Wilbur made a visible fix on directions when the sun came up in the east and knew they were still on the right track. After walking for a couple hours, the children turned petulant and wanted to be carried. They were scolded first, and then toted for a while. Realizing that couldn't continue, he told them, "You all got to be grown up now and walk on your own." The children grudgingly did as they were told.

The second night was much brighter. A moonlit sky overflowed with a blaze of glowing stars. The heavenly sea was telling earth how insignificant it really was. Such a night permitted Wilbur to avoid the road and travel mainly through the woods.

As dawn slowly drew near, they spotted a small farm. It looked rundown and was definitely not operated by the wealthy. Perhaps it was a place where the runaways could spend the day. Being confident they were at least forty miles from the plantation, Wilbur felt they could take this major risk. While Marie and the children hid behind a lean-to, Wilbur approached the door. He gave a short glance through the window and saw an old woman. Her hair was pulled back and tied with a ribbon. She sat in a rocker, a cup in her hand and her eyes closed as she rhythmically swayed to and fro. Wilbur tapped gently at the door.

"What do you want?" she asked, peering through a small aperture in the door.

"We be a free Christian Negro family, walking all night and needing a place to rest. We was wondering if you'd let us rest in your barn."

The old woman caught a glimpse of two children struggling in their mother's grasp. Her initial fears began to subside. Opening the door, she said, "Tell them to come on in."

"Thank you, ma'am, thank you, ma'am," a grateful Wilbur said.

As the family stood before the elderly widow, she said, "Cornbread, chitlins, sow belly, and greens, you all ain't free."

"Yes, ma'am. We be free," Wilber insisted.

"No, you're not. Just look at you. Your clothes give you away. Nothing but rags. You ain't going to get far dressed like that."

"Oh Lord, don't turn us in," he pleaded.

"Slavery ain't right. It ain't Christian not to be free. Me and my husband, bless his soul, probably seen harder times than you all, but at least we were free. I ain't turning nobody in. Just go on over to the barn and be quiet. Don't get many folks coming around since the mister died, so you will be safe."

The widow's barn was neat and dry, giving evidence of good care. No doubt, one of the legacies left by her husband. On one side were unoccupied animal stalls, save one, which appeared to have been used recently. Its inhabitant, a Jersey cow, was currently out in the pasture. Across from the stalls, the implements of agriculture stood idle. A year had gone by since their owner passed away, and some of the tools were beginning to rust from lack of use. For a moment, Wilbur's imagination conjured an image of owning a farm similar to this one. Marie interrupted his reverie when she found a ladder leading up to the hayloft. Sleep came easily once they climbed the ladder and lay down in the hay.

Later in the afternoon, the old woman walked into the barn carrying a large parcel. Standing by the ladder, she called, "Are you all up there?"

"Yes, ma'am, we're here."

"Come on down. I got something for you."

Her parcel contained some of her husband's clothes. Identifying each item, she said, "This suit of the mister's should fit you. You look to be about the same size when he was at your age. He wore it every Sunday 'til we got the one he's buried in. I put in a couple dresses for your wife. All little children run around in rags, or at least they become rags after they have been outside awhile. This other bag has some food in it. Do you see this here hankie? I put some red pepper in it. I've been told if a body covers their tracks with a little of it, hound dogs lose the scent. Tonight, follow the river. It turns north after a while and takes you to a preacher's house 'bout twenty mile or so from here. He's a good man and shares my feeling 'bout slavery. Be real careful, 'cause you know what will happen if you get caught. At best, you'll see the lash. At worst, they'll hang you. I could be arrested and go to jail just for helping you. That's the law. By the way, my name is Sister Sarah. You can tell that to the preacher, but nobody else."

With that she disappeared back into her house. Before the family ate, Wilber gave thanks, saying, "Thank you, Lord, for this food and for Sister Sarah. We know you be watching over us and sure hope you be guiding us to freedom."

When nightfall neared, they changed clothes. That was when Wilber found another bag containing onions.

"Why'd she give us so many onions, Wilbur?" Marie asked.

"I think she meant them for rubbing on our feet so as to throw off the hound dogs-- in case the pepper don't work. Come on, you kids. We be getting ready to do more walking."

Wilbur slowly opened the barn door and felt a draft of warm air blow in. Off in the distance a flash of lightning was followed by a frightening, loud thunderclap, making the hairs on his arms stand up.

"My God, is it ever going to rain, but we can't stay here no longer. Guess we're gonna have to get wet."

The rain might be more fortunate than Wilbur thought. It surely would cover their tracks, and the red pepper could be saved for later. They all made a dash for the woods to hunt for the river. No use worrying about getting wet; they were soaked to the gills already. The treetop canopy kept some of the rain off, but not enough to stop them from receiving a thorough drenching. Progress was at a snail's pace. Their main focus was moving in the right direction, which the ink-black night made increasingly difficult. Each time they reached a small clearing, they quickened their pace, only to slow back down to a crawl once the forest got denser. After four hours, Wilbur surmised they had advanced eight or nine miles and began to keep an eye out for a place to rest. As luck would have it, they stumbled on a makeshift shelter, probably used by hunters when pursuing feral hogs or deer. It offered limited protection from the elements, but had a slant roof made from wood planks.

"It will keep some of the rain off," Wilbur whispered, and with an arm around Marie's waist, he guided her and the children into the shelter. The children had been whimpering most of the way, but they stopped when Wilbur opened the large cloth tote bag and said, "Let's see what the nice lady gave us to eat."

Chapter Fourteen

"Freedom is not a gift bestowed upon us by other men, but a right that belongs to us by the laws of God and nature." ~Benjamin Franklin

"Over here, Mr. Littlefield," someone shouted. "I believe the dogs have picked up their scent."

The runaways were now being pursued. Federal law allowed bounty hunters and citizens to capture escaped slaves in the north, or any other place, and return them to their masters. Littlefield had engaged the services of Caster Fogg, the meanest, most brutal bounty hunter in the south. Nothing was too gross or monstrous for his captious character. Uneducated, violent as a wild boar, and mentally dense, Fogg was convinced Negroes were less than human and fair game if they became fugitives. His recapture rate was exceptionally high, with most of his prisoners hanged for punishment. Man, woman, or child made no difference to Caster Fogg. Today he had engaged three hunting dogs and two bloodhounds, along with two helpers.

Littlefield remained puzzled as to why one of his slaves would want to run away. He took pride in himself for his leniency toward them. They were properly fed and allowed to grow vegetables in their own garden plots. They received a generous supply of clothing, and each family was provided with a wooden cabin. He allowed them to belong to churches, and some were ordained as preachers. A few had learned to read and write. The more trusted could moonlight in their free time. Their physical health was maintained by a qualified physician. True, occasionally families were broken up when members were sold; but never before the age of nine, and he only sold when he had to. He often ostracized cruel slave owners and frowned on miscegenation. Didn't that make him a good slave master?

The rain began to lessen, and with the protection of the forest canopy, the runaway family once again resumed their flight. Wilbur attempted to continue traveling due north but realized that, without a compass, veering one way or the other was a strong possibility. His focus now was to find the river and follow it, looking for the church Sister Sarah had referenced. About three hours later they met the riverbank.

"Praise the Lord, Marie, that be the river the nice lady told us 'bout. We just follow it 'til we see the church." By following the river, they increased their pace without worrying they'd lose their way. A light from the church appeared shortly before dawn.

The pastor of the Friends of Christ church was Sylvester Nash. He and his wife, Rebecca, were childless, a situation they accepted as the will of the Lord. A love of humanity had replaced their parental instincts. They were devout abolitionists, and spoke out against slavery at every occasion. Many of their neighbors suspected them of abetting runaways, but considering the Nashs' position in the community, they decided to let well enough alone. Some agreed with them, while others felt it best not to cause any trouble for the popular pair.

Wilbur found Reverend Nash reading by lamplight and planning the next Sunday's sermon. The pastor was so engrossed that, at first, he didn't hear the tapping on the window. When it registered, he was so startled, his heart skipped a beat. Visitors at this time of morning usually meant one thing.

"Come around to the side door," he whispered.

The pastor opened the door quickly and ushered Wilbur in.

"Who are you?" he asked, staring hard at Wilbur. "What do you want coming around here so early in the morning? The sun isn't even up yet."

Looking down, Wilbur said, "Sister Sarah told us we should come to you."

"We? How many are you?"

"There be my wife and two children hiding outside."

"Tell them to hurry in here and be very quiet."

The others hastened into the house and stood before the pastor, holding one another's hands. The clergyman smiled at Marie and patted Celia on top her head.

"Are you folks hungry? Have you eaten anything this morning?" he asked as he closed the curtains. "I'm going to wake up Rebecca so we all can have some breakfast."

The meal was spare, but warm and tasty. Many church members were cash poor and tithed with their labor and food stuffs, some of which Wilbur and his family consumed at this first blush of dawn.

"Whereabouts you people from?" Rebecca asked.

"We be from the Littlefield plantation. That be southwest of Savannah."

"Did Mr. Littlefield treat you mean?"

"I guess not, ma'am, but he were gonna sell some of us. Most likely either me or Leroy here." Wilbur put his arm around his young son. "Y'all ever think what that does to a family?"

"We certainly have," Rebecca answered frankly. "That's one reason we're going to help you find freedom."

"God bless you," Wilbur murmured, his eyes swimming in tears.

Reverend Nash said, "Right now we need to find the best place for you to spend the daylight hours. I believe we have an excellent spot."

Wilbur and family were escorted to the storm cellar, located in the church basement. Chairs, tables, and church paraphernalia consumed much of the space and hid a door in the back. Behind the door was a small room with a table, chairs, and two cots.

"Not exactly the Peabody Hotel," Rebecca said, "but safe. I'll be around later today with dinner. Get some rest while Sylvester and I try to figure what you need to do next."

Wilbur's head was in a spin. Things were happening too fast for his methodical nature. Self-reliance wasn't enough. He faced the fact that they needed help from outsiders. An unplanned circumstance, but necessary, if their perilous journey was to be successful. Marie and the children slept; she due to being physically exhausted, while the children slumbered with the sleep of innocence.

That evening, Rebecca brought dinner and, after eating, they all began to devise the best plan for moving forward. They knew they would not be safe until they'd crossed the Ohio River and taken refuge in Westfield, Indiana. It was there they'd find another Friends Church. At that point, help would be provided by Riley Moon and his wife, Susannah.

The Moons were connected with the Underground Railroad and had aided many escaped slave families, by hiding them on their farm during the daytime and then helping them on to Canada at night. (Ironically, Riley and Susannah Moon were related to Dutch Moon. The Moon family originally came from Wales. Sir William Moon was an attendant to Queen Victoria. Prior to the American Revolution, two brothers came to America, one family settling in Pennsylvania and the other in North Carolina. The Carolina family moved to Indiana in 1820 and, being the first settlers in the area, built the first log home. Two or three years later, they established residence in Westfield. Dutch's ties to the Friends Church are no coincidence. You may recall he was a singing evangelist when he joined the show.)

"Follow the Ogeechee River all the way to its source," Reverend Nash said. "Take care. The land is heavily forested, but there are many cypress swamps and shoals. Wilbur, we will give you some tools. Best way to travel the swamps is by raft. There's plenty of timber to make one. The river is calm, but the closer you get to its headwater, you'll find some rapids and small falls. Just keep to the west side and you should be okay. Tonight, after traveling about twenty miles or so, you will come to a little town called Jewel. They have a Quaker church. I don't know the minister's name, but I know the way Quakers feel about slavery. I expect your family can spend the day there. And keep using the red pepper along the way."

Chapter Fifteen

The hunting dogs were in a foaming frenzy, snarling and snapping at the air as they attempted to climb the ladder leading to the hayloft.

"I know you're up there. Come down or I'll send the dogs up," Fogg shouted as he motioned his deputy to bring the plank leaning against the barn wall. The dogs could use the plank to climb into the loft.

"This is my last warning," Fogg added. He knew what his dogs could do, having seen them in action before, attacking both man and beast. Trained to be vicious, they either treed or killed their victims. Even a Georgia black bear was frightened of their assault. Delighted at the refusal his captives were making, Fogg sent the dogs up.

The screams turned Littlefield's stomach. As he expelled his breakfast, the bitter taste of bile overwhelmed him. He had to get out of there. He hadn't figured on such a horrible scene. He simply wanted to get his slaves back, that was all. He'd never considered an event such as he'd just witnessed.

Castor Fogg knew he didn't have a snowball's chance in hell of finding whoever was in the loft alive. He always had mixed feelings about that. While he immensely enjoyed the work of his dogs, a sizable sum of cash was lost. The agreed upon bounty for the capture and return of Littlefield's fugitives amounted to about $1,200 dollars, or 25 percent of their market value. Any other runaways captured would normally return a lesser bounty. Fogg, however, was known to illegally sell his catch for larger sums, should the occasion present itself.

Once the dogs were retrieved, the hunting party gathered itself and returned to its original quest. According to Fogg's deputy there wasn't much left of the body to examine. All he could tell was that it was a white man and he was very old.

When night had fully arrived, Wilbur and Marie also resumed their search for freedom. Wilbur had realized they would not reach their goal without assistance from caring individuals outside the racial family. This perplexing fact ran counter to his prior beliefs, leaving him both confused and thankful. Very few runaways reached freedom. Most were caught and returned to their owners, or they went back on their own accord after experiencing the hardship and severity of life on the run. To Wilbur, going back was never an option. The best he could figure, when they got to Jewel, they would have traveled about 120 miles. Each step meant a step closer to freedom. It also meant a step nearer to a Georgia swamp. As the ground got wetter underfoot, he came to the realization that now was the time to build a raft. It turned into a family project, and everyone pitched in. Backtracking several yards, Wilbur found pine trees of the proper size. Aided by a brilliant moon and employing the tools provided by Reverend Nash, he felled one tree and then another, until a proper pontoon took shape. Unfortunately, the prodigious effort consumed a major portion of the night, leaving Wilbur with two choices. Either attempt to hide in the open or travel by daylight.

The raft floated better than his best expectations, and with a hewed pole as its propelling motor, it glided smoothly across the Ogeechee swampland.

They now understood Rebecca Nash's insistence that they cover themselves with a strange substance she provided in a glass jar. The air teemed with morning mosquitoes. Wilbur guided the raft, avoiding nature's obstacles as best he could. Progress was slowed by reed mace and cattails that were grounded well below and extended several feet above the water's surface. The scene, however, was also decorated with a splash of dazzling and intense color. Wildflowers and water lilies contributed to the splendid view.

Marsh birds were actively searching for their morning food. Herons and egrets occupied the edges, while ospreys and a red-shouldered hawk made forays over the water. Negotiating the swamp by raft offered dangers as well. The swampland served as home for various snakes, the most feared of which were the cottonmouth, or water moccasin, and tree snakes. Having a tree snake fall in a raft while passing under a cypress creates a special kind of excitement. And lest not we forget the Georgia alligator, which anticipates that anything in the water is something to eat.

"You young'uns keep your hands outta the water," Wilbur said firmly. "There be things in there that could hurt you."

The water was warm and pleasant to the touch, but Leroy obeyed his father. Pulling Celia's hand out, he wished he at least had some stones to pitch across. Why is it in our nature to skip stones when we come upon a body of water?

Chapter Sixteen

Gladys was preparing the holiday dinner, a responsibility she thoroughly enjoyed and had sustained over the years. Of course, Hattie figured in greatly with most of the preparations. Gladys mainly baked custard pie. Granted, her custard pie was something to die for, and she felt that singular effort gave her justification for claiming responsibility for the entire meal. Naturally, others who lived under the Reno roof knew better, and privately complimented Hattie at the first opportunity. At the table, family and guests displayed a carefree and cheerful mood. And why not? Ed had paid the back taxes and was still financially able to begin another season; Pauline and Dutch were elated, anticipating the forthcoming birth; and Gladys had provided another successful holiday repast.

Still, the specter of the Great Depression loomed in the back of their minds. Unemployment had grown to over 23 percent, making it worse than it had been at this time the previous year. Ed tried not to think about it, hoping his efforts to economize would allow them to turn a profit.

President Roosevelt continued to offer rhetorical optimism. However, his policies seemed to make matters worse. Certain outcomes fed upon each other. The marketplace, stymied by drastically reduced international trade and lack of funding, could not improve. The end result was serious deflation. Roosevelt, distrusting both Wall Street and big business, concentrated remedies on government social programs, which gave some relief but no permanent jobs. The population was stunned and discouraged, with some sensing an apocryphal duration of the bad times. Roosevelt appeared to be their only hope; thus, his popularity endured at the highest levels.

Pauline's baby was due in June. She planned to continue her role with the show, convincing her father it would be for the best if Hattie and Frank joined them. Ed knew Hattie had a calming influence over Pauline, but he left the decision to accompany them up to her. As the weeks passed, Pauline found herself increasingly under Hattie's watchful eye. Without years of formal education, Hattie instinctively understood the need for a proper diet as part of prenatal care. She became as vigilant as a mother hen, looking for anything unusual throughout Pauline's term.

"It be wrong, you smoking while expecting a baby," Hattie said. "You don't want to hurt that child."

"How could that ever hurt someone not even born yet?" Pauline asked.

"Everything you does affects that baby. When I see you smoking, I want to turn you over my knee," Hattie said with conviction.

"How did you get to know so much about having babies?" Pauline asked. "Did you and Frank have children?"

"Yes Miss Pauline, we had a little boy we named Tyrell, after Frank's father," Hattie answered. "He was the sweetest child you ever did see, and made us very proud."

"You've never mentioned him. Does he live here in Georgia?"

With a pained look in her eyes, Hattie explained, "No, Miss Pauline. Tyrell died when he was about six years old. A fever took hold of him and the Lord Jesus came and took him home. The Lord knew how sweet he was and just had to have him."

"Oh, Hattie, you make me cry. You must miss him very much."

"I truly do, but I talk to him every day and that helps. Every night I let him in on things that happened during the day and tell him to be a good boy and mind. He knows all about you having a baby."

Pauline's handkerchief wouldn't hold anymore tears, and she ran from the room to find another.

The English poet and hymnodist William Cowper referred to winter as "the ruler of the inverted year."

During the year 1934, another ruler, Mao Tse-tung, along with 25,000 troops, began a 6,000 mile journey that came to be known as the Long March. His army was one of several others, combining for a total of more than 80,000 soldiers. Because of hunger, sickness, freezing temperatures, desertion, and military casualties, only about 7,000 remained when the destination of Shaanxi in the north of China was reached. It became a significant episode in the history of the Communist Party of China and sealed the personal prestige of Mao Tse-tung.

Here in America, the winter saw justice served as FBI agents killed the notorious bank robbers Pretty Boy Floyd and Baby Face Nelson in shoot-outs. Just prior to Christmas, America heard for the first time "Santa Claus Is Comin' to Town," and lastly, President Roosevelt planned to change the name of Hoover Dam to Boulder Dam, and did so in 1935. (It would be changed back in 1947.)

Georgia winters are usually mild, this one especially so. Any doubt that spring wasn't just around the corner was put to rest by the vernal equinox and brilliant spring flowers. The Blue Ridge Mountains become ablaze with the colors of yellow, red, white, and purple. The lemon-scented primrose and dainty white petals of rocket-shaped shooting stars were now prevalent. Valleys started to demonstrate a blue carpet of veronicas and columbines, with their red exteriors and yellow centers. Ironweed, spiderwort, and sunflowers contributed to the enthusiastic display. The northern migration of monarch butterflies enhanced the scene as they sought milkweed plants in order to continue another generation. In Athens, the moss-draped oaks now had company. Cherokee rose was in bloom, and the cheerful song of the brown thrasher was more readily heard.

The mood of Earth's inhabitants noticeably changed as well. Rarely did a human face pass by without a genuine smile. Mending the canvas, servicing the vehicles, and other routine maintenance was completed in a timely fashion. Ed spent several days writing letters, alerting cast members to the date of departure, and beckoning them to come to Athens a couple weeks ahead of time for rehearsals.

With the time of departure set, Reno's Funmakers would once again open the season in Elberton, then on to Hartwell and Lavonia. Nestled in the foothills of the Blue Ridge Mountains, Lavonia gave newcomers an opportunity to become acquainted with mountain travel. It served to prepare them for later on in North Carolina and Virginia.

The history of the Blue Ridge Mountains is quite interesting. Noted for their bluish color, they form the eastern front of the Appalachians and extend from Georgia to Pennsylvania. Narrow in the east (one to two miles wide), they expanded to up to sixty miles as they enter Georgia. The mountains were formed by geological uplift phases, beginning a billion years ago. In Georgia, the Blue Ridge creates distinctive weather patterns. Valley temperatures are six to eight degrees cooler during summer, and ten to twelve degrees cooler at the mountain tops. Rain and snow is appreciably greater than at lower levels, and the total rainfall is only exceeded by the Pacific coast.

The Spanish explorer Hernando DeSoto is believed to be the first European to reach the Georgia Blue Ridge Mountains, having come upon them while in search of gold in the year 1540. Although others preceded him, the famous American naturalist, William Bartram, visited the Georgia range in 1776 while exploring the Cherokee Nation.

The Cherokee Indians farmed the valleys and hunted in the mountains until the population of Georgia dramatically increased. Indian lands were continuously taken, forcing the Cherokee farther into the frontier. The State of Georgia gave away mountain land via several land lotteries, and in 1828, gold was discovered in the North Georgia Mountains. The Cherokee weren't nomads and had taken to the customs of the settlers. Their reluctance to continue moving resulted in Congress passing the Indian Removal Act, which President Andrew Jackson quickly signed into law. The Cherokee established themselves as an independent nation and took the matter to the Supreme Court. The Court ruled that the Cherokee could not be forced from their land and would have to agree to a removal treaty. By obtaining a treaty, with very few Cherokees in agreement, President Jackson had the legal document he needed. Ratified in Congress by a one-vote margin, the United States began the removal of the Cherokees from Georgia to Oklahoma.

Men, women, and children were uprooted from their land, herded into makeshift forts, and then forced to march a thousand miles. Human loss was extremely high. Chief John Ross finally asked the commanding general, Winfield Scott, to allow his people to lead the tribe west. Chief Ross organized smaller groups, permitting them to forage the forests for food. About 4,000 died as the result of the forced march, later called The Trail of Tears.

Chapter Seventeen

Pauline, now well into her pregnancy, was somewhat limited as to what she could do for the show. Her tap dancing routines would have to wait. She, however, remained active in the plays and comedy routines. One in particular was a vaudeville act in which she played the straight man and her father a freckle-faced, red-haired doofus named Tobey. Ed loved to play the role of Tobey. Besides the red wig, he would blacken his front teeth to give the appearance of some missing. It was an audience favorite. A popular line was when Pauline asked, "Have you ever been made the butt of a rare anecdote?" Tobey responded with, "You bet I have. I've been butted by nanny goats lots of times."

Ed Reno's magic act was the main feature and finale each night. After a complimentary introduction, the houselights would dim and a spotlight focused on one end of the stage. Ed entered, dressed in a dark suit and vest, his famous mane of hair combed straight back, and quickly began a monologue and sleight of hand deception. A bouquet of flowers appeared from nowhere. Large silk handkerchiefs were pushed into the opening of his fist and, presto, disappeared. The beginning part of Ed's magic act continued as the band set the stage for each trick with an exciting musical score, creating mystery, spectacle, and surprise.

"Magic is the age-old story of the hand being quicker than the eye," he said. "Illusions are merely an attitude of mind created by the magician. Or is it really magic? Tonight you will be able to decide for yourself. So now, on with the show."

A cymbal crashed in the band pit, and half the startled audience almost jumped from their chairs.

The son of Reno the Great walked to the front of the stage and held up four metal rings to show those in the reserved seats that the rings were solid. He next called for someone in the audience to come to the stage and examine them himself. A young man took the challenge, and was directed to a chair alongside the magician's worktable. It was agreed that, yes, they were completely solid. Again, walking to the front of the stage, Ed held the rings up. The four of them were linked together. How did it happen? When did it happen? When Ed handed them back to the lad in the chair, the rings were separate again. The audience was asked to give the lad a big hand as he retook his seat.

A covered pan rested on the magician's worktable. Ed removed the lid so everyone could see it was empty. Also on the table were two eggs. He broke them and dropped the raw eggs into the pan.

"We all like to have eggs for breakfast," he said. "But what if we only wanted chicken? All we need to do is reverse the process." Raising a small cruet, he said, "This will give it a better flavor," and sprinkled the liquid over the eggs. He struck a match, flame popped up in the pan, and he put the lid on.

"It only takes three minutes to have our eggs. Let's see if we can have chicken in the same amount of time." He removed the lid, and two beautiful white doves flew out and circled the tent before returning to the table. An assistant appeared, gathered the doves, and left the stage while the spectators began to think real magic was possible.

For well over an hour, the audience was in perpetual awe, and gave each illusion a resounding cheer and applause. As the act drew to its conclusion, Ed approached the front of the stage with a large piece of white cardboard. He turned it front and back to show it was only that. After folding the cardboard into a cone shape, he tapped it with his wand. Reaching in, he began to pull out beautiful silks, so many that his table couldn't hold all of them. Ed showed the audience the cardboard once again, and then rolled it into a cone once more. This time, after a tap of his wand, he pulled out a large rabbit. With each trick, the band played accompanying music.

Finally, Ed made a last cone. He extended his wand. A ribbon appeared at its end, and he twirled the wand until the endless ribbon became a circle, growing larger with each twirl. It became so large that even with Ed's unusual strength, he had trouble maintaining. The band played "Stars and Stripes Forever" and the onlookers, standing in salute, cheered, whistled, and applauded. This was why they came.

Magic can be traced to the beginning of recorded history. Magicians performed in pharaohs' courts in Egypt, and in the streets of ancient Greece and Rome. Later, some claimed Christ was a magician and his miracles only illusions. The famous Indian rope trick was demonstrated six hundred years ago. For that particular trick, a rope, coiled like a snake, uncurls and rises upward vertically. When fully extended, a small boy can climb to the top. Magicians were quite popular throughout history, but not without the danger of their illusions being called witchcraft. We all know what happened to witches. By the mid-1700s modern magic took place at fairs. Once their act caught on with the upper classes, magicians performed in theaters, which led to the great traveling tent show. The long star-covered robe was discarded in favor of a tuxedo with tails. Harry Kellar, the first American-born magician, traveled around the world performing his trade. After 1884, his tour was mostly in the United States. When he retired, fellow magician Howard Thurston took over his show and made it even bigger. During the late 1800s, many magicians got their start in the variety shows of vaudeville. Edward Munn Reno, known as Reno the Great, was a prominent pioneer of the time. Reno would go on to be known worldwide before he finally retired in Kankakee, Illinois. He was also the founder of Reno's Funmakers.

As the season continued, Ed made sure handbills and posters went up in the towns they visited two weeks in advance, and judging by the receipts from the first week, the advertising made a big difference. They played to a packed house every night, and intermission candy sales rose back to pre-Depression numbers. Ed couldn't account for the increase, since times had gotten worse. Actually, FDR's works program had reached northern Georgia. The heads of households were being paid for labor on a multitude of projects, ranging from paving streets to planting trees. They received an hourly wage that was slightly more than relief, and a little less than private employment would provide. Reno's Funmakers experienced similar results in

Hartwell, giving Ed even more encouragement and boding well for the summer.

Pauline couldn't ask for more. The show was profitable, her father was happy, a baby was coming soon, and Hattie was traveling with them.

Chapter Eighteen

"If you want to be free, there is but one way; it is to guarantee an equally full measure of liberty to all your neighbors. There is no other."-Carl Schurz

Wilbur and his family had reached a point where the raft was no longer needed. He had the presence of mind to disassemble his handiwork and scatter the timbers, eliminating any evidence of their original use. They had crossed a swamp in broad daylight, the most perilous moment of the escape thus far. They had no way of knowing whether they had been seen or not; only blind luck had saved them. The daylight hours were drawing to a close, and with a pale moon taking shape, it was turning dark.

The flight to freedom had turned topsy-turvy. They should be traveling at night and hiding during the day. Now, nightfall was upon them and Wilbur sought another place of refuge. He needed advice, he needed rest, he needed to find that doggone church.

The Quaker Church of Jewel was about a mile from where Wilbur stood. Its minister, Ethan Meijer, had moved from the Netherlands to Jewel, where he and his wife Isabella settled after they arrived in the United States. Born and raised in Sweden, they strongly opposed an indifferent attitude when it came to slavery, and took every opportunity to support abolition. Accordingly, they were well aware of current laws when it came to abetting runaway slaves. It came down to their strong beliefs and a law they felt immoral and wrong.

Initially, hearing a gentle tapping at the back door and finding Wilbur standing there, gave them pause. They didn't recognize him. He wasn't from their congregation. The fact that it was daylight indicated he wasn't a runaway slave either.

"Who are you?" the minister asked. "What can we do for you this fine morning?"

"We been traveling the swamp all night," Wilbur answered. "The Reverend Nash said for us to find you."

"Sylvester Nash?"

"Yes, sir. He be the one."

"Come in quickly," Ethan said. He leaned outside, looking from left to right. "You should travel at night, not during the day."

"I knows that, but it got turned 'round 'cause I had to build a raft."

"Well, you're here now and, if you weren't spotted, we can help quite a bit," Ethan said. "This is my wife Isabella. She will show you where your family can spend the remainder of the day. Hopefully, that will give me enough time to arrange the next leg of your liberation. I will need to contact a conductor friend of ours."

Wilbur caught the word "conductor." It was a term he had heard in the fields. It had to do with the railroad, another term he'd heard as well. Up until now, he and Marie had been basically on their own. While goodhearted folks had been instrumental in assisting them this far, the need for partnership with a more formal organization was obvious. They had been traveling in the teeth of Haros and surviving by the fickle whims of destiny. As any gambler will tell you, good luck does not last forever.

Opinions regarding slavery were a mixture of sentiments, ranging from the necessity of it to keep the South, mainly dependent on agriculture, competitive with the more industrialized North; to the religious view that slavery was an aberration before the eyes of God. Significant opposition came from the Christian churches, especially the Religious Society of Friends. Quakers, however, were not alone. Some of the mainstream denominations, along with abolitionists and others sympathetic to their cause, became active in protest and helping runaway slaves find freedom. They used railroad terms like *conductors* for those assisting along the escape route, and *stations* or *depots* for safe houses, where fugitive slaves could hide during the day. The operation became known as the Underground Railroad. It was estimated that by 1850, nearly 100,000 slaves escaped using the railroad. A significant number, yet only less than 1,000 a year from all slave-holding states. (The act prohibiting the importation of slaves became law in 1807, ending the transatlantic slave trade. Slavery, however, continued to grow by the natural increase in slave families. Total slavery amounted to a little over one million people in 1810, and grew to nearly four million by 1860.)

Escaped slaves mostly traveled on foot or occasionally by wagon. Routes were purposely indirect, in order to perplex federal marshals and bounty hunters. At first, the effort was to flee to free states, since their citizens were somewhat indifferent to existing fugitive slave laws. Pursuit mainly consisted of wanted posters and newspaper ads, giving notice of an escapee and the amount of a reward. That all changed with passage of the Fugitive Slave Law in 1850. After its enactment, not only federal marshals, but civilians could lawfully capture runaways in the North. Furthermore, those who aided fugitive slaves were now punishable by law. Such draconian measures were instrumental in bringing about the Underground Railroad, with Canada the primary destination.

One of the most famous American heroes before the Civil War was Harriet Tubman. Born a slave, she rescued more than seventy runaways during a ten- year period. As a slave she was beaten and whipped by various monstrous masters. One of whom threw a metal object at another slave and struck Harriet in the head by mistake. The wound pained her throughout her life, causing seizures, headaches, and hypersomnia. In 1849 she escaped from a plantation near Blackwater River in Madison, Maryland, only to return to free family members. Tubman was instrumental in establishing the Underground Railroad. When the Civil War broke out, she joined the Union Army, serving as a cook, nurse, and scout. In her later years, she became active in promoting women's suffrage. Today Harriet Tubman is an American icon for freedom.

Wilbur and his family spent that evening and the following day in hiding at the church in Jewel. As dusk drew near, Ethan and Isabella returned to talk to them.

Ethan said, "Later tonight a Negro gentleman will arrive with a wagon. Follow his direction explicitly. He will transport you to Crawfordville. At that point you will receive additional instructions. Do you have any money? Here is twenty dollars. It's for you in case of emergencies. Do you understand?"

Wilbur nodded.

"All right then. Be prepared to travel at about eight-thirty or nine o'clock this evening. We'll let you know once everything is ready."

With that, the Meijers left the room. Wilbur looked at Marie, who was embracing the children, and whispered, "I'm kinda scared."

"Me too," Marie quietly replied. "What time do you think it is now?"

"Don't know for sure, but it's been dark for a spell."

Sometime later a knock sounded on the door, and Marie found Isabella standing on the other side.

"It's that time," Isabella said.

Once outside, they saw a sturdy farm wagon covered by well-worn gray canvas. The rectangular wagon, a favorite on plantations, was comprised of flat boards with four large spoked wheels, twelve spokes in front and fourteen on the rear. Harnessed to the wagon were two grizzled horses that gave an occasional snort and nicker, anticipating the night of work ahead.

Perched atop the wagon sat an older black man. His face, what wasn't covered by a salt and pepper beard, was lined with wisdom wrinkles. The crow's feet at the corners of each eye became even more prevalent when he smiled.

"'Evening, folks," he said. "Just climb in back an' cover up with the canvas. It's gonna be chilly tonight an' it'll keep you warm."

Wilbur gave Marie a boost into the wagon, and then handed up Celia and Leroy before standing on a wheel spoke and lifting himself in.

"My name be Henry," the driver said as he flipped the reins. The wagon gave a slight jerk, and they were on their way.

Chapter Nineteen

The incident back at the barn and the arduousness of perpetual pursuit forced Littlefield to lose interest in the hunt. At least in actively participating. He returned to the plantation and the comfort of his day-to-day responsibilities. Castor Fogg, on the other hand, renewed his zeal each day like a form of madness. Infuriated at not being able to locate the runaways, he tried to consider all possibilities. His dogs hadn't detected a significant scent. Either these slaves were more intelligent than those he'd previously captured, or they were getting help. And that was against the law, a point he'd take up in the next town they came to.

Fogg and his deputies stopped in Louisville. The town was named in honor of King Louis XVI of France, who had supported fledgling America during the Revolutionary War. Louisville was the capitol of Georgia from 1796 until 1806. Since then it had remained the Jefferson county seat and a virtual hotbed of slave traffic in the state. As they rode toward the sheriff's office, they passed the market house, located in the center of town. The adjoining bell tower would ring out to announce the sale of almost everything. Whether it was a sale of land or agriculture and cotton commodities, or, more frequently, the sale of slaves, the market house stood ready to serve. Many of the slave sales were illegal, with Fogg a frequent participant. The sheriff, Bascom "Bad Ass" Johnson, was a friend of Fogg's and a willing partner in the illegal sales.

"What you're saying is the Littlefield Negroes are getting away," Bascom said to Fogg, while pouring more rye whiskey in their glasses, raising the level another three inches.

"I can't figure it out," Fogg said. "There's six of 'em counting the kids, and no sign of 'em for two weeks now. The dogs ain't picked up any scent either. They gotta be getting help from somebody. Littlefield says none of 'em can read or write, and they ain't supposed to be very smart."

"You know them Quaker bastards are famous for hiding runaways and they're always being tight lipped about it. Seems to me, old pal, you ain't discovered the route their taking. Hell, they could be a hundred miles away by now."

They had been discussing the fugitives for nearly two hours. Fogg took a healthy swallow of rye and blew out an extended breath. At first the potent liquid had burned so much, his eyes watered. It was going down easy now. Unfortunately, Bascom's words were getting fuzzy and hard to understand. Fogg laid his head on the table and told himself to remember "the route" as he passed out.

The following morning Fogg awoke in one of the sheriff's cells.

"There's hot coffee on the stove," Bascom shouted from the outer office.

Fogg entered the room, rubbing his eyes, and walked over to pour himself a cup. It was hot and bitter, just what he needed. "Last night you said something about the route they are traveling on. You got any ideas?" he asked.

Bascom replied, "Yeah, I've given it some thought. Most likely they would follow the Ogeechee River and look for help along the way. If they're as dumb as you say, they wouldn't use the north star for bearings, so following the river would keep them from getting lost."

"That would mean they'd have to cross swamps and shit. They might be gator food now."

"That's a chance you'd have to take. If it was me, I'd follow that river and look for Quaker churches."

The more Fogg thought about it, the more sense it made. Nothing else had worked. After he and his deputies mounted their horses, they headed west to find the river. It took over two days before they arrived in Jewel, a delay due to the need to circumvent the swamp. The detour had compelled the bounty hunters to travel through dense forest, too difficult to traverse on horseback. They were forced to continue on foot and lead the animals. Once they arrived in Jewel, Fogg immediately began looking for the Society of Friends church.

The minister's cottage was located adjacent to the church. A path led directly from the side door of the manse to the sanctuary. Fogg took the parsonage path and rapped on the clergyman's door.

"How may I help thee, friend?" the minister asked.

"My name is Castor Fogg. I'm looking for some fugitive slaves that might have passed this way a week or two ago."

"And what business of thee makes such a question asked?" Reverend Meijer returned calmly.

"I represent the owner for one, and for another it's against the law. And for another," he added, his voice rising and his face getting red, "I'm told you people know a lot about that sort of thing. So answer me right, or you risk pissing me off."

"I've no wish to anger thee, friend. Perhaps thee may describe those of which thee seek."

"Describe 'em? Describe 'em? They're runaway Negroes. That's enough. That describes 'em," Fogg shouted, his voice rising to a higher pitch.

"If thee truly want my help, thee need to give me some type of description of those thee seek, anything."

"They all look alike," the slave hunter yelled.

"That's not true, friend. The Chinese believe all whites look alike, and that's not true either," Meijer said drily.

"I'll get the sheriff and he'll let my dogs go in and look around, and they'll tell me what I want to know. They'll tell me if runaways were here or not, you snotty son of a bitch." Fogg was boiling with rage.

"That wouldn't prove a thing. Both slave families and free Negroes attend services. Thy dogs will only prove me right," the minister said honestly.

"Then let me ask you in a different way. Has any Negro strangers been here?" Fogg asked tersely.

"Even thou art not a stranger to my eyes. And in the eyes of the Lord, there are no strangers. Inside is the house of the Lord. Would thee care to come inside and pray with me, friend?"

Fogg stalked away, wanting to burn the church down. He knew the dogs wouldn't prove anything and he knew the preacher was lying. He was so sure, he and the other slave chasers stayed in town a couple days in an attempt to learn more. They interviewed several people, along with keeping a watchful eye on the church, but without results. Finally, drawing a blank, they renewed their hunt and rode north.

Chapter Twenty

By now Reno's Funmakers had given performances in Pendleton and Greer, South Carolina, Newton and Boone, North Carolina, and were heading for Big Stone Gap, Virginia. The attendance was greatly improved and, thanks to President Roosevelt, those in the audience could even jingle their pockets. The time was also drawing near for Pauline. With Hattie's constant urging, it was decided she should deliver in a hospital. The closest of any size was in Bluefield, West Virginia. On June 6, a nervous Dutch, Pauline, and Hattie drove to Bluefield. No one on earth could keep Hattie from being there, and Pauline would have insisted on it anyhow. During the pregnancy, Hattie had had such a calming effect on young Pauline, Pauline couldn't imagine having done this without her.

The following day, Pauline was registered, in her room, and in labor. The delivery was difficult and serious. For all of that day and most of the next, progress was nil. At last the doctors decided to help the baby along with a forced delivery. Using forceps, the doctor delivered the baby, but left deep impressions on each side of the skull and broke an arm. When newborn wailed, another of the Lord's miracles was performed before the eyes of mankind. The exhausted doctor walked into the waiting room and announced the birth of a boy. He told Dutch he could visit his wife, but only for a short while. Hattie quickly brushed past the doctor. Dutch stayed, shook hands with the doctor, thanked him and thanked God, and nearly fainted. They named the ten-and-a-half-pound baby George Edward, after his father and grandfather. Over time the indentations faded and the broken arm healed.

The Reno's Funmakers show arrived the following week, on their way to give a performance in Welsh, West Virginia. This time, they made the trip with the addition of a new baby in the cast.

Hattie appointed herself chief security officer and refused admittance to anyone other than immediate family. When well-wishers wanted to see the baby, she told them, not for one full week. She wanted George Edward to get a good start in life before any germs were brought around.

Once, an unadmitted canvas man asked, "Is there anything wrong with him?"

Hattie replied, "Who say that? Who say that? There ain't nothing wrong with that child. He be perfect."

After the "Hattie week" ended, a few were allowed in to visit Pauline, bring gifts, and view the baby. Still, it was only those who passed Hattie's muster.

"Oh, Hattie, please don't be so strict with visitors," Pauline said.

"Miss Pauline, the child is a gift from God. He be telling the world everything is okay, so it can continue to go on. I'm not gonna let just anybody come in and ruin the work of the Lord," was her reply.

Pauline, not wanting to upset Hattie, let the matter drop.

Hattie had her rocker brought over, and during the baby's fitful periods, she became the only one who could quiet him to sleep. Pauline, amazed by it, wasn't going to look a gift horse in the mouth. And so it went for the rest of the season.

The arrival of a baby seemed to brighten everybody in the Funmakers' traveling troupe. The presence of a new life, like the advent of spring, has a way of rubbing off on others. Northern bookings ended in West Virginia. Therefore, preparations were made to travel back and play the returning schedule on the way to Athens. The first stop was Wise, Virginia, and then they continued on to Lenoir, North Carolina. Turnout and gate receipts continued to be robust. Ed was in a position to pay off the majority of the Kirksville loan, and planned to remit a certified check at the first chance. He was confident the balance would be cleared before they got back to Georgia, leaving him enough to see them through the winter and begin the season next year. Life was good.

One of the last engagements on the return schedule was Lonesome Pine, where Ed and Dutch had made that fortunate sales call two years earlier. Although the mayor, Chester White, had a little larceny in his soul, he turned out to be a decent sort, and he promoted the Funmakers at every chance. It was like old home week when the showmen were ushered in. Chester White shook hands as if he were campaigning and appeared sincerely happy to see them again. It couldn't be for the lot rent, because that had been reduced to $5, and waived completely the previous year. Something else was causing such good humor, and Ed would learn about it shortly.

"How is everybody doing?" he asked. "Tell me about the summer thus far. This damn Depression just won't go away. I think it's going to be a way of life from now on."

"Well, we didn't come in here with our begging bowls," Ed said laughing. "Seriously, this year is a hell of a lot better than last. From what I see, you've got to give a lot of credit to Roosevelt and the Works Progress Administration. More people are working and earning money."

"The problem with the WPA is they don't care what kind of work it is. It only creates work for the government, but no permanent jobs. Until America starts making and selling things, this economy is never going to improve," the mayor said gravely. Changing the subject, White then stated, "What you and I think doesn't mean a thing. Opinions are like assholes. Everybody's got one."

"That's the truth for sure," Ed agreed. "What's happening with you and Lonesome Pine?"

"Plenty. That is, plenty with me, not so much with Lonesome Pine. You've never met my daughter, have you? Well, needless to say, without her sunshine, there never would be morning in my family."

"She sounds like a remarkable girl."

"That ain't the half of it. She and her husband Walter had a little boy in February. Yep, you're looking at a grandpa."

"Chet, I know exactly how you feel. I've just recently became a grandfather as well. My daughter had a baby boy this June. I guess we're both a couple of proud grandpas."

"Are you thinking about putting him in the show?"

"Thinking about it? Hell, he came out doing a magic act," Ed said jokingly.

"I hope you and Dutch can stick around for a while. My daughter's bringing lunch over and I can show off my grandson."

Always the politician, Ed said, "We wouldn't miss it for the world."

Genuine smiles were broadening on the three faces in the room. What started out as a purely business acquaintance, over time, grew into honesty and friendship. By knowing the mayor better, they began to like him.

We are all three individuals—who we think we are, who others think we are, and who we really are.

Kindness is like a strange cat. If you give it milk, it will always come back to you. Should the clerks who worked in the mayor's office ever learn that, they'd look forward to each day, just to go to work.

At that moment, a young man and woman were struggling to get a stroller up the front steps of the Lonesome Pine courthouse.

"Your daughter's here," a clerk shouted from the foyer.

"Show her in," the mayor called back.

George Sand was right when she said, "There is one only happiness in life, to love and be loved." The presence of love seemed to fill the air as Chester greeted his family. The emotion did not escape Ed and Dutch, who were caught up in it. They were both aware that the center of the mayor's family, a new baby, also resided with their family.

Hoisting his grandchild in his arms, the mayor said, "This is Carson." Nodding toward the mother and father, he added, "My daughter Teresa and her husband Walter."

He introduced Ed and Dutch, explaining they were the owners of Reno's Funmakers.

"We're very pleased to meet you," Ed said. "You'll never guess it, but your father speaks quite highly of Carson."

Teresa laughed. "Really? That comes as a complete surprise to me."

"Teresa is as talented as she is beautiful," White said. "A year ago she was in Hollywood trying to get in pictures. I think she got homesick and had to come back. Probably missing her daddy too much."

"I'm sure that was it," Teresa said.. "Missing Walter surely couldn't have had anything to do with it."

Putting jokes aside, White asked, "Ed, do you still have a talent contest on Thursdays?"

"Sure do. That's become a part of the show now."

"I'll try to get Teresa to sign up. She can sing like a whippoorwill."

Teresa's cheeks got hot and red with embarrassment.

When asked to stay for lunch, Ed and Dutch made their excuses. "We'd like nothing better," Ed said, "but unfortunately, we must to get back to the show."

Ed left a small stack of free passes on their way out.

Upon returning to the show, the first thing Dutch did was hold George Edward and thank God again for the miracle. So thankful was he that when he closed his eyes, tears ran down both cheeks.

Again, attendance for the week was well ahead of the previous year. Expectations for Thursday and the talent show ran high, especially since Teresa White Collins had agreed to participate. Rumor and innuendo had circulated quietly among the community regarding her mysterious return from California. Upon learning she would take part in the talent show, the same gossipers made sure they had reserved seating. So the stage was set. The mood was lively after a burlesque comedy act, in which Ed, playing the character of Tobey, had been too embarrassed to answer when Pauline asked him, "What does a man do standing up, a woman sitting down, and a dog on three legs?" Pauline scolded him for refusing to answer and said, "Why, shake hands, of course."

Many in the talent contest were giving it their best, but the audience was relentless in their judgment, generally responding with roars of laughter. They found more humor the harder a contestant tried and were cocked and primed when Teresa was announced. She chose to sing "Smoke Gets in Your Eyes," a new song first heard the previous year. The house lights lowered, and sitting on a chair in center stage, the spotlight on her, she began to strum a guitar and sing.

"They asked me how I knew, my true love was true."

The raucous crowd chose to be silent. In fact, except for the voice of a blond angel, you could hear a pin drop.

"I of course replied, something here inside cannot be denied."

When the song ended, the big top vibrated from the booming applause, which lasted for several minutes. If anything was proven that night, it was that the girl had talent. Questions regarding her return from Hollywood would remain unanswered from that point forward. After collecting first prize—a diamond ring—she and her husband drove back to the farm. Teresa knew that sitting next to Walter with his arm around her, was as close to heaven as she could be here on earth.

Love is what's left after being in love fades away. That alone still isn't enough. We need trust and honesty along with it. These things don't happen overnight. It takes a long time, and you have to work at it.

A successful season had concluded, and Reno's Funmakers was back in Athens. The winter routine was unchanged with one exception—the bills were paid. Gladys and Pauline were awaiting a package from the Kirksville bank, and Frank and Hattie (who was now a full-time babysitter) had resumed their former duties. From all indications, the winter would be enjoyable.

During one of Gladys's social events, she learned that a young expectant mother, unable to raise another child, was considering putting the baby up for adoption. The wheels in Gladys's mind began to turn. She recalled her pride and high self-esteem after Pauline was born, and how it was repeated with Pauline having George Edward. The more she thought about it, the more she wanted the baby, so she told Ed about it.

"I just don't understand you, Sylvie. At this time in our lives and with a new grandchild, you want another baby in the family? Isn't George Edward enough? How do you think Pauline will feel about it?"

"Pauline is wrapped up with George Edward, and Hattie has him every spare minute. They treat me like I'm not around," Gladys lamented.

"I think they just don't want you disturbed," Ed answered dryly.

"How about somebody thinking about me for a change?" Gladys was adamant.

The next day Ed inquired into obtaining legal adoption papers.

The day Sylvia Gladys was brought home, the Renos' lives were changed forever.

Chapter Twenty-One

The wagon moved along an irregular route for about two hours, before Wilbur spoke to Henry.

"Is you a slave too?" Wilbur asked.

"No, sir. I used to be one, but I got set free. Don't rightly know what good it do me. Still do the same ole thing," Henry replied.

"Why'd they set you free?"

"Don't know for sure. One day the Master, he come to me and says, you is free. They called it manumission. Don't mean nothing, though, 'cause I still got to work. It do let me travel a lot more."

"You still live and work on the plantation?"

Henry laughed. "That's about the size of it."

"Have you ever been stopped when taking folks like us?" a concerned Wilbur asked.

"Sure enough. Lots a times. I always tells them that I be taking slaves, out on loan, back to the plantation. When I tells them what plantation it be, they always let me go."

"What one is that?"

"That be the Rotterman place. Ole man Rotterman is the nastiest, meanest white man the devil ever made. I seen him once horsewhip a fella near to death, and he was white. They all scared shitless of him, and he got four boys that might be meaner. They be so afraid I would tell Master Rotterman that they looked in his wagon, they let me go, right pronto, and wish me good day to boot." Henry grinned.

They encountered no one that night, and they reached Crawfordville well before dawn. The station was a small farm just outside of town. There, Wilbur and Marie learned their next stop would be Madison, and once again they would travel by wagon.

At that point, the runaways had traveled over 160 miles. As summer turned to fall, and the farther north they went, the cooler each evening would become. This was not overlooked by the railroad helpers. Accordingly, the Littlefield runaways were given heavier clothing, since what they currently wore wasn't made for the winters in northern Georgia.

The new conductor arrived on schedule and loaded his cargo immediately. There was no movement in the night air. Apparently captivated by the cacophony of the locusts, it refused to stir. Even with the temperature dropping, the horses perspired and needed to be moving in order to cool down. The open box wagon was similar to the one Henry had driven the previous day. Fully laden, it gave the appearance of ferrying items on their way for delivery.

The conductor wore a stoic expression and a wide-brimmed black hat. While appearing to be unfriendly, he merely had a no-nonsense personality that hid his truly altruistic nature. Wilbur misunderstood that, and after sinking beneath the canvas cover, whispered only in conversation with Marie and the children.

The safe house in Madison was similar to those before. However, the journey to the next station was done on foot.

They hiked mainly through dense forest, with the Apalachee River due east of them for bearing. Their guide followed a trail quite familiar to him, and circumventing an occasional shoal, they easily reached the Good Hope church before sunrise. The Methodist church would shelter them until nightfall.

The fugitive slaves learned they would be transported next by an actual railroad. A short line had been established to carry agricultural products between Madison and Clermont. New Hope had a depot and was a routine stop. They were to board the freight during a short delay and ride north to Clermont. To continue farther by rail might draw attention, as unknown people would be involved in the cargo transfer. Wilbur met both the engineer and fireman shortly before departure. Both were avid abolitionists and well-experienced in working the Underground Railroad.

"We have a rail car assigned to you and your family," the engineer said. "Once you get comfortable, I'll close and secure the door with a padlock. The door won't be opened until we reach Clermont. At that point, another man will take you to the safe house. Are there any questions?"

A frightened Wilbur could only shake his head no. Emotions were running high in the fugitive family. Wilbur was nervous, Marie was fearful, Celia was frightened, and Leroy was excited, celebrating the adventure with a grin from ear to ear. He was actually going to ride on a train. What boy, or man for that matter, isn't fascinated by that massive machine of power called the iron horse? What soul isn't affected by that mournful whistle, heard late at night, off in the distance? The emotions aroused in Leroy were then, and are now, increasing human heartbeats around the world.

Chapter Twenty-Two

The events of 1936, like those the year before, not only define the times, but altered our lives as well.

At the Berlin Olympics, American sports hero Jesse Owens destroyed Adolph Hitler's vision of Aryan superiority by setting world records and winning four gold medals. Actually, Hitler was infuriated by Owens's stellar performance, and discontinued shaking hands with gold medal winners. He only waved to Owens.

Back home in the United States, neither President Roosevelt nor Harry Truman proffered White House invitations or public honors to Owens. It wasn't until Dwight Eisenhower became president that Owens received the invitation and honors he so rightfully deserved.

Hitler also broke the treaty of Versailles by sending troops into the Rhineland; and creating a new air force, the Luftwaffe, under the command of Reichsmarschall Herman Göring. He also deprived German Jews of citizenship. His actions did not go unnoticed. They were observed by the world community, which chose appeasement over confrontation.

Here at home, the Great Plains fell victim to a relentless harmattan, a swirling black blizzard that turned day into night and blew away huge clouds of topsoil. The incessant winds came in the midst of a drought and record stifling heat. Steele, North Dakota, and Alton, Kansas, recorded temperatures of 121° F. Even in Wisconsin Dells, Wisconsin, the temperature hit 114°F on July 13. The unrelenting heat lasted for weeks, leaving devastation in its wake.

On a brighter side, Roosevelt was reelected in a landslide; Margaret Mitchell's *Gone With the Wind* was published; seventeen-year-old Bob Feller struck out fifteen in his first game for the Cleveland Indians; and Reno's Funmakers opened another new season.

And so life went on and the Great Depression continued. Due to federal spending, the GNP improved and unemployment was reduced to 17 percent. The highest tax rate was raised to 79 percent. While these were signs of encouragement, the situation basically remained the same.

Ed introduced new illusions into his act. One involved the disappearance of water and the other levitation, in which a globe rose beneath a silk cloth and floated, independent of anyone on stage. Both were well received by a fascinated audience. Dutch and Pauline became a popular duet à la Fred Astaire and Ginger Rogers. And new plays included Hattie, much to her outward reluctance and inward pleasure.

Frank Keagan, the show's booking agent, fancied himself a great chef, which sometimes resulted in clashes with Hattie. Their cookhouse arguments always involved each other's recipes. While Hattie's kitchen prowess was never questioned, Frank Keagan, to his credit, had a recipe or two that were unequaled. One that comes to mind is his spaghetti sauce. He only gave it to Pauline with a promise that she never reveal its ingredients. She kept that promise throughout her life. However, she couldn't avoid being observed while she made it. To the best of my recollection it was something like this:

> Ingredients:
> 1 28 oz. can whole tomatoes
> 1 15 oz. can tomato sauce
> 1 12 oz. can tomato paste
> 1 medium yellow onion, diced
> 1 garlic clove, diced
> ½ pound bacon
> 4 pork ribs
> 1 tablespoon oregano leaves
> 1½ pounds lean ground beef
> 1 oz. extra virgin olive oil
> Vegetable oil

Directions, first day:

Add tomatoes, sauce, and paste to large stainless steel kettle. Add the extra virgin olive oil.

Sauté onions and garlic in vegetable oil, using fry pan. Add to kettle when they become translucent.

Fry bacon until crisp but not burnt. Add to kettle.

Add oregano and light salt and pepper.

Cook for the rest of the day, stirring occasionally. Boiling can be avoided by using a diffuser. Turn off the heat before going to bed and let the kettle sit covered on the stove.

Directions, second day:

Heat the sauce and add the 4 pork spare ribs. Cook on simmer for the remainder of the day, until the meat comes off the bones. Stir occasionally to avoid boiling. Remove the bones.

Prepare meatballs using the ground beef. Roll into balls 1 inch in diameter. Cover with plastic wrap and store in refrigerator until next day.

Directions, third day:

Add meatballs and simmer the sauce, cooking until done, usually 2 to 3 hours. The sauce is now ready. Prepare spaghetti pasta per instructions on the box. Serves six people.

I know this recipe takes three days, but it is well worth it.

Hattie always criticized the time required and then had two helpings.

For Reno's Funmakers, the main topic of cookhouse conversation was storms. Tornadoes were always in the forefront of thought whenever a big top tent was involved. That spring, besides the torrid heat, tornadoes were a major preoccupation.

The weather is a frequent topic of conversation most everywhere. That is especially so in the South, and for good reason. Most people tend to train their eyes skyward whenever ominous dark clouds appear.

When warm air and cool air collide, the result can be weather mayhem. Such was the case in the spring of 1936. After the coldest winter in United States history, the summer brought record-setting heat, records that still stand today. In the midst of the Great Depression, high unemployment, drought, and crop failures, human beings seemed to be tested to their limits of endurance. Unfortunately, that usually is when the next shoe falls. And that was the case in Gainesville, Georgia.

Combining temperatures created the worst weather-related disasters ever, and Gainesville found itself in the center of it all. After sweeping through Tupelo, Mississippi, and other towns in their path, multiple tornados struck Gainesville. Terrible devastation and death resulted when the Cooper Pants factory collapsed, killing those who, ironically, were lucky enough to have a job. Schoolchildren died as other structures met a similar fate, and over 750 homes were destroyed by the tempest winds and resulting fires. All told, over 500 died and nearly 2,000 were injured. Without question the numbers were actually greater, since Negroes were not included in the count.

Chapter Twenty-Three

Sparkling jewels once again graced Gladys and Pauline, proof that Ed's loan was paid in full. They were only material things, true, but each represented a treasured memory. Where Pauline was concerned, it was a diamond ring for each of her teenage years; and for Gladys, the anniversaries of her marriage, which began December 19, 1913.

Even though it would be a year between performances at the various towns, the traveling repertory show needed to refresh its theatrical content. Something new had to be added in order to avoid appearing stale or blasé. Ed called for a meeting of the cast and crew to brainstorm fresh ideas. The input from Frank Keagan was vital in such settings, since he usually had his thumb on the pulse when booking the show in advance. Town officials routinely asked him if there is "anything new this year."

"We probably have more talent than any show our size playing today," Ed said to the group. "I feel a great deal of it hasn't been tapped. Do any of you have ideas, or know someone you think would fit in and improve what we now have?"

He turned to Frank. "How about you, Frank. What do they say when you set up the schedule?"

"For the most part, they ask about the magic act and plays. It's very important to have a couple new ones each year," Frank answered.

Ed looked at his daughter and smiled., "You've got to keep writing new plays, honey. I know George Edward takes up a lot of your time, but you can buy plays from Variety or Playbill. I think," he added, joking, "we've got a lot of people on the show who can read. All kidding aside, Funmakers isn't a circus, but we do have former high-wire acts with us. I'm wondering if there is a way to work in Sylvie with, let's see, the rolling globe. Maybe a little juggling on the side. You get the picture."

Gladys was the first to speak up. "I don't see how I can find time for practice with the new baby and all. It's been years since I've walked the globe or juggled. That takes practice, and lots of it."

"We would just figure out a way to give you more time," Ed replied. "Maybe Hattie would be willing to watch both kids."

"Next thing you know, you'll want to me hang by my teeth again," Gladys said sarcastically. "Like you said, this ain't no damn circus."

"Now don't get yourself upset. We're only kicking around some ideas. You might not be able to do either one anymore."

Gladys's cheek was twitching. That comment made her mad. "I'll do the act next week," she said. "You just find the damn globe."

Ed was smiling. He not only found the globe, but the Indian clubs for her juggling act as well.

Practice time for Gladys gradually served as the ice breaker for Pauline with her adopted sister. While technically Hattie was watching both babies, she took every opportunity to have Pauline hold the new baby girl.

"Hold your baby sister while I tend to George Edward," Hattie, like a fox, would demand as she handed Pauline the warm little bundle.

Most women are genetically wired for maternal love. Few things are more rewarding than looking into the innocent face of a newborn cherub and receiving a smile. Such was the case when Pauline first held Sylvia.

"I think she's smiling for me," Pauline said.

"That more likely be gas, honey," Hattie replied.

"Come look and then tell me that."

"You might be right. It sure do look like she be smiling," Hattie finally agreed with a twinkle in her eye and self-satisfaction.

"She doesn't seem to cry very much. Do you think something's wrong?" Pauline asked.

"Ain't nothing wrong, honey, she's just content. She be happy to have her big sister hold her. I'll take her now," Hattie said, holding out her hands.

"That's okay. I'll hold her until she gets too fussy," Pauline said.

Hattie returned to her rocker and began swaying to and fro while knitting an outfit for George Edward.

Pauline observed her for a while, and then said, "You might as well make one for Sylvia when that one is finished."

Her eyes focused on her work, the wise Hattie murmured, "Mm-hmm."

True to her word, Gladys performed before a live audience the following week. She was featured in an acrobatic act in which she walked astride the rolling sphere while juggling. Appearing to be a simple matter, in reality walking the globe is very difficult. Just standing on the ball requires exceptional balance; traveling on it, special talent; and juggling as you do so is nearly impossible. Put it all together with musical accompaniment, a glittering costume, and a pursuing spotlight, and you have created great excitement for the people gathering under the big top.

Additions to Ed's magic act garnered the same result. His patter and the manner in which he presented each new illusion improved with every performance.

Pauline had purchased a new play from Playbill, and it also shared equal success. The rural audience, disheartened by the times, responded most often to plays with a moral value, ones in which the mistreated underdog wins out in the end thanks to steadfast faith, prayer, and an unsuspected hero within the family. Vaguely abstract and philosophical stories needed to wait a little longer for improved conditions and a more joyful atmosphere.

Pauline also began to look forward to taking care of her sister. At times she offered before being asked. Sylvia was a happy little innocent, rarely complaining except when hungry. She differed from George Edward in ways her big sister found thoroughly delightful.

The summer season seemed to fly by, and before the cast and crew knew it, plans were being made for returning home for the winter. The earnings were not as good as the previous year, but all in all, Reno's Funmakers remained profitable. Ed kept his father informed by letter and an occasional phone call, and was reassured each time with an offer of a home in Kankakee.

Chapter Twenty-Four

The steady sway of the boxcar and clicking of its wheels had a soothing effect on those inside. As the train rolled on and the miles passed by, Wilbur began to relax. Looking at his family, he saw that Celia had fallen asleep. Marie, her back against a cotton bale, had her eyes closed but remained awake; and Leroy was still smiling. Wilbur wondered what kind of life awaited them if their escape was successful. He was confident in his ability to work hard, as well as Marie. Even Leroy was near the age of being productive. Still, none had experienced labor as free individuals ... an exciting and daunting thought. Wilbur contemplated those left behind in his family, and Marie's family as well. He wondered about Patrick and Ben. Were they safe, did they get away? So many thoughts, his head began to throb. Then, after shutting his eyes, his thoughts turned into dreams.

Hearing a rattling at the boxcar's sliding door, Wilbur awoke with a start. The fog of sleep quickly vanished as he realized they'd arrived at their destination. It was still dark outside, and a voice from the shadows ordered them to come quickly and be silent. Still somewhat confused by the interruption of deep sleep, he followed in a gradually fading stupor. They were led to another horse-drawn wagon.

"Climb in, we've got a ways to go before morning," said the driver.

The next destination was the church between Ivy Log and Blairsville, about twenty-five miles from where they stood. Without mishap, it would be reached ahead of sunup and daylight.

"How did the train ride go?" the driver asked.

Wilbur answered, "I was little scared at first, but seems like it turned out okay. My son Leroy here thinks it be great."

"Most young'uns feels the same way. I guess it's pretty exciting for 'em. Gotta be careful now, though. The law has caught on and sometimes inspects the train. The one you guys was on is private owned, so it'd take a court order, but that can be got beforehand if they're suspicious. Just sit back while I get my team into a trot. We make better time when they canter along and don't get too tired."

"What kind of church is it?" Wilbur asked.

"Don't really know if it's got a name. Not much of a church either. It's a cabin up in the gold fields. But the preacher is against slavery. That I do know."

The area Wilbur and his family had arrived in was known as Union County. It came about as the result of the Georgia land lottery in 1832. The Cherokee Indian territory, later declared Cherokee County, was apportioned into lots and offered to lottery winners. If a winner did not wish to purchase the land, it was sold to the highest bidder. Because most people cared little about land, the Scotch-Irish of the Appalachian Mountains, though very poor, were able to buy lots for next to nothing. These mountaineers were hardened by poverty, strengthened by their Christian faith, and pro-Union in their patriotism. Differing from their neighbors farther south, they generally were also against slavery. The gold fields operated within Union County until 1900, at which time they were no longer profitable.

The minister of the cabin church was Fredrick Crabtree. He and his wife, Mildred, had moved to the gold fields to save souls from the temptations of greed. Their job was easier than they'd expected. Little wealth was gained by individual miners, who came to the fields seeking gold and left disappointed. Their church not only served its purpose, but had another important function as well. It acted as halfway house for runaway slaves.

Shortly after daybreak, Wilbur Littlefield and family became part of that category. They were treated to mountain food, consisting of deer stew, boiled potatoes, yams, maize bread, and crabapple pie, proving once again that hunger is the best seasoning. As you might think, they went easiest on the venison.

"You all be safe here," Fredrick said. "We ain't seen no slave catchers in over a year. I guess they don't like being shot at very much," he added dryly as he passed more pie to Leroy. "From this point you'll be traveling over the mountains and mostly on foot, so we got to make sure you got some heavy clothes."

"We were given heavier clothes the last place we stayed at," Wilbur replied.

"I'm talking about coats and the like. Nights in the mountains gets real cold. I mean devilish cold. You all gonna need boots, mittens, and something to put on your ears. Don't worry none. We got everything you need."

Their conductor was a true mountain man named Tobias Taylor. He stood nearly six and a half feet tall and wore a bearskin coat. His complexion, darkened by both hard weather and sun, was partially hidden by a full beard. Perhaps his most striking characteristic was the Long Tom rifle straddling his forearm. He gave the impression of one who could easily survive in the mountains, or anywhere else, if need be. Living his whole life in the mountains, he had learned the hidden Indian trails and secret passages in order to travel unnoticed. With him as guide, they would journey at times during the day. That would be the case that day, since the Spartan conductor arrived at the first cockcrow.

Before starting, Tobias said, "Ain't no use rushing things. Mountain travel be slow at best, so we gonna pace ourselves so as not get pooped too soon."

After an hour on the trail, the fugitives realized the dense forest and undulating terrain were slowing their pace. Wherever the destination, it could only be reached by deliberate speed and not a minute sooner. Due to their age and agility, the children were handling the march best of all—excluding Tobias Taylor, naturally, who moved with ease of a mountain goat.

Once satisfied with their progress, the mountaineer called a halt, saying, "Best we stop here for a while and rest up. You children find us some wood to build a fire so's we can cook something to eat."

Wilbur was shocked and said, "Won't somebody see a fire?"

"Sure they can," Tobias answered in a relaxed manner.

"Won't that be dangerous?"

"Seeing is one thing, but finding us is another. They might see the fire, but ain't nobody able to get to us."

The path to where the group rested was a secret Indian trail. Without knowledge of such routes, pursuers were not only unable to reach them, but would likely end up lost if they tried. Nevertheless, after eating warm food, Wilbur was anxious to resume the trek.

They continued in the monotony of their long walk, until a grunting sound was heard coming from a raspberry thicket up ahead. Tobias raised his hand, signaling for them to stop.

"What is it?" Leroy whispered.

"Nobody move," was all Tobias said.

As the group stood holding their breath, the raspberry thicket began to shake. Then, to the surprise of the Littlefields, a tiny black bear cub scurried into the path, followed by another.

"Just let 'em pass," the mountaineer said hoarsely. No sooner had he spoken, the black bear sow ambled into view. She charged for a short distance toward the hikers and then came to a bouncing stop, slamming her front paws hard on the ground. No one was confused by her actions. It was a warning to leave her cubs alone. Tobias led them in a wide arc, giving the bear ample space to continue her foraging.

What was old hat for the conductor was a startling experience for everyone else. The runaways had never seen a live bear, let alone one with two cubs. The occasion would never be forgotten, and would be recalled many times in future conversations.

By the time nightfall approached, the fugitives were flagging. They had driven hard over alien terrain, and welcomed an opportunity to sit down and rest.

"What's it like being a slave?" the mountain man asked Wilbur. "I know it ain't natural, but what does it feel like?"

"It takes away most natural feelings, so you end up not feeling nothing," Wilbur slowly answered. "Oh, you got your wife and family, but you can't do for them like a man. I guess it just takes away your manhood."

"A mountain man could never be a slave. Being made to stay in one place would kill us. Being told what to do and shit like that wouldn't set for a mountain man."

"It don't set for anybody, Tobias, if you gets a choice, but slaves can only put their faith in the Lord and dream about freedom. We don't get no choice about it."

"Well, you doing something about it now, and it makes me proud to be a helping you," Tobias said as he stretched out and leaned back against a tree. "Hey, Leroy come over here," he called. "Look up in that tree and tell me what you see."

"Looks like a big bird," Leroy responded.

"It's a big bird all right. That be a giant owl. The Indians say it brings good luck. I don't reckon you ever heard that before. Another thing, his feathers weigh more than he does."

"I think you be spoofin' me," Leroy answered with a grin. "Feathers weigh next to nothing."

"It's a fact, it's a fact," Tobias said as he lit his pipe.

He also authorized another fire as the temperature began to dip. After they had eaten, he told his fellow travelers, "Best we get 'bout four hours sleep, or least 'til the moon gets a little brighter."

These were welcome words to Wilbur and his family. Once they got comfortable, Leroy whispered to his father, "When I get free, I want to be like Tobias." The young boy had found a hero.

His father smiled. "And here I thought you wanted to drive a locomotive on a train."

Chapter Twenty-Five

The late '30s were disastrous times around the globe. In Russia, shortly after the death of Vladimir Lenin, Joseph Stalin emerged as the principal power broker and, after gaining control of the country, created his own brand of communism. Using a variety of excuses, such as the expected war with Germany and saboteurs in the midst of the new Communist Party, he set about to eliminate any resistance to his rule. Opposing groups were declared "enemies of the people," with over 400,000 expelled from the party. During 1936-1938, nearly a million individuals perished from either starvation or by execution. Besides those who were shot, others were deported or exiled to gulag prison camps, where they disappeared and died. These atrocities became known as The Great Purge, and included people from all walks of life, anyone Stalin thought could challenge his authority.

Also indefensible was the failure of news correspondents to accurately report these outrages. For the most part they accepted testimony from discredited witnesses and reported mendacities.

The other threat to the world was, of course, Adolf Hitler. After being appointed chancellor of Germany, he pursued his goal of seizing "living space" for the Aryan people. He felt the Versailles Peace Treaty was unfair, only agreed to by corrupt politicians, and systematically violated its provisions.

The Treaty demilitarized the Rhineland and recreated Poland. It forbade Germany from having armed forces—no air force, no submarines, and a domestic army of only 100,000 soldiers, with no conscription. All of which Hitler ignored as he began to build up the military. While doing so, he approved of numerous violent acts, resulting in the murder of seventeen million civilians, including six million Jews in the Holocaust. His Nazi Party showed no mercy to the disabled, homosexuals, most religious groups, and political opponents. The rest of the world accepted his argument that all this was necessary in order to keep the peace. In fact, Great Britain signed an agreement that allowed Germany to increase its naval tonnage up to 35 percent of the British navy. Nonaggression pacts were signed with Germany until 1939, when he invaded Poland. England and France, who had nonaggression treaties with Poland, were forced to declare war on Germany; exactly what Hitler wanted, and within three years Germany occupied most of Europe. France surrendered in 1940, and England was bombed nearly every night.

On June 22, 1941, Hitler undertook what would be the turning point of the war. With three million soldiers, he invaded the Soviet Union, breaking another nonaggression pact that had been signed two years earlier. His initial victories faded as the battles became increasingly more difficult to win. The Russians fought fiercely and the Russian winter took its toll. Subsequently, a defeated German army began a freezing death march in retreat.

On December 7, 1941, Japan, an ally of Germany, attacked Pearl Harbor in Hawaii, forcing Hitler to declare war against the United States, the greatest industrial complex in the world. I've always believed that the action by Japan could never have been condoned by Hitler. Accordingly, he must have known that now his dream was at its end. And so it was, four years later.

(Looking back, one wonders how the world could have stood by while so many atrocities were taking place. Why something wasn't done to intercede. If we were to go back, would we change anything? Probably not. When considered as a group, we humans would choose debate rather than confrontation. The world is changed by strong individuals, not any group alone. I'm reminded by the saying that a camel is a horse designed by committee. One only has to look to the United Nations to see that group-think is usually at a stalemate.)

In America during 1937, the worst school disaster in US history took place in New London, Texas. An explosion, due to a natural gas leak beneath the building, resulted in the death of over three hundred children and teachers. The total could possibly be even more, since many workers in nearby oil fields were itinerant and their families may not have been recorded.

President Roosevelt's effort to stack the Supreme Court was rejected by the Senate. Amelia Earhart and her copilot, Fred Noonan, disappeared over the Pacific Ocean, on the last leg of her effort to fly around the world. *Snow White*, the first feature-length cartoon in color and sound, premiered. Spinster Ida May Fuller received the first monthly Social Security payment of $22.54, after working only three years.

* * * * *

As Reno's Funmakers prepared to launch another season, Ed Reno received a telephone call from David Shirkie, asking if it would be okay to visit the show in May. He was looking forward to see everybody again, especially the new infants.

David's visits were always joyous events. His friendly nature and occasional zany antics never failed to put a smile on the faces of those around him. Family visitors also knew they would participate in the nightly theater programs, because with a traveling repertory show, everybody works. Most look forward to it and are disappointed if their role is trivial or insignificant. David, on the other hand, relished any role, as if it made him the headliner. As a result, Ed attempted to incorporate all of his talents, from dramatic acting to playing the piano. The practice of employing family members worked out well, considering the economic times.

The Depression was taking its toll on the traveling tent shows. Several were forced to shut down, and prospects for the rest weren't very good. Ed began the season with less money than the year before, but hoped the gate would sustain them as the weeks went on.

Receipts from the initial stops in Georgia were encouraging enough for him to take a short side track and visit Wallace Brothers Circus in York, South Carolina, their winter quarters. He was friends with the previous manager, Jess Adkins, but had yet to meet the new owner. Jess had formed another circus called Cole Brothers and had persuaded Clyde Beatty, the famous lion tamer, to join him. Beatty had been a headliner with Wallace Brothers for ten years and was sorely missed.

"What was the turnout like when you opened?" Ray Rogers, the new owner, asked. "The reason I'm asking is we plan to open next week in Valdosta, then work our way north."

"It was pretty good for us, about the same as last year," Ed replied.

"You guys do it right. The big top circus has tremendous overhead, but we need it, along with all the ballyhoo, to attract the customers. With the economy the way it is, ticket prices are practically frozen, while costs for salaries, maintenance of the animals, and travel keep going up. You can remember when the circuses traveled by rail. That's been cut down to just a couple now. Even by truck and wagon, you can't imagine what the costs are."

Ed nodded. "This Depression is hurting everybody."

"It's not only that, Ed. Radio and movies are probably hurting us even more," Rogers lamented.

"How bad has Clyde Beatty's leaving hurt?" Ed asked.

"I wouldn't say this to anyone else, but that hurts like hell. We do have a feature star now. Tom Tyler, the cowboy movie actor, is with us, but he doesn't care that much for circus work. I'd like you to meet him before you go back. Would you guys like to take a tour?"

It was a time of uncertainty for the big top circus. Earlier successes could not be sustained. Failure of the touring circuses resulted not only from the Great Depression, but several other significant factors as well. The circus's physical presence diminished as talking pictures became a more interesting form of entertainment, with movie houses opening in nearly every city. If a small town was isolated and didn't have one, another was located only a short distance away, easily reached by car. Circus day, formally a major event in a community, became less significant, to the point that the morning street parade was discontinued. No longer having a monopoly on entertainment, circuses saw audience numbers decline. People were able to choose how they spent their limited dollars from a menu of other types of entertainment. Many circuses had to shut down completely, while others merged with a former competitor in order to survive. The handwriting was on the wall—the great American circus years was gone forever.

After finding Tom Tyler in the stable tent, Rogers introduced the two men. "Tom, this is Ed Reno, the owner of Reno's Funmakers tent show. You may have heard of his father, Reno the Great Magician."

"I think everybody has heard of your father, it's nice to meet you," Tyler said.

"It's good to finally meet you. I've been a fan of yours ever since Bob Robinson told me to see your movies. Do you know Bob Robinson?"

"Sure do. Bob gets lots of work in the westerns. He just looks the part. I bet he's been in more movies than I have," said Tyler.

"How do you like circus work?" Ed asked.

"It's okay, but my first love is the movies. I need the money since movie roles have dried up, and Ray was kind enough to offer me a job."

"Tom, my grandson is here with me and I was wondering if I could get a picture of him with you."

"No problem, I'll hold him while I sit on Tony here."

Tony was the white horse Tom Tyler chose in most of his Western movies. Tom was a popular star of both silent and early sound Westerns. While most of his movies were the bottom half of a double feature, his career stretched from the1920s to the 1950s. By mainly making low budget B-movies, he lived on modest salaries and never got rich.

Born into a Polish-American family in 1903, Vincent Markowski worked at several jobs before landing in Los Angeles as a movie extra and stuntman. Because of his good looks and athletic physique (he was a champion weight lifter and acclaimed to be the strongest man in the world), he was offered the lead in a series of silent Western films under the stage name of Bill Burns. His name would later be changed to Tom Tyler. Working hard to lose his Lithuanian accent, he made a smooth transition into talking pictures. After the competition in Westerns became fierce, he was forced to take supporting roles in larger budget films. Perhaps his most famous role was that of Captain Marvel in the serial film, *Adventures of Captain Marvel*. That success was parleyed into portraying the Phantom in a similar genre within three years. Eventually, rheumatoid arthritis crippled him to the point that he was only able to play an occasional bit part. He appeared in several supporting roles until his health forced his return to Michigan and live with his sister. Finally, when he was fifty, the curtain came down for the last time. Tom Tyler died of heart failure.

The photograph of George Edward on Tom Tyler's horse became a family favorite.

Driving back to the Funmaker's big top, Ed reflected on the visit and became depressed. The thought of the American circuses ultimate end was a bitter pill, too hard to swallow. He knew Wallace Brothers wouldn't last much longer, and wondered when Reno's Funmakers would face a similar circumstance.

Gladys noticed that George Edward was developing a vocabulary. Though still one of an infant, she needed to talk to Dutch and Pauline about it. One thing she would not tolerate was being called Grandma. Being called Grandma or Grandpa would diminish her and Ed's theatrical images with the audience. The perception of their being old was something many actors tried to avoid.

"If he can't call you Grandma, what do you want him to call you?" Pauline was hurt again.

"He can call me Nan, and since he'll probably call Dutch Dad, he can call Ed Big Dad."

"I don't know why you get so worked up about it," Pauline said. "Isn't it natural for a grandson to call his grandmother Grandma? Everybody's going to know you're his grandmother, and the same with Daddy. What does Daddy think about it?"

"It doesn't make any difference what Ed thinks, just do as I say."

Actually, ever since George Edward had been born, Ed carried on endlessly about his grandson. He started with the first person he met and hadn't stopped yet. Nevertheless, for the rest of their lives, George Edward called his grandparents Big Dad and Nannie. Nannie, instead of Nan, became the only exception requested by Gladys.

Later, when Dutch returned to their trailer, Pauline repeated what her mother had said.

"Your mother was only thinking about her role with the show. If we were in a different business, she wouldn't care," Dutch said consolingly. "I'm sure it wasn't for any other reason."

"Don't bet on it," Pauline said snidely. "It just hurts to make George Edward call them something that isn't natural for him."

"Sweetheart, you wear your heart on your sleeve. Try not to take these things so personal. Life isn't always a bed of roses. If this is the biggest problem we ever have, we'll be the luckiest couple that ever lived. Why don't you mention it to Hattie and see how she feels about it?"

Along with everything else, Hattie was the family arbiter. She was also due any minute to watch George Edward, so Pauline could rehearse her routine for the evening performance. The familiar knock heralded her arrival, and Pauline quickly opened the door.

"Guess what Mother wants now? She told me to not let George Edward call her Grandma and Daddy has to be called Big Dad, but I don't think he knows anything about it," Pauline said as soon as Hattie settled in.

"Is the baby asleep?"

"Yes, he's taking a nap," answered Pauline. "But what do you think about what Mama said?"

"Honey, that all depends on why she says it," Hattie replied.

"I think she said it out of pride so she can appear younger. She's too proud to be a grandmother."

"Miss Pauline, there's nothing wrong with being proud. You be proud of little George Edward just like I was proud of Tyrell. That kind of pride is our own opinion of ourselves. Vanity is a different matter. That be concern of what others think of us. Vanity goes way beyond pride. The Bible tells us that pride goes before a fall, so you can imagine what the Lord thinks about vanity. Now I don't know why Miss Gladys say that, and I can't criticize something I don't know. I always try to believe the best in everybody. It helps me sleep at night. I do know that most arguments between a mother and daughter are about as important as a straw in the wind."

"Miss Pauline, you best dry your tears 'cause what Miss Gladys did was the will of the Lord. In fact, honey, everything we humans does is in God's plan. We can't know why and we can't change it. We all just have to accept it and go on with our lives. Be thankful for the blessings He done give you. You got a husband that loves you and the most beautiful baby boy. Besides, you still a daddy's girl to Mr. Ed."

"He probably won't wake up, but if he does, there's a fresh made bottle in the icebox," Pauline said as she left for the big top, still a little miffed.

That night she sang the Al Jolson song, "Sonny Boy." When she finished, it was impossible to determine who was crying the most, Pauline or the audience. The rest of the show came off like clockwork. As with most family disagreements, the morning was, to a certain extent, pardoning.

Dave Shirkie's arrival raised the spirits of everyone, especially Pauline. It gave her the opportunity to vent her thoughts to a more sympathetic ear. She wasted no time in doing so, even before George Edward was presented to Dave. Dave was in total agreement with his cousin, but asked not to have his opinion revealed, for fear that Uncle Ed might take it wrong. That was okay with her, being satisfied she was right all along.

The relationship between Pauline and her mother became merely cordial, as if each was afraid to relate her thoughts. A deep hurt dwelled in the daughter's consciousness. Sometimes it brought forth anger, but most often it caused tears. The concealed rift demanded an airing that never happened.

The next evening, when the final curtain closed, Gladys and Ed had visitors back stage. The performance had been lively with extended applause and several encores. For the actors, that was what it was all about—seeing and hearing firsthand success in what you do. Two of the visitors were Reverend Eli Brinkman and his wife, Toni. Reverend Brinkman was pastor of the local Methodist church. Though parishioners praised the show, he was unsure if Reno's Funmakers was acceptable fare for the youngsters in the church, and had come to see for himself. He secretly loved magic acts, but never would reveal that as the reason for his presence that night.

"How do you do?" he said to Ed. "My name is Eli Brinkman, and this is my wife Toni. We pastor the Asbury Methodist church here in town. We just had to tell you how much we enjoyed the performance this evening. It's so good to see a show with what we like to call clean entertainment. One that's suitable for the whole family."

"Thank you very much," Ed said. "We try to present a show for the entire family. My daughter writes most of our plays, and we prefer those with a happy ending and a moral."

"I especially liked the magic act. How in the world did you make those doves vanish and then reappear?" the minister asked, hoping for an explanation.

Ed laughed. "All I can say is, it must have been magic."

Toni looked at her husband as if to say, I told you so, then turned to Gladys. "Gladys, we have a ladies group at the church that does charity work, and each month we have a luncheon. It so happens Thursday is scheduled for this month's affair. On behalf of our group, I want to extend an invitation for you to come. I always try to have an interesting guest, and the ladies would be thrilled to have you there."

Although Gladys wasn't that keen about attending, she knew the importance of good public relations and how it affected the show's turnout. "I'd be pleased to attend. What time do you wish me to arrive?"

"Oh, don't worry about a ride. I'll pick you up here at say eleven o'clock. That will give us a little time to talk before everybody comes."

That night as they lay in bed, Ed whispered, "I wonder what you'll have for lunch," followed by his familiar laughing hiss through his teeth.

Toni Brinkman pulled up at eleven on the dot. You could see by her smiling face that she relished this kind of event, and beamed a welcome to Gladys. The manner in which she drove to the church, overemphasizing every motoring step, gave evidence she was a beginning driver. It was also apparent, she enjoyed every minute of it.

The basement of the Methodist church had a kitchen on one end with a few rows of picnic tables. It obviously was arranged for church potlucks and the like. The other end of the room was designed to accommodate the youngsters in the church. Besides a couple of Ping-Pong tables, several pairs of roller skates hung along the wall. The concrete floor at that end was freshly painted gray. Roller skating isn't the most friendly pastime for a painted floor.

The menu for that day consisted of tuna sandwiches with lettuce and pickles, hot coffee, and a fruit salad for dessert. Naturally, each table had a pitcher of water. Gladys heard the din of conversations as the ladies filed in and took their places. The meal began with a prayer of thanks, and immediately the women started picking at the fruit salad.

"Have you always been in the theater?" asked one of the women.

"Yes, to a certain extent," Gladys answered. "When I met my husband, I was performing as a trapeze artist and walking the high wire."

"Isn't that dangerous?" asked another.

"Yes, and it requires a great deal of practice. Even then there's always concern for one's safety. The more dangerous, the more exciting the act becomes."

"Please don't take this wrong," a third woman said, "but, you seem so normal to have such excitement in your life."

"It's only a job in my chosen field, the same as any of you ladies if you work outside of the home."

"I work at a millinery shop," a heavy-set woman said, "and there isn't anything dangerous or exciting about it."

"How about when the boss walks in and catches you writing letters?" Toni said jokingly.

Several women giggled.

"Well, maybe that was exciting, but never dangerous."

With that, everyone had a good laugh.

"Seriously," Toni said to Gladys, "practically all of us have seen the Funmakers show at least once, and we wondered who that cute little boy is who sings and dances. We all thought him such a dear and so young."

"That is my grandson, George Edward, my daughter's son."

"Your grandson," they all exclaimed in surprise. "You look too young to be a grandmother."

At that moment, pride triumphed over vanity. So much for the narcissism of youth. That myth was now exposed. Nevertheless, the name Nannie stayed forever.

With their summer tour nearly over, one thing was proven to Ed. You will never get rich owning a traveling tent show. In those times, the best you could hope for was just to break even. The attendance and gate receipts held pretty steadily, but profits were slim and not enough to cover all the expenses. More cash was needed for repairs and upkeep. Plus, the annual taxes on the Athens property added to the overall burden. Ed, feeling against the wall, could only see one solution. Once again the family jewels would have to travel to John Cornelius and the Kirksville bank.

That winter in Athens turned out to be a sad one for the Reno's Funmakers family. Frank Robinson's brother-in-law suddenly died, leaving Frank's sister, Ethel, with five young children and a small gas station to run by herself. Ethel turned to Frank for help. Hattie and Frank were like family, and the thought of them leaving left a hole in the Renos' hearts, which could only be filled with sadness. For Pauline and Dutch, Hattie was the third leg of a three-legged stool. For Pauline herself, Hattie's smile had stopped a thousand tears and made her a better person. She would grieve and be sorrow struck the longest.

"Frank, I haven't met a man better than you," Ed said honestly. "If there is anything I can do, don't hesitate to ask."

"I appreciate that Mr. Ed. This is the hardest thing Hattie and me has ever had to do. My little sister is in trouble and needs me to help her. I think you know that I got to go and be with her."

Ed put his arm around him and said, "I would be surprised if you didn't do the right thing."

Hattie made sure she said her good-byes to Pauline when Dutch was present. That way she thought emotions would be better controlled. She thought of Pauline as a daughter, and little George Edward helped relieve the sorrow left by Tyrell's death. As she knocked on the door, she took a deep breath. Once in the room, all her plans vanished like smoke in a windstorm. As she hugged Pauline, tears flowed from both women.

"What am I going to do without you?" Pauline asked between sobs.

"You'll be just fine, baby," Hattie reassured her. "You got Dutch and my little man George Edward to keep an eye on you while I'm gone."

"I'm never going to see you again. I just know it," Pauline said gravely.

"Now don't you be interfering with what the Lord got planned," Hattie scolded her. "If the Lord wants it, our paths will cross again for sure."

And so it was, on that winter day in Georgia, Hattie and Frank walked out of the lives of the Funmaker family forever. For the longest time it was difficult to find humor in any antic performed by those attempting to cheer them up. Eventually, the balm of time began to heal the wounds of sorrow, and the Renos began making plans for the coming season.

Chapter Twenty-Six

In 1938, Adolph Hitler's exploits portended a dire preview for the future of Europe. Though born in Braunau, Austria, Hitler always considered himself a German. Once in control of the army, he assigned Nazis to top positions and began his plan to annex Austria as a German state. In February 1938, he gave Austrian Chancellor Schuschnigg a list of demands, one of which was to make Seyss-Inquart, an Austrian Nazi, minister of the interior. Schuschnigg suggested putting the annex decision to a vote. That infuriated Hitler, and he threatened to bomb Vienna. Schuschnigg and his cabinet resigned, leaving Seyss-Inquart as the sole member of the Austrian government. In March 1938, he invited the German troops into Austria.

It now became evident the führer had no intention of abiding by the dictates of the Treaty of Versailles, in which the annexation was strictly forbidden. Immediately, the Nazis initiated anti-Jewish policies throughout the country. The Anschluss (annexation) resulted in synagogues and Jewish-owned buildings being plundered and destroyed. Many Jews were killed during the riots. Those wanting to emigrate out of Austria were hindered by needing to have visas and documents authorizing their departure. Anything of value had to be left in Austria.

Elsewhere, the Church of England accepted the theory of evolution.

Benny Goodman played jazz at Carnegie Hall.

Federal minimum wage was set at 40¢ per hour.

Instant coffee was invented.

Blood tests for syphilis were required to obtain a marriage license.

Mexican courts ordered foreign oil companies to provide back pay to striking workers. The oil companies refused. Because of the stalemate, Mexico's President, Lázaro Cárdenas, nationalized all foreign oil properties, including those of the United States and Britain.

Orson Welles panicked the nation when "The War of the Worlds" was broadcast. Nearly two million listeners believed it to be true, and some actually armed themselves and rushed to the fictional scene of events.

New England was struck by the most massive hurricane recorded since 1869. Eastern Long Island, NY, received the most damage when hammered with wind gusts of one hundred miles per hour. The storm killed nearly 800 people, destroyed over 57,000 homes, and property losses were estimated at $306 million dollars. (A little under $5 billion in 2010 dollars.) A movie theater in Westhampton was swept out to sea with about twenty people at the matinee, including the projectionist. It landed two miles into the Atlantic, drowning fifteen.

Douglas "Wrong Way" Corrigan left New York for Los Angeles and wound up in Ireland.

Reno's Funmakers had a new act. Pauline had taught the children to tap dance and they practiced during the winter. They were quite accomplished, considering their ages. They usually took turns being critical of each other, as three-year-olds sometime do, but more importantly, they loved to perform. The audience readily accepted two cherubs tripping the light fantastic. By then, George Edward was affectionately calling Sylvia, Dodo. It was later modified by her friends into Dodé, a nickname she carries to this day.

That summer, when Dave Shirkie-Reno made his annual visit, he brought with him an 8mm movie camera. It became a big novelty for the whole family. Movies were taken of the children, the entire Funmaker group, and everything else that happened to appear in its viewfinder. Dave had an ulterior motive. Now he could have movies taken of him, acting out various dramatic scenes, and send them to Hollywood in hopes of being discovered.

In the field where the big top was erected, ran a clever little brook. Twisting and turning as it found its way, it created a curious attraction for the children. The water gently flowed over a sandy bottom and smooth stones. Anyone who has ever walked in such a stream understands the sensation one gets feeling the sand between their toes and the water ripple against their legs. It is a simple pleasure in life, perhaps unknown by the urban community.

With the movie camera in hand, Dave decided the creek would be a dandy subject, and set the stage by having the children play in it. Dutch had made a toy boat for George Edward to float, and Dodo insisted on bringing her doll with her. So, with the camera rolling, they tiptoed down the slight embankment. That is, Dodo tiptoed. George Edward was too cautious to rush into a stream at least four inches deep. After much encouragement, he managed to go down backward and stuck a toe in the water. That was all it took for him to determine the danger was too great for him to precede with such foolishness. By that time Dodo was splashing upstream, turning over pebbles. Finally, Dutch decided to take a run and leap over the creek, after first making sure it would be caught on camera. You can guess what happened next. Dutch's mighty leap landed him in the water. To his credit, he almost made it across. As he headed back to change trousers, Dave assured him it had all been caught on film. For some reason, that wasn't that important to Dutch anymore.

"Pauline," Dave said to his cousin, "I'd like you to take a movie of me acting out some dramatic scenes so I can send it to Hollywood."

"I've never used a movie camera before," she reminded him

"Don't worry about it. I'll show you how, it's easy."

About every kind of scene you can think of was filmed, even a scene in which Dave used a gun and played the heavy.

Vanity was filling the air as Dutch returned, dressed in his tuxedo for the evening performance. Having been told he resembled John Barrymore and John Boles, he asked to have his profile shot on film.

Then Pauline wanted a movie taken with her in a swimsuit. Shakespeare got it right when the mischievous fairy Puck said, "Lord, what fools these mortals be!"

However, the story doesn't end there. Dave took the film to be developed, and when he got it back, he set up the projector. The whole family sat in anticipation as the rectangular light appeared on the screen. First came the brook with Dodo splashing her doll in the water, and then George Edward's refusal to enter, followed by Dutch's leap into midstream, bringing smiles all around. Dave anxiously awaited the shots of him in the various scenes. When they appeared, alas, every frame showed Dave only from the neck down.

* * * * *

While Reno's Funmakers entertained a week in Lenoir, North Carolina, a boyhood pal of Ed's paid a visit. Joie Ray came over from Boone where he took part in public relations for the Appalachian University track and field program. It was obvious the two were delighted to see each other. Both had grown up in Kankakee, attended Steuben school, and participated in sports. Joie was quite a bit smaller than Ed, standing only five foot five and weighing 118 pounds. Nevertheless, he never missed the chance to tell Ed that he would have beat him in the ring if only he were six inches taller and fifty pounds heavier. After which, Ed would pick him up and bounce him until he said uncle.

Joie Ray may have been small in stature, but not in courage. He was the holder of seven world records in racing. Among them, the world record in the one and two mile distances. In addition, he participated in three Olympic Games, won the Wanamaker mile seven out of eight tries, and earned over 950 medals in an illustrious career in track.

Sickly and anemic as a child, Joie had such poor health, he was taken out of school at nine years old to live on his grandfather's farm. A few months of farm work did wonders, and he soon regained his strength. Joie credited much of his success to the years spent in the YMCA, where he boxed and wrestled with other athletes. It was there he gained personal confidence and discovered his ability to run. He would brag about how he was going to beat the famous runners in a race, and then went ahead and did it. Sportswriters started to call him "Chesty," and soon he became a crowd favorite. When his career began to fade, Joie remained in the news for many other exploits, some of which were zany. He once lasted 1,730 hours in a marathon dance contest, entered snowshoe races in Canada, and competed in the roller derby. Each year he ran the mile on his birthday. At the age of seventy, he ran it with a time of 6:11.5.

When together, Ed and Joie were like a couple of kids, two grown men going through a second childhood and having more fun this time. It revealed a side of Ed rarely seen by outsiders. The immense responsibilities of managing a tent show in the midst of the worst Depression in the history of the country left few opportunities for Ed to let loose his lighthearted and genial side. Those fortunate enough to see him in rare good humor came away with a different understanding of the magic man from Kankakee. Wanting to introduce Joie to everyone, Ed requested that a dinner be held in the cookhouse tent with all the Funmaker crew invited. It truly was a gay affair, with stories told by both Ed and Joie that brought the house down with endless laughter.

Joie had become a member of the Seventh-Day Adventist Church and held firm to their precepts regarding healthy food. As an athlete, he already was careful with his diet, so a church rule in this area posed no hardship. Except perhaps when Ed called the pork roast beef and passed it down the table. Joie, always suspicious of his buddy, took a small piece but didn't eat it, concentrating primarily on the vegetables.

Joie remained for the evening performance and received standing applause when introduced to the audience. He returned to Boone with a vow to keep in touch. True to his word, he made several visits from Gary, Indiana, to Kankakee as the years rolled by. Looking back, it seems that time is a relentless wind that blows gentle when we are young; and then, when least expected, becomes a windstorm like a tornado. It leaves us to wonder where the years have gone and where we were as they passed.

Chapter Twenty-Seven

Arriving on the outskirts of a village community that would later be called Cleveland, meant the party was now in Tennessee. Tobias turned to Wilbur and said, "You be meeting a fellow named Jack Leffingwell. All I know is he has the boat that'll take you all across Chickamauga Lake. Ain't got no church here, just a meeting house. We're gonna wait till it turns dark, and he's supposed to come stand by that big oak tree over yonder."

According to plan, as the moon came in view, a dark figure could be seen leaning against the mighty oak.

"You all wait here while I go see if he be the right man," Tobias said, being cautious. He hadn't worked with Leffingwell for awhile and had to make certain things were going according to plan. As it turned out, Jack Leffingwell had ferried more than one hundred slaves across the lake and taken them safely to the next station.

"I hope you folks know how to ride a horse," Jack said with a smile. "If you don't, it don't matter much, 'cause once you get atop, the horse does the rest."

Wow! thought Leroy. Escape was much more fun than he'd ever suspected.

The boat was a typical flat-bottom craft, large enough to carry five passengers. With only a slight breeze, the water remained tranquil, and they seemed to glide with very little effort from the oars. It was apparent Jack had made the journey many times before. He didn't speak but hummed a tune barely audible to the others. Leroy let the boat pull his hand through the water, as he pretended it was a rudder, while nobody noticed.

"Is this a good fishing lake?" Wilbur finally asked.

"You bet it is. And I plan to do some fishing when I come back this way," Jack answered.

"If I ever get free, I plan to do a lot of fishing," Wilbur stated.

"I suspect you will," Jack said with a smile.

With the reflection of a bright moon glistening on the water, Jack put the boat in at a sandy spot and then dragged it up to higher ground.

"The horses are a short piece ahead," he said. "We only got four, so the young'uns gotta ride double."

To Leroy, it was like someone had shoved a dagger in his back. He had to take his first ride on a horse with Celia hanging on behind him.

The horses were kept in a small barn alongside a rough-hewn cabin. Its proprietor, Luc Langlois, was a weathered mountain man who eked out a modest living trapping beaver as well as other varmints. Originally from Canada, Luc had been drawn to the Appalachian gold fields, but soon realized mining was not for him. The solitary life in the mountains suited him well, and the popularity of fur clothing allowed him to earn a little cash. He had built the cabin by himself, as well as the barn used to house the horses. Jack Leffingwell paid about $2 a month to keep the horses there, the money provided by the Underground Railroad. Luc's feelings about slavery were what you would expect from a man who loved freedom.

Jack Leffingwell led a somewhat similar and equally dangerous life. His survival depended on both physical strength and personal bravery. He had to master the use of firearms, horsemanship, and swimming, and have wilderness skills necessary to live through the hardship of long, lonely winters.

Jack had gotten the horses from a Choctaw Indian named Yalata, using tobacco as trade. The Choctaw, along with several other Indian tribes, made up a group known as the Chickamauga Confederacy. Indians from various tribes had come together to resist the influx of settlers taking their land. After fighting a losing battle for years, they finally retreated to the south Cumberland Plateau, where they were able to retain a portion of the territory.

The escape route would lead the runaway slaves in a northwest direction, through the Cumberland Plateau and Indian Territory. The horses were small but sturdy, perfectly suited for travel over rough mountainous terrain. Luc had saddled them just when the sun went down in anticipation of their nighttime arrival. After making certain they were properly cinched, Jack announced, "Let's mount up. I want to get to the next stop afore daylight."

He knew that wasn't possible, but figured once they were in Indian Territory, they would be safe from bounty hunters and the law. Both were unpopular with the Indians. The procession began in single file with Wilbur bringing up the rear, and it didn't take long for the novice riders to learn how to move their bodies with the motion of the animals. Lulled by the groan and squeak of the leather saddles, they continued for two hours before Jack signaled for them to stop.

"Best give them a little rest," he said as he dismounted. He had chosen an area well concealed by trees, with several large rocks on which they could sit and rest themselves.

"We don't have too far to go now to reach the Choctaw village and my friend Yalata," Jack said, passing the water canteen around. "You'll be spending the day with his family, then tonight we head for Cardwell Mountain. There are enough caves under that mountain to hide a whole army, and that's where the next contact will meet us."

Jack had been to the village several times while conducting for the railroad. He had first become friends with Yalata when he initially entered with a gift—a deer tied across his saddle. Each of his subsequent visits had been while assisting runaway slaves. The Indian tribes were suspicious of all government men and any potential settler. They soon learned Jack Leffingwell was a friend who posed no threat. Aiyana, Yalata's wife, was a Cherokee. Their marriage, though not uncommon in the Chickamauga Confederacy, had required approval from several people, since Aiyana was also the daughter of a chief.

As they entered the village, the group was met by a number of small children, who ran ahead to announce their arrival. Wilbur hadn't expected the village to look as it did. Instead of wigwams or tepees, the dwellings were composed of log cabins with outbuildings. Farming was, obviously, the major industry. Large sections of the land were devoted to raising crops and feed for the cattle. European influence had transformed the once proud warrior hunter into an agrarian and cattleman. The proud warrior still existed, but it rested beneath the passive surface, requiring only to be summoned should the need arise.

Yalata did not smile. He acknowledged Jack only by narrowing his eyes, then motioning the group to his home. Once inside, the Littlefields discovered the work of a craftsman. There was a fireplace on one end of the main room with iron ladles hanging by hooks on either side of it. Iron kettles rested in front on the stone slab floor, and a rifle was cradled on top of the mantel. Marie noticed a spinning wheel near one wall and a butter churn sitting by another. A long handmade dining table with two benches stood nearby. All were polished to a shine. Wilbur observed that the cabin had puncheon floors, giving it a rich and pleasant appearance. Wilbur etched the various images of this home in his mind and in the hopes he would put them to use at a later date.

Aiyana spoke some English, enough to put her guests at ease, and offered them hot food and water. They sat on each side of the table while Aiyana, refusing help from Marie, served the meal. Everything consumed that day had either been raised or farmed by Yalata, Aiyana, and their children. At their host's request, Wilbur related the story of their life as slaves and their escape for freedom. His tale fell on sympathetic ears, since many Indians had been forced to give up their land and been marched, against their will, to unfamiliar reservations. Occasionally joined by runaway slaves, they had fought a losing war of resistance for years. The government, realizing the difficulty in capturing those in the Cumberland Plateau, lost interest. Over time the tribes were assimilated into the dominant society.

Yalata would accompany them to Cardwell Mountain. He was respected by the other tribes, and his presence would make it safer should they meet any hostile renegades. The destination for the Underground Railroad conductors would now be the McMinnville area and Cumberland Caverns beneath Caldwell Mountain. Their journey there would cross the path the Cherokees took along the Trail of Tears. Thousands had camped in the area to rest, grind their corn, and tend to their sick. The graves of several hundred who had suffered and died were there. Tears always streaked Yalata's impassive face whenever he passed those graves.

The caravan drew little attention during the thirty-mile trip on horseback. Once or twice they ran into a group of mounted Indians, but they were only curious and Yalata explained the situation. On one occasion, after talking to Yalata, several rode in a circle around the fugitive slaves, each one reaching over and tapping them before galloping off. Wilbur never found out what that meant.

Over thirty miles of caves meander under the mountain, providing excellent hiding places for those not wishing to be found. The grottoes can also be dangerous, should anyone attempt to pursue their prey in there. A wrong turn guaranteed confusion, raising the risk of a person never finding his way out, but spending what remained of his life in total blackness.

Yalata stayed with the Littlefields while Jack rode to an area where mining took place. Nitrates had been mined there since 1812, providing saltpeter for the manufacture of gun powder. Having made friends with some of the miners, he visited them on each trip, sharing news. This time he alerted them to the fact he was joined by Yalata. Miners' concerns about renegades forced them to consider firearms as another work tool.

In the event the next conductor failed to show, Jack would take the fugitives to the Baptist church in Statesville. Two days passed, and it appeared as though plan B needed to be executed. Just when Jack was about to explain the situation to Wilbur and his family, a horse and box wagon pulled up. The driver's hat brim was turned down and coat collar turned up, hiding the driver's face. Jack walked toward the wagon to get a better look, and a woman's voice asked, "Are you Jack Leffingwell?"

"I might be. Then again I might not be. Who the hell are you?"

"My name is Abigail Adams. I am Deacon Adams's daughter. My father couldn't make the trip. The good Lord took Pastor Simmons day before yesterday, and the council had to meet for succession talk. I volunteered to take his place."

Jack tilted his head to see her face better. "You people must be crazy. There are renegade Indians between here and there. Nobody risks a trip like that alone."

"I ain't actually alone," she said, holding up a rifle in one hand and pistol in the other. "And I can use them better than most men."

Jack saw he had ruffled her feathers and replied, "I suppose you could. Let's go meet the folks you'll be taking to Statesville."

Even though Abigail tried to hide her face, Jack saw enough to determine she had handsome looks. In fact, he found her pretty. After she took off her hat to wipe her brow, he saw she was beautiful.

"Your husband couldn't make the trip either?" he asked.

"I'm not married, but if I was, he wouldn't need to come along. I can take care of myself."

Jack had made up his mind. He wanted to get better acquainted. So he decided to join them on the trip back. Various excuses ran through his mind. He knew if any of them offended her, she wouldn't allow him to come along

"I understand Statesville is where all the cotton mills are located," he said casually.

"Yep, and that ain't all. We got seven stores, three blacksmiths, wood shop harness, boot and shoe shop as well. We also got probably what you'd like most of all—five saloons."

"The saloons don't interest me none, since I don't drink hard liquor," he lied. "But I sure would like to see the boot maker. These old brogans are about to give out, and there ain't any good cobblers where I come from."

"Statesville has a good one."

"Would you mind if I tagged along on the way back? I need to have a pair made."

"Can't see where it'll hurt anything," she replied.

That little statement made Jack Leffingwell's day. After introducing Abigail to her passengers, he went to tell Yalata the change of plans. They were going to do some hunting and fishing on the way back. Now Yalata would travel back alone. The tawny Indian only smiled when Jack told him, knowing full well the real reason. They would hunt together at a later time. After receiving his railroad payment and tobacco, he turned his pony and trotted south with three horses in tow.

Abigail planned to take the same trail back that she had used to get there. It was basically known only to settlers, who traveled it in order to elude renegade Indians and various highwaymen. Without mishap, she figured it would take two days. Three at the most.

Jack gathered necessary provisions and, with the passengers situated in the wagon, they departed. The well-fed team of horses would get extended rest periods along the route, making up for not resting a day before the return trip. By now, the runaways have been traveling for over two months, and though fatigue overwhelmed them, their resolve had been only strengthened. They were encouraged by the knowledge that their Beulah Land lay ahead.

Jack brought his horse alongside Abigail and said, "I never knew this trail was here. I mainly take the other one and just kept my eyes open for bounty hunters. Indians didn't bother us much with Yalata along."

"Well, you ain't got Yalata with you now," she said without taking her gaze off the path.

Jack kicked his horse and galloped ahead for a while, trying to figure a way to break the ice with such a stubborn woman. Temporarily giving up, he slowed his mount and talked with Wilbur and Leroy.

The first stop to rest the horses came when the sun began to pale in the west. The traveling party also took the opportunity to relieve themselves and stretch their legs. By traveling northwest, on the edge of the Cumberland Plateau, the Littlefields were exposed to some of nature's most awesome beauty. They saw verdant valleys and rocky ridges created by water over them for thousands of years. The uplands, covered with stately pine trees and a kaleidoscope of beautiful wildflowers, announced how insignificant humans truly were.

Abigail began unloading provisions and instructed the others to begin setting up camp for the evening. Where they camped offered a view of the immediate area below, and building a fire was deemed safe enough. Jack mentally agreed with her actions and marveled even more at this confident female.

"Best I can do tonight is beans, bread, and coffee," she said. "Where I plan to stop tomorrow will give us a chance to catch some fish, and I promise you all a better meal."

Since they'd had no breakfast and had traveled all day, Jack and the Littlefields were so hungry, the hot beans were the best they ever tasted. After eating, Jack unhooked the team and walked them to a grassy span beneath a nearby copse. Abigail had overlooked that task, and mentally chided herself while pretending not to notice. The women slept in the wagon while the men spread out their bed rolls close to the fire. Their faint conversation lasted a short while, but was soon replaced with the soft snoring of two tired men. Suppressed laughter could be heard from the wagon a little longer, but eventually, that too ceased.

Jack was awake before sunrise. A foggy mist lay over the valley. He loved this time of day and welcomed it with deep breaths, making his chest feel cold and refreshed. He stoked the fire, and soon coffee was steaming from the pot. He was working on his second cup when the rest began to rise and shine.

"I don't usually sleep this late," Abigail said as she poured a cup of coffee and stared into the fire. "Have you been up long?"

"Not really. Don't usually wake up so early," Jack said in an attempt to make her feel better.

"I got some bacon in the wagon. That ought to make everybody feel good before we start on the trail again."

"Sounds good to me," Jack said. "I'll harness the team while the bacon is cooking."

After breakfast, the journey continued. Once on the road Wilbur asked Marie about the laughter he'd heard coming from the wagon.

"Oh, mainly girl talk," she answered.

"But what was so funny?"

"We found humor in the way Mr. Leffingwell keeps trying to impress Abigail," Marie finally confessed.

"What did she say?" asked Wilbur.

"She says that he's just a backwoods dummy and better leave her alone," Marie whispered. Wilbur couldn't help from smiling.

The day turned out to be unseasonably warm, and with a cloudless sky, the sun shone full on the group. Initially, its brightness raised their spirits. However, as the day progressed, the intense warming took its effect. Horses required more rest breaks, and water consumption doubled. While offering Abigail the water canteen, Jack asked, "How soon do you think we'll reach that spot you've been talking about?"

"Don't worry, Mr. Leffingwell. I'm sure you'll be able to tough it out 'til we get there."

"I was only thinking of the others," he said tersely. To himself he added, *Damn that woman.*

In the late afternoon, Abigail guided the team off the trail and up a slight incline, to a location overlooking a waterfall and rivulet beneath.

The cascade formed a swell similar to a small lake, before flowing on its winding way in search of a larger body of water. Oak and other hardwoods forested the grassy site, and the gurgle of the stream could be heard from where they set up camp.

"I got fishing poles in the wagon," Abigail said, "if anybody wants to try their luck in the stream."

"I do," shouted an enthusiastic Leroy. "Come on, Dad, let's go fishin'."

"Jack, you coming too?" Wilbur asked.

"Maybe Mr. Leffingwell doesn't fish," Marie said.

"Oh, I've done a little fishing in my time," Jack said. "Guess I'll give it a try. But let's build a fire first. Wilbur, you and Leroy gather some of that hardwood. I'll get the rocks to make the fire circle."

No sooner had Leroy begun looking for the wood, than he heard the splash of a fish hitting the surface to eat a floating insect. He had an armful of firewood before his father had picked up his first stick.

The poles were made of bamboo and the line was heavy, with a large hook and lead sinker. A moveable cork was fashioned to float on the surface and indicate if there was a bite. Jack doubted if that kind of gear would work in a mountain stream. While Wilbur and Leroy dug for worms, Jack refashioned his line to troll just beneath the surface. He made a lure out of bird feathers and set about to fish for mountain trout.

That night they lazed around after eating their fill of the speckled fare. The sky remained clear, and a million stars brightened the heavens. Abigail lay back on a grassy slope and said her nightly prayers, while Jack took the liberty to sit beside her.

"Do you read the Bible much, Mr. Leffingwell?" she asked quietly.

"I got one in my saddle bags, but can't say I read it a lot," he replied. "Parts of it are hard for me to understand."

"I'm surprised you carry one," she said. "When I see the heavens all starlit like this, I think of the book of Psalms. 'The heavens declare the glory of God; and the firmament sheweth his handiwork.' Psalms 19:1.

"He telleth the number of the stars; he calleth them all by their names. Great is our Lord, and of great power: his understanding is infinite.' Psalm 147:4-5."

Jack was impressed. "You sure do know your Bible, ma'am."

"Do you know your verses, Mr. Leffingwell?" she asked.

"No, ma'am. I only learned one poem my whole life, because it be the most fitting for me. Would you like to hear it?"

"I suppose so," she said.

> *"Bright Star! Would I were stedfast as thou art —*
> *Not in lone splendor hung aloft the night*
> *And watching, with eternal lids apart,*
> *Like nature's patient, sleepless Eremite,*
> *The moving waters at their priestlike task*
> *Of pure ablution round earth's human shores,*
> *Or gazing on the new soft-fallen mask*
> *Of snow upon the mountains and the moors.*
> *No — yet still stedfast, still unchangeable,*
> *Pillow'd upon my fair love's ripening breast,*
> *To feel for ever its soft fall and swell,*
> *Awake for ever in a sweet unrest,*
> *Still, still to hear tender-taken breath,*
> *And so live ever — or else swoon to death."*

"I can't say where I first heard it," Jack said, "or even who wrote it. But it just seems to be fitting."

The silence seemed to last forever before Abigail, with moistened eyes, finally said, "Would you mind if I called you Jack?"

Chapter Twenty-Eight

Hitler demanded Czechoslovakia cede the Sudetenland. England and France met with him in Munich and agreed to his claim that German Nationals were being mistreated. Subsequently, they pressed Czechoslovakia until she acquiesced. German troops marched in and took control of the country. Hitler was fulfilling his goals like clockwork.

He next turned to Poland with the same argument. The UK and France had signed a nonaggression pact with Poland to defend her from enemy invasion. Hitler had previously agreed with Stalin to partition Poland and divide it. As a result, when he invaded Poland, Britain and France declared war on Germany. In actuality, though, they offered little help to Poland. At the same time, Russia invaded Poland from the east. It was getting confusing to determine who was friend and who was foe.

Hitler announced to the German parliament his plans to eradicate Jews from Europe. Joining the Hitler Youth group became mandatory for Aryan teenage boys, and the mentally ill were exterminated. The ambitions of the fanatical German leader had made the world a dangerous place. Newspapers and radio constantly kept the populace informed, yet some remained indifferent to the tragic treatment of Jews. Many believed the stories were untrue.

Here in the States, a politically radical Roman Catholic priest, Charles Coughlin, influenced the attitude of many with his radio program. Coughlin initially supported President Roosevelt's New

Deal, but gradually found himself against it. Claiming it wasn't liberal enough, he took to the airways to speak out against certain aspects that he felt lacked social justice. In addition, he agreed with some of Hitler's policies, and believed the Jews were a major part of the problems facing the world. The bishops lacked the courage to confront him, out of fear of a schism and losing Catholic followers. Phenomenally popular, his radio program and brand of anti-Semitism influenced 30 million listeners. In fact, Gustav Schröder, captain of the German liner MS *St. Louis*, sailed to America seeking asylum for 930 Jewish refugees. They were refused entry and forced to return to Europe, only to be murdered as the war progressed. It left one to wonder whether Coughlin's radio rants had a part in our refusal to accept them.

The advent of a world war wasn't the only calamity taking place around the globe. Consolidated brush fires in the State of Victoria, Australia, burned nearly five million acres, entirely destroying several towns. Over 3,700 buildings and 1,300 homes were turned to ashes. Seventy-one people died.

In Chile an 8.3 magnitude earthquake left 50,000 dead and 60,000 more injured, mostly due to falling buildings.

On the lighter side, Ernie Hausen, using the techniques he perfected while working as a butcher at McMillen's Meat Market, won the National Chicken Picking Championship by plucking a chicken in 3.5 seconds.

Peruvian Lina Medina gave birth to a baby boy at the age of five years, seven months, and twenty-three days, making her the youngest mother on record. The father was never known.

Errol Flynn celebrated his thirtieth birthday.

Lou Gehrig, diagnosed with amyotrophic lateral sclerosis, retired from baseball. The movie *Gone With the Wind* premiered, and *The Wizard of Oz* opened at Loew's Capitol Theater in New York.

Frank Sinatra recorded his first hit, Ted Williams collected his first hit, and Lou Gehrig said, "Yet today I consider myself the luckiest man on the face of the earth." He died a year later.

* * * * *

In 1939, the United States continued to be mired in the Great Depression. Having over 17 percent of the citizens unemployed seemed like a way of life. The mood was solemn and spiritless, with little confidence in the future. And now there was another worry—the goings-on in Europe. President Roosevelt signed a Neutrality Treaty, hoping to lessen fear and improve morale. Most people felt it was just a matter of time before a world war broke out and engulfed the US.

* * * * *

Ed Reno opened the season with a contracted Reno's Funmakers tent theater. With operating cash in short supply, and all avenues to obtain more apparently closed, the expenses were down to bare bones. Only immediate family made up the acting cast; canvas men would be hired locally; and for many of the repairs and erecting the big top, Ed and Dutch would be part of the crew. Ed knew these cost-saving cuts were beginning to show. The big top required new canvas, scenery and props had faded over time, the curtain looked ragged, and some of the audience seats were broken. Outwardly, Ed refused to accept the inevitable, but in quiet moments, he acknowledged reality. He also knew most tent shows had finally gone out of business, and that specter followed him like his shadow. The economy hadn't improved in several years, and a world war loomed in Europe. He knew America would eventually become part of it, dampening the future even more.

This would probably be the last year for Reno's Funmakers, or at least until a brighter future returned. He planned to play the most popular bookings, trusting in the loyalty of older fans. With house lights turned low, they might see with their memories more than their eyes.

Ed and Gladys were having breakfast when the subject of closing came up.

"I'm at the end of my rope, Sylvie. We are about to lose everything. Your jewels are gone, and the house in Athens can't be maintained any longer. I've had to beg, borrow, and steal in order to open the season, and if the gate is bad, we won't make it through the whole year." As he spoke, he couldn't meet his wife's eyes.

"This ain't the end of the world," Gladys said reassuringly. "Look on the bright side. We got our health, we got the kids, and we got a place to stay in Kankakee."

Pouring more coffee, she reminded him, "Those jewels have been with Mr. Cornelius more than me and Pauline. A little longer won't hurt a bit. As far as the house in Athens goes, it's only bricks and wood."

After stirring her coffee awhile longer, she added, "Damn nice bricks and wood, though."

That comment lightened the situation, and Ed walked over to Pauline and Dutch's trailer whistling "Stardust" through his teeth.

Answering the knock at the door, Pauline greeted him. "Hi, Daddy. You're up kind of early. Come on in and have some breakfast."

"No thanks, honey. Your mom and I just finished. I want to talk to you and Dutch about where we stand with the show."

The three of them took chairs around the breakfast table. Pauline poured her father a cup of coffee and reheated Dutch's by adding a little more. Since their marriage, Pauline had become the official family worrier, mainly because the easy-going Dutch never seemed to let most problems bother him. The truth of the matter was that Pauline viewed all issues as major complications, while Dutch viewed most as only minor setbacks. While Pauline stewed and fretted herself into a dither, Dutch quietly solved the problem.

Ed continued, "It looks like there's a strong possibility we'll have to close the show until things pick up. Should that happen, we plan to go to Kankakee and take up residence in the house Granddad offered us."

"You mean we'll give up show business?" Pauline asked with a quivering voice.

"Not at all. Only until conditions get better," Ed said. "Times are bad right now, and if there's a war, it'll get even worse."

"When will all this happen?" she asked.

"Well, we will continue the season and see how things go, but if we run out of money, that's when we shut down and head north."

After Ed finished his coffee, he left Pauline and Dutch and inspected the big top tent. After he determined the setup was correct, he turned his thoughts to the evening performance.

Pauline was in a state of shock. Agonizing over what her father had told them, she said to Dutch, "What are we going to do? All I know is show business. We're going to need to find other work. This will be terrible, and think about George Edward."

"Hold on, sweetheart. Having to seek different employment isn't going to be hard. And as far as George Edward is concerned, he will start school in Kankakee instead of being homeschooled on the road."

While Pauline saw major tasks ahead, Dutch only included them in his trivial category and spent the afternoon consoling his wife.

Surprisingly, the opening night receipts were very good. That and a robust cashbox helped to push back the memory of the discussion earlier in the day.

Dutch could sleep all day. Pauline woke when the alarm clock began to ring and jangle on the nightstand. George Edward, however, was a different matter. He woke before the rooster found his voice and would climb out of his crib, go to the bathroom, get dressed, and silently open the front door. His destination: his grandfather's trailer.

To that earliest of risers, Big Dad walked on water. Many times Ed would awaken with a little face a few inches away, peering down at him, asking when he was going to get up. Once, while George Edward was eating an onion he found in the ice box, it was the onion that struck Ed as the most humorous. He just had to tell Pauline. Gladys wanted to lock their door at night, but Ed left it open so his grandson could get in. He didn't want him roaming around the big top alone. Ed wasn't worried about other intruders, because his pit bull, Jack, slept by the bed each night. No one came near without Jack sounding the alarm. However, the only alarm that sounded when George Edward arrived was Jack's tail wagging against the floor.

Dutch solved the problem of George Edward's early morning wanderings by removing their door handle that night. Much to his chagrin, he was roused the next morning by his son, alerting him to the shocking fact that somebody had stolen the door. Pauline explained to him that he shouldn't go outside until she got up. This only resulted in Ed getting a little more sleep in the morning, since he continued to leave his door unlocked.

Little George Edward had been potty trained at the age of seven months, with only one memorable accident. Scolding him for that embarrassing incident, his mother said, "Even little Dodo never peed her pants." A humiliated George Edward responded, "Yes, but her ain't got no hincus." That became a story the family recalled several times during the years ahead. Another was when George Edward watched his grandfather clipping wire with a pair of pliers. Ed told his grandson, "Look here, son. Your granddad can cut this big wire with only one hand."

"My daddy can do it with both hands," was the youngster's reply.

Chapter Twenty-Nine

Maintaining a positive front was vitally important to Ed and the Funmaker troupe. He always took a firm line with appearances and often was heard saying, "Never let them see you cry or think that you're down."

The big top theater had fallen on tough times and operated on very thin ice. From outward appearances, however, things couldn't be better. That was just the way Ed wanted it. Weekly revenue allowed them to keep going from town to town, but survival was uncertain. Ed planned for the worst while hoping for the best. He had recently talked to his sister Emily about staying with them that winter. He knew she had a large house with spare bedrooms that would give the family shelter, allowing him time to dispose of Funmaker equipment and schedule the move north.

Emily and Harry Gilbert lived in Georgia, near Athens. Harry was Ed's sister's second husband. She had originally married Arthur Argus-Burdene, while both performed in the circus traveling the Redpath Lyceum circuit. Argus—his stage name—was a Cherokee Indian and the son of the tribe's chief. They had four children, three of whom died shortly after birth. Their daughter, Auline, became known as Princess Nonie and lived to be seventeen. After Emily and Arthur Argus-Burdene divorced in 1922, she continued performing in the circus with a new partner. They called themselves Gilbert and Burdene.

Shortly after Princess Nonie died, Emily and Harry adopted a little girl, eight years old, and changed her name to Emilie.

Having been in show business themselves, they were sympathetic to Ed and graciously offered their help. Ed promised to keep them informed.

That night the family gathered around the kitchen table while Gladys counted attendance receipts. Pauline had previously reported the dismal results for candy sales. Final totals revealed the take was just enough to continue operations.

"I don't get it," Dutch said. "The Depression has been going on for years, and sales were never this bad before."

Ed gave an extended sigh and agreed. "People are scared and afraid to spend money in the face of a potential war. They know it's only a matter of time before we're in it. They spend all day with their ear to the radio, and the news ain't good. We're probably crazy trying to buck the trend. The Depression is one thing, but when people have their sons and husbands fighting somewhere across the ocean, they won't be interested in coming to the show."

"Do you really think we're going to get into the war?" asked Gladys.

Ed replied, "I sure do, and it's only a matter of time. When that happens, all bets are off. The show has to close down."

Pauline, with her elbows on the table and chin on her hands, said, "Daddy, you seemed real nervous during your magic act. Didn't you feel good?"

"The pressure's getting to me, honey, that's all. I was so nervous, I damn near ruined some of the tricks."

Gladys ended the session by saying, "It's late, and we have to pack up in the morning and travel to the next town. A good night's sleep will do a world of good."

Reno's Funmakers just seemed to go through the motions the rest of the summer as they performed at the remaining prearranged engagements. For the audiences that did attend, they enjoyed a pleasurable evening and went away feeling their money was well spent. Problem was, there just weren't enough of them.

Frank Keagan had a little money put away. Being a bachelor with few vices allowed him to continue the job he loved and save a portion of whatever he was paid. He now willingly worked for no pay, primarily because of respect for Ed and compassion for the rest of the troupe. As the summer ended, his last official act was to find a buyer for the big top tent and equipment. Wilson Brothers, a small carnival, could use the tent and paid a fair price. It gave Ed more than enough to last the winter and take the family north to Kankakee.

Chapter Thirty

Abigail made certain their arrival coincided with twilight. Her cargo would be staying in Statesville at a newly erected log cabin Baptist church. With the passing of Reverend Simmons, the church deacons elected Abigail's father, Hyrum Adams, as the new pastor. Hyrum Adams was a staunch abolitionist and an active participant in the Underground Railroad. Short in stature, the new pastor was elevated by his love of the Lord and a fiery trust in the Bible.

"How was your journey?" he asked his daughter.

"I encountered no problems either going or coming back," she replied. "Oh, yes, a fellow conductor by the name of Jack Leffingwell joined us on the return trip, and I found him quite helpful on occasion. His knowledge of the territory was useful."

"Where is he now? Has he returned?" her father asked.

"He's still here. He wants to have some boots made before going back."

"And where is he now, daughter?"

"He's outside with the Littlefield family."

Hyrum noticed it immediately. Abigail was acting too indifferent regarding her escort home. Never doubting his daughter's character, he could tell the man affected her.

"Bring the wagon around back," he said, "and have them come inside. I need to talk to them about the next leg of their journey. And ask Mr. Leffingwell to come in as well," Pastor Adams added as he perceived a twitch in his daughter's left eye.

The log cabin church was built with both a loft and a cellar. Either could serve to harbor the runaways. The Pastor chose the loft. Unnoticed from below, the entry door was covered by a faux ceiling panel. When the panel was slid back, a rope fell. Pulling on the rope made steps drop down. The congregation understood the purpose of the cellar, but few were aware of the loft. All the builders knew was that both the late Pastor Simmons and Pastor Adams asked that the church be built that way. Obviously, Pastor Simmons had shared Adams's feelings about slavery.

"We're going to ask you to stay in the church loft until the next conductor arrives," Pastor Adams said to the runaways. "You will be perfectly safe there, and Abigail will bring you food. Now there's a chamber pot in the corner with a rope tied to it. I'll be back this evening to see how you're doing, and you can lower it down to me. I'll empty it for you. Do you have any questions?"

"How long will we be up there?" asked Wilbur.

"The rest of today and until tomorrow evening. That's when I expect the escort to arrive."

"Tell them about the Bible meeting," Abigail added.

"I almost forgot. We're holding the weekly Bible meeting tomorrow morning at ten. You'll hear them come in, so just be quiet. It will last a little over an hour and Abigail is the instructor."

Jack Leffingwell thought, *I wonder why I knew she would be the teacher.*

After Wilbur and his family were secured in the loft, Parson Adams invited Jack to come to the house. He was curious why his daughter acted strangely whenever Jack's name came up. For her part, Abigail was torn between joining the men and preparing the meal for the Littlefields and themselves. Pastor Adams resolved the issue by telling her to fix supper while he and Mr. Leffingwell had a chat.

"Tell me about yourself, Jack," the pastor said to the other man as they settled in the parlor. "Have you been with the Railroad long?"

"I've been a conductor for three years now. Never could accept the idea of a man being a slave. Freedom is very important to me. You probably can tell I value my independence."

"That being so, I suppose you're not married," the pastor commented.

"I never found the right woman. At least, not yet anyhow," Jack replied.

"Marriage might interfere with your independence," the pastor said frankly.

"You seem to be an independent man. Did your marriage interfere?" Jack asked.

"Not in the least. Abigail's mother, bless her soul, was everything I ever hoped for, and we were like two peas in a pod when it came to the important issues."

Jack nodded. "That's the kind of woman I'm looking for." He smiled. "When I find her, I'll ask her to marry me."

"You born in Tennessee?" Pastor Adams asked.

"No, sir. I was born in the Appalachian mountains of Georgia. My folks originally came from Pennsylvania. Dad moved us to Georgia because of the gold fields. He didn't find much gold, but kept at it until he got killed. After that, my mother remarried and moved back to Pennsylvania. I stayed in the mountains doing odd jobs—hunting, fishing, and trapping. I got to know most of the trails, and one day I met a fellow by the name of Tobias Taylor. He talked about the Underground Railroad and slavery and all. The rest is history. I don't have much formal education, but I've got knowledge about most everything else. I do read the Bible on occasion, and I can't say I understand all that's in it, but I do let it evaluate me as a person."

"I'm impressed. And I think the girl you ask to marry you will be a very lucky woman," the pastor said truthfully. "I understand you're looking for a good cobbler. If I be so bold, I'd take pleasure in introducing you to those here in town."

* * * * *

The next stop for the Littlefields was a small farm a mile or so beyond Carthage, Tennessee. Their escorts, Albert and Geneva Beardsley, had fallen in love with the property at first sight and purchased the land without hesitation. In recent years, they had spent considerable time making improvements. Ideally located by two clear water creeks, the soil produced a plethora of crops, and provided enough feed for a small herd of cattle. The Beardsleys had previously lived in Ohio, when they had been involved with the Underground Railroad. They continued their participation shortly after buying the farm. Over time, they became very influential in the area, and were able to ferry across the Cumberland River without unnecessary interference or mischievous prying.

The Beardsleys were introduced to the Littlefields and explained to them the next phase of their journey, which would begin that evening. They would travel by wagon to the Cumberland River and be transported across the water on Walton's ferryboat. The ferryboat captain was a friend and was expecting them in the wee hours of the morning. Once across they would travel to the farm and spend the day there incognito. The next conductor was scheduled to arrive that evening. In the event he was delayed, they would stay at the farm another day.

By now, Wilbur and family were conditioned to the routine. Each phase of their journey meant a step closer to freedom. They were also appreciative of the manner in which the Beardsleys explained the next stage. It lessened confusion and tended to make the trip more tranquil. Not knowing why certain things happened and whether or not events were going as planned created a great deal of stress. Knowledge of the plan lessened much of their anxiety.

"I believe we're ready to take off," Geneva said. "Wilbur, get your family in the wagon and use the tarp to cover up. It's a nice clear night, so we can clip right along."

Leroy made a point to shake hands with Jack Leffingwell, the best fisherman he ever met. All farewells being said, Albert made a clicking sound and snapped the reins. With a slight jolt, the wagon began to roll down the darkened road.

The air was cool and crisp, and the dirt road muffled the creaking sound of turning wagon wheels. Wilbur took the occasion to finish the sleep that had been disrupted by their departure. The monotonous jangle of the harness served as an effective sedative. He awoke when the Beardsleys stopped to rest the horses.

"Everything all right?" he asked.

"Just fine," Geneva replied. "We're resting the team for a while. Do you folks need anything?" she asked, passing a water canteen to Marie.

"The water be all we need," said Marie.

"I love this time of year," Geneva said. "Crops are ready for harvest and the air is clean and fresh. You folks come off a plantation?"

"Yes, ma'am," Marie said. "We be from the Littlefield plantation. They let us use a plot of ground they couldn't grow nothing on. We made that our garden and grew the only vegetables we had. Growing stuff was my solitary joy, except the children, of course. Once we be free, I'm gonna have a real garden."

"Whereabouts is the Littlefield spread located?" Albert asked Wilbur.

"A few miles from Savannah, Georgia," Wilbur answered.

"My, my, you folks have come a long way," Geneva said gravely.

The horses shied as a mother raccoon scurried across the road, followed by three kits.

Albert chuckled. "Just some raccoons. They're cute little fellows, but sometimes they're a pest, especially around the henhouse."

Being nocturnal animals, the raccoons were probably on the hunt for food. Raccoons eat almost anything. They don't hibernate in winter, but if the weather gets too cold, they might sleep for several days. The familiar mask around their eyes actually serves a purpose. It reflexes glare and enhances their night vision. Like most critters, they can spook horses.

"I'd like to have me one of those babies and raise it as a pet," Leroy said.

"They don't make good pets, son," Albert said. "Best you leave them to the wild where they belong. A good hound dog is what you need. It'll follow you everywhere and be as loyal as Christ's disciples. Eleven of them, that is to say."

Even in total darkness, the ferry operator recognized the Beardsley wagon. He walked over to the barge and dropped the gate. The main ferry boat stood at anchor, but considering this was one of the narrowest spans across the Cumberland, he chose to use the ferry barge. Albert coaxed the horses on board, and the gate was quietly replaced. When they reached the other side of the river, the operator dropped the gate again, and the Beardsley wagon continued on its way. Not a single word broke the silence. Albert knew a road that circumvented the tiny community of Carthage. After about a mile, he turned the wagon onto his lane and pulled up by the barn.

"Don't light any lamps until you get situated inside," he said to Geneva. "I'll unhook the team and put them to bed. They already have plenty of hay and water in their stalls. I'll be there in short order."

Geneva, taking Marie's hand, led her into the lightless house. The others followed closely behind. Once safely inside, she told them, "Just stay right here for a second while I cover the windows."

Lamplight revealed a comfortable living room with well-made accouterments. Handcrafted furniture announced the talent of the artisan, while the arrangement reflected good taste. The sight of it all was a jaw-dropper for Marie. To the young woman, the house seemed straight out of a fairy tale. It took a while before Marie could catch her breath and utter a word. Finally she said, "Your home is beautiful."

"Thank you, dear," Geneva said. "It didn't happen overnight. We went years with only a makeshift table and empty kegs for chairs. Back then the land came first and our comfort came second. The Lord has been good to us. That's one of the reasons we do what we do, to thank Him for our blessings."

The sound of a door closing meant Albert was back. From somewhere on the farm, a rooster crowed.

"We all need some breakfast," Geneva said, "but I can't cook a thing until the road dust is washed off. Come with me, Marie, and bring Celia. We've got a little laundry room by the kitchen, and I'll get some water heating. You men can go with Albert. He washes in the creek unless there's snow on the ground."

The water in the Beardsleys' creek came up to Wilbur's knees. It ran clear, cold, and swift over a sandy bottom. It felt icy at first, but seemed to warm up as they got used to it. They tossed a bar of homemade lye soap to one another, and Wilbur and Leroy recorded one of the fastest baths on record, while Albert happily splashed like an otter.

"There's a spare bedroom at the end of the hallway," Albert told the Littlefields when they had finished breakfast. "You're welcome to it if you want to rest up. It's best you stay inside during the day in case some busybodies come poking around."

That was agreeable to all except Leroy. It dashed his hopes of investigating the farm, especially the cattle.

That evening the next conductor appeared, ready to transport the group to a church in Westmoreland.

Chapter Thirty-One

Ed Reno and family were now back in Georgia and staying the winter with his sister Emily and her husband Harry. The big top tent was gone, along with most of the traveling equipment and vehicles. The only things he'd kept were his magic paraphernalia and, at Gladys's insistence, the large globe she walked on in her juggling act. Keeping the globe baffled everyone, but she was adamant.

"Do you think Reno's Funmakers will ever be back?" Harry asked Ed.

"Yes, I do, but not until all this uncertainty is over. We all plan to return to the road bigger and better. Once the economy comes back and the war scare is gone, we'll resume the life we love best."

Harry was convinced, but wondered how long that would be. "I think we will be in the war sooner than later. The problem I have is, how long will it last? "

"It won't last very long once we're in it," Ed insisted. "How's it going over there? I haven't heard the radio for a couple days."

"Not very good from what I hear," Harry replied. "It seems like Germany is knocking the crap out of everybody."

"That'll stop when we get in it," Ed said, with assurance.

The talk of the war continued until Emily entered the room to announce dinner was ready. Emily thoroughly enjoyed having her brother and Gladys with them, yet she couldn't help overhearing Ed's phone calls to their father in Kankakee. They would be leaving soon, and heaven only knew when they would see each other again. To Emily, good things in her life never seemed to last. Their leaving saddened her, and brought back memories of losing her first three children, and then Princess Nonie as a teenager. Their adopted daughter Emilie was now in her twenties and on her own. Emily and Harry remained active in show business. Jobs were scarce, though, and the closing of Reno's Funmakers didn't make prospects any better. Ed had always been their fallback whenever they found themselves between jobs.

During the winter, Ed managed a few auditorium performances of magic in the area schools. Pauline and Dutch provided accompaniment with songs and piano music. The act was successful, but the prolonged time between shows seriously reduced their revenue.

As the leaves on the Georgia trees budded out, the Funmaker family began their pilgrimage north. The journey proceeded without incident and ended in Kankakee, Illinois.

The house in Kankakee had three bedrooms and, with proper arranging, accommodated the two families. It was obvious improvements were needed, but those would have to wait until jobs were found.

The only experience they had was in entertainment, not much in demand in Kankakee. Dutch did learn of possible employment with a radio station in Peoria, a town about a hundred miles to the south. He went there on a lark and ended up with his own show three days a week. It was a matinee program, in which callers tried to stump him with songs. If he didn't know it and couldn't play it, the caller received a dozen roses from a local florist. The show became quite popular and brought the station more advertisers.

The announcer would say, "The time is eleven o'clock." Then a voice in the background would ask, as though he hadn't heard, "What time is it?" The announcer would answer, "It's time to stump the piano player."

Dutch opened with playing an oldie, and when he finished, people would call in. Mostly women callers asked for songs such as "Night and Day," "Over the Rainbow," "How Deep is the Ocean," and "Cheek to Cheek." One lady asked for "Back in the Saddle Again," a song made popular by cowboy Gene Autry. For the most part, Dutch knew the songs and played the chorus. Occasionally, one would puzzle him and the happy caller got the roses. It kept the staff busy looking up some of the melodies to make certain the song existed and wasn't a bogus title.

About the only one who didn't like the show was Pauline. It required too much time traveling back and forth. At times Dutch was needed at the station for promotional events and was forced to spend the night, incurring additional expenses. His absence from Pauline made her unhappy and worried. That settled the issue for Dutch.

Refusing a raise in salary, he chose to please his wife and began another job search in Kankakee. His college education paid off. A local manufacturing company needed a supervisor, and Dutch was hired. Unfortunately, it was for the second shift, but again, that only bothered Pauline. As far as Dutch was concerned, he was used to working at night, and it afforded him the benefit of sleeping until noon. After a few weeks on the job, Dutch was able to get Ed hired. Until then Ed had been only able to find employment for short durations. Their new employer had received government contracts and was expanding. Each week, Dutch found a check for $37.50 in his pay envelope. Ed received slightly less, but together it was more than enough income to begin renovations on the house.

The first project concerned heating. At present, the house was heated by a large coal-burning stove in the living room. Ideally, it should be located in the basement. Unfortunately, they had no basement. Accordingly, digging a basement became their first major task.

The consequences of war had brought dark days for many people around the world. Since it came on the heels of a global economic depression, most had little solace when planning for the future. Each day was taken as it came. Uncertainty hampered any planning and slowly shattered future goals. Such was the case with Reno's Funmakers. In mortgaging the life they treasured most, they now, fundamentally, had to go through the paces with a portion of their self-importance lost. The only way to avoid despair was convincing themselves that, once the war was over and the economy improved, they would go back on the road. We all tend to compensate the present with dreams of something better in the future. For many, in the complexities of life, such thoughts are the only thing that sustains them. Perhaps another term for their dreams is hope.

At present, the war in Europe looked bleak, for the Nazis appeared unstoppable. Hitler, intoxicated with success, made continuous demands on neighboring countries, and they complied mostly out of fear. Almost immediately after the invasion of Poland, the ethnic cleansing, or mass execution, of Poles began. Patients from mental asylums were gassed to death, and Polish Jews were dispatched by shootings, hangings, and gassing as well.

Allied resistance in France failed to restrain the German juggernaut, and eventually found itself in a losing defense at Dunkirk. For some unknown reason, Hitler signed off on the order to halt the German armored advance and assigned the attack to the Luftwaffe and infantry. Complete devastation of the Allied forces was averted, and 338,226 troops managed to escape across the channel. Still, the Allies suffered serious losses. They were outnumbered two to one, and over 30,000 troops were either killed or wounded. Another 30,000 were missing or captured. In addition, the loss of materiel on the beaches was enormous. Left behind were massive supplies of ammunition, nearly 900 field guns, over 300 large caliber guns, 700 tanks, 20,000 motorcycles, and 45,000 trucks and other vehicles. England was left with only enough materiel for two divisions. On the beaches in France, materiel for ten divisions was abandoned. It would take months for England to replace those losses.

The appeasement fostered by Neville Chamberlain proved devastatingly wrong, forcing his resignation. Winston Churchill, correct in his active opposition to Hitler, became prime minister and the singular inspiration to hold the country together. And now the unrelenting bombing of England began.

Chapter Thirty-Two

Pastor Hyrum Adams had grown fond of Jack Leffingwell, while his daughter Abigail feigned indifference. The recommended cobbler took measurements and told Jack there would be about a one-week waiting period for the new boots. He had offered a special sole material that hadn't arrived yet, though it was expected any day. Hyrum felt somewhat responsible for the delay, since he had recommended this particular craftsman. Assuring Jack the delay was well worth it, he helped him find lodging at the home of one of the parishioners. He also offered to come by and take him to church services on Sunday. Jack wasn't about to refuse and at 9:30 sharp Sunday morning, the carriage pulled up, with Abigail as a front-seat passenger.

"Good morning, Brother Jack," Hyrum said. "Did you sleep well last night?"

"Couldn't have slept better, considering that bed has a feather tick mattress. First time for someone used to sleeping on the ground," Jack said as he climbed aboard next to Abigail. "I hope this isn't too crowded for you, Miss Adams. I could sit in the back."

"It's only for a short distance," she said.

Once inside the church, Hyrum said, "Would you mind giving us a hand, Jack? We need to get set up for services. Abigail will show you what to do."

Jack found himself placing hymnals along each pew while Abigail practiced a gospel song on the organ, a recent addition, much to the pride of the pastor.

"Now when folks start coming in," Hyrum said to Jack, "just hand each one a schedule of today's service. It's that stack of white sheets there by the door. Sorry to say, you'll just have to sit back there by the door."

Thank God for little blessings, Jack thought.

He found it hard to follow the service, since he was distracted by Abigail and the sound of the beautiful hymns she created. Even though he tried to focus on the pastor, his eyes had different ideas and continuously moved in her direction. When the service ended, Hyrum walked from the podium to where Jack stood and gave a benediction. After the church emptied, Jack reversed the pre-service procedure. He gathered up the hymnals and placed them in a cabinet by the organ. Abigail collected the white schedule sheets. Jack never did see where they ended up.

Hyrum usually was jovial when Sunday services were completed; today was no exception. He cheerfully said to Jack, "You will make the preacher happy if you join us for an early Sunday dinner."

"That's not necessary, Pastor Adams. You've done too much for me already."

"I insist, Jack, and please call me Hyrum. If it's all right with you, I'd like to consider you my friend."

"I'd be honored," Jack replied. Turning to Abigail, he said, "I hope I won't inconvenience you."

"Mr. Leffingwell, there is always room for one more at every dinner."

Jack sensed she must be annoyed, because she didn't call him by his first name.

When they entered the home, Abigail suggested the men relax in the parlor while she prepared the meal. As soon as Hyrum sat down, he unlaced his Sunday shoes to let his feet breathe. Jack noticed how comfortable he felt around Hyrum. It was like they have known each other for years instead of days.

"Have you ever considered settling down?" Hyrum asked him. "Have you ever thought about where you'd like to be if you ever did?"

"If I said I've never thought about it, I'd be lying. I guess the right opportunity never came up. My independent life suits me fine. I can go where I want, do what I want, and if I'm willing to fight, say what I want." That made both men laugh.

"Hypothetically speaking," Hyrum went on, "what would you do if the right woman came along and wanted to stay put? Stay and build a farm, for example."

"I guess if she was the right woman, I'd do what she wanted and live the boring life."

"You'd learn in short order that building a farm is the furthest thing from boredom you can find," Hyrum said. "Building a cabin to live in, clearing the field for planting, fighting the weather, raising cattle and maybe a child or two, you'd find out there isn't any time to be bored."

"Do you think I might squeeze in the time to do a little hunting and fishing?" Jack jokingly asked.

Hyrum laughed. "How would I know? You'd have to ask your wife."

"What's so funny?" Abigail asked as she entered the room to announce dinner.

The following day Jack checked with the cobbler and learned that the awaited material had just arrived. The cobbler would cut the patterns for his new boots the next day, and he should have the boots by the end of the week. Good news put a spring in his step, and he decided to go to the Adams farm and curry his horse. Before making the two-mile walk, he stopped by the church in hopes of possibly getting a ride. As he approached, the sight of the Adams carriage justified his decision. The closer Jack got to the church, the better he heard powerful, soul-stirring music being played on the organ. The deep mournful notes exploded in volume when he opened the door. Abigail Adams was totally enrapt with the music, and Jack stood there for several minutes before she noticed him.

"You startled me," she said.

"That music was amazing. What was it?" Jack asked.

"Bach," she answered. "His Toccata and Fugue in D Minor. Father doesn't like it very well, so I come here and play it when he's away."

"Your father is away?"

"Not exactly. He travels once a week to visit the shut-ins. He should be home by now. Did you want to see him?"

"To be honest, I was looking for a ride to your farm. I want to curry my horse."

"I'm ready to go back. I can give you a lift."

When the carriage reached the farm, they noticed Hyrum had already returned. The evidence was his horse in the corral just off the barn.

"If you like," Jack said to Abigail, "I can take the harness off and put the horse in her stall."

"That would be nice of you," she answered.

Jack was putting the currycomb to use when Hyrum appeared at the barn door. The way the sun illuminated the opening, his image appeared black with a lighter glow on the periphery.

"Is that you, Hyrum?" Jack asked.

"It's me."

As Jack walked toward him, Hyrum's silhouette became more distinct and developed color.

"I bet your horse appreciates your attention," Hyrum said.

"It's been a while, and I don't have much else to do. By the way, my boots will be ready by the end of the week."

"That's one of the things I'd like to talk about. Today, I've been out calling on the members that can't make it to church regularly. Some are sick and others too feeble to leave their homes. A lady by the name of Rosenthal owns the land next to us and wants to sell off a hundred acres. She's up there in age. Heavens, must be over ninety now. Well, I took a look at what she offers and it reminds me of the land my wife and I bought when we first arrived here. About sixty-five acres is ready for tilling and the rest needs to be cleared. Twenty acres or so is in standing timber, some pine, but a great deal of hardwood. There's a pretty good size creek that winds through the place. She's asking $100 for the tillable land and will throw in the woods."

"Why are you telling me this, Hyrum?" Jack asked as he returned to his grooming.

Hyrum took a deep breath. "Well, I was thinking about our conversation regarding marriage and independent freedom, and it came to me that a man with his own house and a good farm could marry about any girl in the area, and the right one is likely to be among them."

"You old fox," Jack said. "You're trying like the dickens to get me to give up my independent life."

"If it's a problem with the money, that can be worked out," Hyrum said.

"It's not the money, I've got the money. The problem is giving up my independence and finding the right woman."

"Now don't get your britches too tight. Just think about it, that's all I'm asking." Sensing he had struck a chord, Hyrum changed the subject. "How about a tall glass of cold lemonade?"

That night Jack dreamed through a restless sleep. He kept cutting down trees. Finally giving up on the sleep, he got out of bed. As dawn broke, he found himself hiking to the Adams farm. Apparently no one was up, and he saddled his horse and followed the creek. The morning air was cool and refreshing, and his mount nickered and romped happily along the way. Jack wasn't totally sure why he'd taken this route. In fact, he hadn't been totally sure about anything the past few days. Entering a stretch of grass wet with morning dew, he noticed a cabin in the far distance. The windows were illuminated by lamplight, and Jack guided the horse in that direction.

Like most older people, the widow Rosenthal rose before sunup. The pre-dawn morning provided time for her to read her Bible and reminisce about her youth. Blessed with good eyesight and keen hearing, she heard Jack Leffingwell's approach before he dismounted.

"Good morning, ma'am," he said when she opened her door. "Is it too early to be having a conversation about the land you're selling?"

"You must be the young fellow Pastor Adams talked to me about."

"I suppose I am. My name is Jack Leffingwell."

"Come in and sit a spell," the widow said politely. "Are you interested in buying the land?"

"From what I can see in the morning fog, it looks fine. I would like to take a better look once the fog is burnt off."

"That won't take too long now," she said. "Join me with a cup of tea while you wait. Tell me about yourself. Have you farmed before?"

"No, ma'am. Not with a big spread. My life has been spent hunting, trapping, and fishing. Do you need any help fixing the tea?"

"You just sit still, young man. I can handle this very well. It's nice to have the company. I haven't felt too good lately. That's why Pastor Adams stopped by to visit me."

"Hope it's not serious," Jack said.

"Everything's serious at my age, but I'm feeling much better now. It was probably just a cold."

If Yalata could only see me now, Jack thought, *drinking tea like an Englishman.*

Minnie Rosenthal could talk for hours and loved to have company. Jack, after refusing another cup of tea, excused himself and explored the property in the bright sunlight. He was quite impressed with the creek; it provided a natural water supply for raising cattle and horses. A couple hours later, he rode back to the widow's cabin.

"I understand the asking price is $100. I'd like to buy the land. My money is in the bank in McMinnville. I'll have it sent to Statesville, and it should get here in a week or so. Would you like to receive your money as a bank draft, or do you prefer cash?" "I'd like to have it put into my account in Statesville," she said.

"I'll see to it. There's one other thing, Mrs. Rosenthal. For personal reasons, I want the sale to be held in confidence for a while."

Chapter Thirty-Three

Ed Reno and Dutch were digging the basement by hand. Working after their shift at the factory and on weekends made progress on the excavation rather slow. The removed soil was collected in a wheelbarrow and pushed to the rear of the lot. By now a good-sized mound had formed. Enterprising Ed found a buyer for the black earth, and when there was enough for a pickup truck load, the buyer came over with two of his sons and loaded the truck bed. Whether it was used for fill or resold, Ed never took the time to find out.

Various passersby continuously made suggestions. One in particular struck the two men as kind of funny. The man suggested they move the house. Then they could dig unimpeded, make the forms, and pour the cement. After it set up, they could move the house back. The more Ed and Dutch labored and the longer it took, the more that suggestion sounded pretty good. In the end, it took almost a year before the basement was finished and the furnace could be installed. Many a night afterward, they would sit around the kitchen table, shaking their heads and saying, "How the hell did we ever complete that job?"

A show-business frame of mind was ever present in the Renos and Moons, lying just beneath the surface of the foreign life in which they resided. Show business was what they knew best. It was what they excelled in, and, it was what they loved most. Their current life was temporary, they told themselves, as they await the mythical return of better times.

Ed came up with the idea to show movies in the smaller communities, those that didn't have theaters of their own. He believed wartime conditions would soon limit gasoline, forcing more people to stay closer to home. When that happened, the weekend movie would be a popular form of entertainment. Accordingly, he acquired a 16mm projector and found a source for the movie films. Next, he and Dutch called on the mayors of the surrounding communities. The price they quoted must have been too low, because in three days, summer weekends were booked for the rest of the year.

They didn't show the movies on a screen, but against the outside wall of a local building. White, flat, and no windows were the only requirements. Many buildings qualified, so they always had several to choose from. They preferred one with a central location and easily accessed electricity. Most of the movies they showed were Westerns, and those featuring Tex Ritter and Hopalong Cassidy proved favorites. In a way it was rather enchanting—a warm summer evening, friends and neighbors gathered on lawn chairs and benches, the images of moths dancing across the picture as they circled the projector's flickering light, and Tex Ritter telling the saloon keeper, "When he wakes up, tell him I still ain't a'rollin'."

On occasion, Ed was able to perform his magic act, usually at a school. Pauline and Dutch presented him with the same introduction they used on the road. They sang a song first, then Dutch provided background music to accentuate the drama of each trick.

The Wildwood Avenue house now had a basement with a coal-burning furnace. One of the first pieces of furniture they purchased was a used upright piano. It served as the center of family entertainment. During that first year Gladys learned to play the accordion and became quite proficient, but refused to play in public.

Nevertheless, living close to Chicago made it easier for Dave Reno-Shirkie to visit his uncle Ed. Dave was entertaining at a Chicago nightspot, and occasionally brought a fellow entertainer with him. In that regard, most visitors were either family or someone in show business or both. The get-togethers consisted of conversations about life on the road and concern over the war. After dinner, the remainder of the evening was musical entertainment until the wee hours of the morning. Visitors ended up sleeping in their chairs, on cots, or sometimes on the floor with blankets and pillows.

On one occasion Dave brought a singer with him. He had bragged about him on previous visits, and finally things worked out so they both could come down. Dutch and Dave took turns playing the piano, with Gladys on the accordion and Dave's friend singing. Everyone joined in, including the children, making it a joyful evening. Dave's enthusiasm was dampened somewhat when he asked his uncle Ed what he thought of the singer. Ed told him that he didn't care for him that much, and thought he was just a hog caller. Fortunately, others had a different opinion and were less critical. Frankie Laine went on to have a great career.

* * * * *

As summer days quickly passed, it became time for Pauline to enroll George Edward in school. Steuben School was conveniently located less than three blocks south of the house. Holding her little boy's hand, she made her way to the school, up the steps, and into the principal's office.

"From what you tell me," Mrs. Redfield, the principal, said, "your son hasn't received any formal education."

"Yes, but he knows his numbers and can read and write," Pauline answered.

Mrs. Redfield replied condescendingly, "Yes, my dear, but formal education is more than reading and writing. Considering his age, we can try him in first grade. Keep in mind, if he has problems keeping up, he could be held back."

When the school bell rang George Edward found himself in first grade. Before the week was out, he was moved to second grade.

* * * * *

In November 1940, Franklin Delano Roosevelt defeated Wendell Willkie for an unprecedented third term. The majority of American voters were locked in with Roosevelt, even though they were distressed over the Great Depression and unemployment stood at 15 percent. The opposing party, under the delusion of the discredited Herbert Hoover, failed to present an alternative electable candidate.

The electorate, already despondent over dismal conditions that had lasted years, were given something else to add to their worry list. In response to Hitler's victories in Europe, President Roosevelt signed into law the first peacetime draft in United States history. Under the terms of the act, all males between the ages of twenty-one and thirty-five had to register for the draft, with selection to be conducted by lottery. Later FDR asked Congress to extend the length of service. The peacetime draft, in itself, was unpopular. Extending the length of service caused turmoil and national debate for several months, which ended when Japan attacked America at Pearl Harbor. The United States, from the Pacific to the Atlantic, from San Francisco to Boston, from the mountains of Virginia to the cotton fields of Dixie, was now at war.

Chapter Thirty-Four

The Littlefields were told that the trip to Westmoreland would take about a day and a half. Actually, their destination was midway between Westmoreland and Lafayette. The Railroad conductors were tobacco farmers, Samuel P. Butler and his eldest son, Linas. The Butlers owned one of the largest tobacco farms in the area. Once slaveholders, they had given their slaves freedom several years earlier. Ironically, the free slaves continued living and working on the farm. But now there were two differences. One, they were paid for their work; and two, and most importantly, they were free. Tobacco was a valuable cash crop, and it made Samuel P. Butler a rich man. In addition to the vast fields, his property contained greenhouses and large warehouses.

Growing tobacco began with sowing seeds in hot beds located in part of the greenhouses. That allowed for a good start, and protected the seedlings from insects and spring chills. Young plants were then transferred to another section of the greenhouse. When mature enough, they were transplanted in the fields. After the plants were fully grown, they were harvested and taken to the warehouses for curing. Finally, the finished product was sold to tobacco buyers. While tobacco had other uses, most buyers wanted it for recreational consumption.

Wilbur, Marie, and their children rode in a wagon loaded with tobacco. The large leaves provided perfect cover for those hiding beneath. The aroma was pleasing to Wilbur. Marie and Celia didn't mind at first. However, after a few hours, they became nauseous and had to stick their heads out for fresh air.

"What's wrong, ladies?" Linas asked, laughing. He and his father had seen this response before, mostly by women.

"It's just the smell gets to us after a while," said Marie.

"I know what you mean, ma'am," Samuel P. said. "This trip is usually pretty quiet, so you all can ride uncovered. Just remember, get under when I tell you to."

Marie and Celia enjoyed the ride a lot more then. Wilbur, however, chose to savor the aroma and dream about a good cigar. The Butlers took turns driving the team, stopping only to rest and water the animals. Each rest stop allowed everyone to stretch their legs and visit the coppice, usually located just off the road. The journey was without incident. Marie and Celia only had to duck under a couple times, and even then, they suspected Linas was just having a little fun. Turning onto his property, Samuel P. negotiated a side road that led to a cabin with a light in the window. The family inside was anticipating visitors and quickly ushered the runaways through the door.

"You all will be staying here until I find out when the next train is due," Samuel P. said. He had worked with the Underground Railroad ever since he saw the light and freed his slaves. Never a tyrant and always concerned with what he called the slaves' lot in life, he operated his farm more as a supervisor or steward than a southern plantation owner. That was until the day a traveling preacher stopped by for a drink of water. They talked for hours. The preacher stayed for dinner. He and Samuel P. talked some more and prayed; and after the man of God rode away, Samuel P. Butler freed his slaves. He got involved with the Railroad shortly thereafter, but found it hard to use the Railroad terminology. It just seemed silly.

The occupants of the cabin were Solomon Brown and his wife Betsey, former slaves.

"Now you folks jus' make yourselves at home," Betsey said, "while I whip up something to eat."

Marie slowly looked around the large room. Observing the furnishings and windows with bright curtains, she said, "Thank you. I apologize for snooping, but your house is so nice, I just couldn't help it."

"Solomon and I are very proud of it as well. We purchased a lot of the furnishings from in town. Mr. Butler let us use the wagon to haul it back to the farm."

Wilbur turned to Solomon and asked, "You all be free, but still stay here and work on the farm?"

"That's right, doing practically the same things as I did before," replied Solomon.

"How come you all ain't working now?"

Solomon flashed a big smile. "Seems like we be expecting company and Mr. Butler gave me the day off. Been getting a lot more days off lately, if you know what I mean."

Their conversation continued after the meal, with each family answering the other's questions. Wilbur learned more about Mr. Butler and Solomon's role in helping slaves find freedom. He also learned that being free still had dangers. Bounty hunters were known to kidnap free black people and sell them again in the south. That was the main reason Solomon wasn't allowed to help away from the farm. Even trips to town were chaperoned by one of the Butlers. The grandfather clock against the wall chimed three times, announcing it was three in the morning, before the evening ended.

Linas Butler knocked on the door at noon, bringing news of the next conductor. Plans called for a journey, on foot, to a station near Franklin, Kentucky. Those in the traveling party must be ready to start at nine that night. Marie's heart raced each time she learned about their next journey. It always took a few minutes before she settled down and made appropriate arrangements.

When the appointed time arrived, they were surprised to find that Linas was their conductor. Naturally, Solomon and Betsey were aware of that, but such actions were still unlawful, and security required revealing as little information as possible.

At 9:15 that evening, Wilbur and family were on their way over the rolling hills to the Commonwealth of Kentucky. Linas proved to be an enjoyable traveling partner, besides an astute guide. His joking and easy attitude kept smiles on the fugitives' faces.

"Kentucky's a funny state," Linas said to Wilbur. "Folks claim to be southern, but they hold northern beliefs."

"Ain't Kentucky a slave state?" asked Wilbur.

"Yeah, I guess it is, but ain't nothing like the Deep South," Linas said. "First of all, they don't raise cotton, and the farms are a lot smaller. Nowadays, Kentucky's selling their slaves to the plantations down south. My father has the right idea. Free the slaves and hire them to work for you."

"Solomon told me about that. Seems to work for him and Betsey."

"Don't get me wrong, a lot of folk still believe in slavery and admire plantation owners," Linas said honestly. "I've also heard people brag about having bluegrass here in Kentucky. It's supposed to make their horses run real fast. Well, one thing I do know. There ain't no bluegrass around here. We're heading for the coal fields."

"Do they work slaves in the coal fields?" Wilbur asked.

"Some do. That's the funniest thing you ever did see. You can't tell who is slave and who is white. Both look alike when they come out of a mine."

For the next couple hours, no one talked as they tramped on. Finally, Linas said, "We're going to be looking for a church near Dimple."

Dimple was more a populated area than a village or town. A nearby Baptist church served that portion of Butler County. Once the passengers arrived at the church, word was immediately sent out for a new freedom train schedule and the cargo's next destination. After rest stops in station depots at Cool Springs and Pleasant Ridge, the travelers reached Owensboro and the Ohio River. The Underground Railroad sometimes called it the River Jordan, because Indiana, a slave-free state, lay on the other side. Their passengers were anxious at that point, but had to wait patiently while the railroad made arrangements for their ticket to liberty.

It was now apparent to Wilbur that they would never have found freedom solely on their own. Only because of their chance meeting with the widow, Sister Sarah, had they come in contact with the Underground Railroad. Without the assistance of that elderly lady, they would have been captured, returned to the Littlefield plantation, and punished. Beulah Land would be nothing but a hopeless dream. As the book of John recalls, Jesus said, "The wind bloweth where it listeth, and thou hearest the sound thereof, but canst not tell whence it cometh, and wither it goeth: so is every one who is born of the Spirit."

And so it was with the runaway family, huddled together, giving thanks for blessings bestowed on them by the Lord.

Chapter Thirty-Five

Sundays after church, the Reno's Funmakers family frequently visited Edward Munn Reno and his wife Minnie. Edward, always an early riser, preferred attending the early service. Dutch, on the other hand, was better able to be present at the second service at 11:00. As things worked out, the visit to Ed's father would include lunch, with Gladys and Pauline bringing a covered dish. Most conversations centered on the Depression and economic times, but now the war in Europe was included. That the United States was building Liberty ships had captured Edward's attention. He viewed it as a prelude to the States joining the war.

"We're building them to replace British ships sunk by German submarines," he told Ed frankly.

"I heard on the radio they were ordered by England as cargo-carrying merchant ships," his son replied.

"That might be true, but look at it this way: they're being made with cheap steel, only expected to last five years, and produced as fast as we can build them. That tells me they're designed for war. When a German submarine sank the SS *Robin Moore*, our cargo ship, all we did was issue a formal complaint. If that's all we're going to do, you know damn well they're going to hit us again. Eventually we've got to get in it."

"I suppose you're right," Ed said. "Roosevelt wants us to take part. So far, Congress is standing for neutrality. One thing's for sure. It would finally get us out of this Depression."

"Yeah, all the unemployed will be in the army," Edward said sarcastically. "There is something else I want to tell you, but it can wait until after we eat. Don't let me forget."

Conversations got brighter during the meal, except when Minnie complained about rationing, should war break out. Turning to George Edward and Sylvia, she exclaimed, "My heavens, you kids are growing like weeds."

Like most children their age, they were embarrassed by compliments and just looked down at their plates.

"Did you listen to President Roosevelt's four freedoms speech?" Pauline asked her grandfather.

"I heard it," he answered tersely.

"Did you like it?"

"He made it part of the State of the Union address. In general, it was okay, considering the fact we've been in a Depression for ten years. But a couple of his freedoms I didn't care for."

"Why not?" Pauline asked.

Aware that his father could pontificate for hours, given the chance, Ed began to get a little nervous. He gave his daughter a familiar look.

"I'll tell you why not," Edward said. "Here we are with about ten million people unemployed, and another five or six million on some sort of relief, and he's talking about everybody around the world has a right to economic security. That's socialism, pure and simple, and it ought to scare hell out of every American citizen. That bunch he's got in his administration wouldn't like anything better than to see us a socialist country. Also, that freedom from fear baloney is nothing but a pipe dream. There's always going to be somebody or some country opposed to something, and it'll attack the other and—"

"Who's ready for a piece of pie?" Minnie interrupted.

After the meal, Edward took the family outside to visit his petite menagerie. Everyone acted as if it were their first time. Satisfied with the presentation, Edward was ready to go back to the house.

"Dad, you want me to remind you about something," Ed said to his father.

"That's right. While I was in the bank the other day, a friend told me about a piece of property that can be purchased at a good price."

"Did you buy it?" Ed asked.

"No, I've got enough property right now. I did think about buying it and reselling, though. But then I thought about Pauline and Dutch. Dutch has a good job and it's got to be cramped living with you guys."

"We're perfectly content the way things are," Ed said comfortably. "Another house would just complicate things when we go back on the road."

"What's wrong with you, son? There's a war coming. It's going to be years before you go back on the road, if you ever do. Pauline and Dutch need to look at the house. A family can't own too much real estate," Edward stated with conviction.

Unlike immature men, Ed was adult enough to hear what his father told him.

Pauline and Dutch inspected the house the following week. It was the last house on Croswell Street, adjacent to the old Electric Park, now called Waterman Park. It had five rooms with a bathroom and an oversized yard that extended farther east to the road. Originally priced at $2,900, the owner sold it to them for $2,500. It had belonged to his mother, who had recently passed away. He lived in Ohio, so he needed to sell. The First Trust Bank of Kankakee loaned Dutch the money at 3 percent interest for fifteen years.

At first, Pauline was torn at having the house. To her, it seemed like the family had split up. Ed explained that it didn't represent any parting of the ways. It was a family opportunity, and it would be a mistake to let it slip away.

In short order, Pauline was busy decorating. Making curtains and painting the living room walls occupied a lot of her time. Also, she wanted George Edward to continue to be enrolled in Steuben School. That required her dropping him off in the morning and picking him up later at her mother's. For George Edward, it was only a two-block walk to his grandmother's house. That system worked well during the week. A day or so every week, George Edward spent the night at his grandparents'. Sylvia was only one year behind him in school, so they walked home together most of the time.

George Edward began to make friends with neighborhood kids, so any concern over him being lonely was soon dismissed.

The large yard was a main attraction. Privet hedges and peony bushes served as a fence along the boundaries, and Dutch planted a garden. On the north side of the yard stood an arbor loaded with Concord grapes. They never ran short of grape jelly and jam.

George Edward's birthday parties were celebrated on that verdant enclosure with family and guests at picnic tables—children at one, adults at the other. Perhaps the most popular boy in the neighborhood was Larry Krause, an accurate rock thrower. Larry was reputed to be able to knock a squirrel from a tree with one toss. Obviously, no one ever picked a fight with Larry, even though he was the smallest in George Edward's gang of friends. Games were played for prizes. The most popular was one in which children stood on a chair and tried to drop clothespins into an empty milk bottle.

* * * * *

Even with the terrible war raging in Europe and the grim prospect that the United States would be involved, sooner rather than later, America took time out to be entertained by her popular troubadours. To a country disheartened by years of economic depression and plagued by an uncertain future, the radio gave a much needed diversion. The likes of Frank Sinatra, the Dorsey Brothers, Duke Ellington, Xavier Cugat, and Glen Miller helped take our minds off the daily grind. Each day was filled with news of another tragic event, and we blindly pressed forward to that most fearful day of all.

Chapter Thirty-Six

Hyrum entered his house, overflowing with excitement. While depositing the collection from Sunday's service, he happened to overhear comments about money arriving from McMinnville to be placed in Minnie Rosenthal's account. It could only mean one thing—Jack Leffingwell bought the land.

"Abigail, where are you?" he shouted with excitement.

"I'm here, Father. What are you so excited about?"

"I just heard that Jack Leffingwell bought the land widow Rosenthal was selling. I think I'll go over there and help him stake out the property lines."

"No need to do that," she snapped. "He'll probably just pee on the trees."

"Why do you criticize him so much? Makes me think you're in love with him. No woman acts the way you do unless that's the cause. Jack's always been a perfect gentleman where you're concerned. He's done nothing to deserve your wrath." He looked closely at his daughter. "Has he ever expressed any feelings for you?"

"No, and he better not. There have been plenty of men in Statesville that have. I'm just not ready for that kind of talk."

"You haven't found the right one, that's all. Maybe someday Jack Leffingwell will propose to you."

"He better not, and that's all I have to say about it," Abigail insisted.

"Your mother and I didn't raise any dummies. You're too smart to let him get away. As Shakespeare wrote, 'the lady doth protest too much,' and to me, with the way you're carrying on, you've lost all credibility."

A few weeks later, Hyrum secured his horse's harness to the carriage and leisurely trotted over to the Leffingwell work site. Reluctantly, Abigail joined him. Construction had moved right along. Which was surprising, since Jack was doing most of the work by himself.

Finding Jack on the roof, they sat and observed him for quite a while before he finally noticed them.

"Thought you might want something cold to drink," Hyrum shouted up to him. "Abigail made lemonade." He omitted the fact that she had done so unwillingly.

"Sounds good to me, I'll be right down," Jack replied as he crawled over to the ladder.

Jack had worked shirtless, and his tanned body glistened with perspiration as he raised the glass and downed the lemonade in one long drink. The sight of him made Abigail uneasy. It was difficult for her to look directly at him, and she constantly averted her eyes.

"Do you want another glass?" Hyrum asked. "We brought plenty."

The first glass had quenched his thirst. Jack savored the second one for its flavor. "Would you care to look inside?"

The structure was presently just one large room, but future walls were marked in chalk on the floor. Openings for windows were provided on each side, and he'd marked off space for a loft at one end.

"I see you are planning a loft," Hyrum remarked.

"A little more than that. I plan to build a second story over one end. The stairs will be located over there." Jack pointed in the direction that faced a stand of trees.

"I don't think I ever saw a cabin like this before," said Hyrum.

"It's my own design. I was sitting here one day, looking things over, and it just came to me."

"You've been coming to church on a regular basis now, so if you don't mind, I plan to discuss the cabin with the parishioners. Next week, I believe, you're going to have a lot of helpers."

Hyrum was prophetic. Jack received so much help, it taxed his brain just to make assignments.

Returning from one of his routine visits, Hyrum found Abigail peeling potatoes for supper.

"You never did tell me what you thought about Jack's house," he said.

"It's built to last a tornado, but it's too rough inside. He's missing a more gentle touch," she said.

"Well, there's a constant parade of buggies and bonnets, so it won't be too long before he's gets lots of help in that area. I'll bet he spends the winter there putting up curtains."

Abigail wrinkled her brow at that thought, and she carelessly cut her finger. She knew Maryellen Riberty had her sights set for Jack and that farm. She bragged about it all over town. Abigail also felt Jack knew nothing about Maryellen and her reputation when it came to men. At first, she decided to just let it go. It was none of her business. That worked for a while, but then it began to weigh heavily on her mind. Finally, she concluded the proper thing to do was to ride over, under some pretense, and talk to Jack in person. Halfway there she wanted to turn back. By mustering her courage, telling herself it was her Christian duty, she continued forward.

Jack greeted her with a smile, saying, "What do I owe for the pleasure of your company this afternoon?"

"Don't get yourself excited. Father wanted me to see the progress the congregation has made," she said, still straddling her horse.

"Hop down and I'll take you for a tour," Jack said. He reached up to help her dismount.

Once inside, Abigail noticed the fireplace against the living room wall. The hearth consisted of flat marble slabs, and the rest of the fireplace was built with perfectly matched stonework and a mantelpiece above. The chimney, also covered with stone, extended through the second floor and out the roof.

Abigail didn't know what to say. She was greatly impressed, but didn't want to let on. "It's really nice," she said. At that moment, she caught sight of the curtains and realized, at once, that he didn't make them.

"Who made your curtains?" she asked innocently.

"Maryellen Riberty."

"I'm not surprised. Decent men avoid her like the plague. She's bragged about sleeping with most men in Statesville. It figures you would take to her."

"I don't know about any of that. She's been nice to me. She offered to make the curtains, and I viewed that as a kind gesture. The rest of that stuff I don't care to hear about."

"You've probably slept with her yourself!"

"For your information, that I haven't done. But I'll tell you one thing. At least, she's not a tight-assed bitch that works overtime to insult me and everything I do!"

Abigail was in a state of shock. It was the first time anyone had used profanity to discipline her or had referred to her in that manner. Her heart was pounding and her face was hot from an angry flush. It seemed like an eternity passed, and still she couldn't speak. At that moment, Jack took her left wrist and pulled her to him. Her breath escaped her as he tightened the embrace. She was unable to move as he bent his head down and kissed her. The kiss was hard. She tasted his passion and became weaker yet. She had been kissed before, but not that fiercely, not that passionately, and certainly not for that length of time. When he pulled away, she wiped her mouth with the back of her hand and saw that her lip was bleeding. She still couldn't speak. All she was able to do was turn around, walk outside, climb on her horse, and race home in a gallop.

On Sunday Abigail failed to attend church services, telling her father she had a fever and might be coming down with something. The next week she was melancholy and moped around the house. Hyrum knew something was wrong, but felt his daughter would eventually come to him.

"Have you visited Jack Leffingwell lately?" she finally asked.

"Yes, I was over there yesterday for a short time," answered Hyrum. "Why do you ask?"

"No reason. I just was curious as to how the house was coming along."

"Now that you ask, I did notice something kind of strange. All the curtains were gone. I plan to take him a couple bales of hay tomorrow. Would you like to come along?"

"No thanks. I've got too much laundry to wash," she lied.

Hyrum found Jack building stalls in the newly erected barn. He guided his horse, pulling a wagon with three bales of hay, through the barn door. Jack laid down his hammer down and walked over to Hyrum.

"Brought the hay we talked about," Hyrum said.

"You didn't have to do that. Everybody's been too kind," Jack said. "If I live to be a hundred, I can never repay you all."

"You ought to know by now, Jack, it's the Lord that does the repaying."

While Hyrum tossed the bales from the wagon, he admitted, "There is something you possibly can shed a little light on."

Carrying a bale to the corner of a stall, Jack asked nervously, "What's that, Hyrum?"

"My daughter is acting strangely," Hyrum said, climbing down from the wagon. "And it seems it started after the last time you two were together. I thought maybe you might know what's bothering her."

Jack faced the older man. "I believe I do, and it's within your rights to horsewhip me about it. Abigail has cause to hate me the rest of her life. Up till now I've never considered myself a bad man, but the last time Abigail was here, I forced myself on her and kissed her."

"I knew it, I knew it," Hyrum said. "And I knew something was wrong. What you confessed just now makes a great deal of sense. I'm sorry things haven't worked out more civilized between you. And you do deserve to be horsewhipped, but that's not a good enough punishment. Your price of penance is to marry her. I want you to go to the house, while I'm here, and ask Abigail to be your wife."

"I'd rather be whipped," Jack said.

"No, you wouldn't. I know more about both your feelings than you do yourselves," Hyrum said with conviction. "Do as I say and God help you both."

Abigail had been crying when she heard the knock on the door. Quickly drying her eyes, she opened it. Standing before her was the remorseful mountaineer.

"May I come in?" he asked after removing his hat. "There's something I need to say."

"I can't ask you to sit down. My father isn't here," Abigail responded, though she moved aside so he could enter.

Standing before her, Jack began losing his nerve. His eyes also began to fill with tears and his body trembled. "I want you to know how sorry I am for what I said and did. Abigail, I've been in love with you ever since that first day when you pulled back your hat. Maybe I'm not as smart as others who have sought after you, but I'm honest, faithful, and hardworking. I couldn't go on living without asking your forgiveness—and one more thing. Will you marry me?"

They were married the following spring, with Hyrum performing the ceremony. Abigail wore her mother's wedding dress. Jack wore a big smile and his new boots. The boots that had delayed his return to McMinnville, the boots that were responsible for his friendship with Hyrum, the boots that were instrumental in him surrendering his independence. The boots that changed his life forever.

One last thing. A small parlor organ had been ordered out of Pennsylvania to surprise Abigail on her birthday.

Chapter Thirty-Seven

Perhaps the most dangerous time for slaves escaping from the Deep South took place at the shores of the Ohio River. The river served as a natural barricade, preventing access to the slave-free states beyond. Bounty hunters and lawmen, aware of that fact, made it the final focus of their hunt. They gathered in suspected portal areas, interviewing any who might have knowledge of a runaway's presence. So it was for Castor Fogg. Driven by his obsession to capture Wilbur and his family, he had traveled hundreds of miles in frustrated pursuit. It was no longer the reward he sought. Revenge for the many times he'd felt thwarted had compelled him to the Ohio shore. Castor Fogg was no newcomer to the area or the river. Many times he and his cohorts had captured innocent free blacks and used the Ohio River to transport them to New Orleans to be resold. Castor's purse weighed heavily with the ill-gotten profits.

Fortunately for the Littlefields, the Underground Railroad at the Ohio River had an enterprising stationmaster. Vernon De Groat was one of the most popular and influential lawyers in Owensboro. His unconventional maneuvers in the courtroom had garnered him many victories, and his approach as a stationmaster had similar results. This time the challenge was greater. He wasn't planning the escape of a single runaway. Now it was four. Complicating it further, two of them were children.

It had been nearly two weeks since Wilbur had heard anything encouraging. Although the family was comfortable in a safe house, each passing day heightened the ever present tension and fear.

At last, De Groat came to visit them. He was ready to discuss his plan to get them to Indiana, the slave-free state.

"Does anyone suffer from claustrophobia?" he asked Wilbur.

He could tell by Wilbur's expression, he had no idea what it meant. "Can you tolerate being enclosed in a large wooden barrel for an hour or two?"

"Would it have breathing holes?" Wilbur asked.

"Of course. Don't concern yourself about that. Will you all be able to stand it over a period of time?"

"We'll do what we have to," Wilbur answered with conviction.

"Good, here's the plan. There's a steamer boat that transports whiskey to southern Indiana. It carries bourbon made by the Beam family, who routinely lease the boat. I have the captain on board, no pun intended, and also the distiller's representative, who will supervise the cargo being loaded. You folks will be the last barrels loaded. That makes you the first barrels to come off on the other side.

Taking time to look each member in the eye, De Groat explained further, "Once unloaded, you will be met by Pastor Milford Moon and taken to the Society of Friends Church. The Moon family will line up the depots that lead the way to Canada."

"When will all this begin?" Wilbur asked.

"Someone will pick you all up at five tomorrow morning."

Only the children slept that night. Wilbur and Marie remained awake, discussing the forthcoming ride in a wooden barrel. Like most evenings spent in pensive conversation, sleep came shortly before it was time to waken. They were roused by the anticipated visitor and taken by wagon to a riverfront warehouse. Wilbur, being the largest, was asked to assess the fit inside one of the selected barrels. Once he was inside, the lid was put in place. His voice muffled, Wilbur said, "I fit okay."

An hour later, four drums with their human content were loaded topside on a ship destined to make its first port of call less than a mile away.

Not surprisingly, Castor Fogg was drawn to any vessel carrying bourbon whiskey. He observed each keg being placed on board, and while his thirst increased barrel by barrel, his precious prey escaped before his very eyes.

The River Jordan was crossed, and with deliberate speed, the first four kegs were transferred to a wagon waiting by the dock. From all appearances, the driver could be a tavern owner receiving fresh stock. This wagon master, however, didn't care for that kind of spirits. After traveling a short distance, Pastor Milford Moon pulled the team to a stop and removed the lid from each cask.

"Please remain where you are for a little while longer. We will be at the farm shortly," he said.

The stationhouse, or farm, was located in Spencer County and was only four miles away. Abraham Lincoln once lived in Spencer County, when his family moved from Kentucky in 1816. In fact, he first studied law there, before relocating to Illinois.

Pastor Moon and his wife, Margaret, had made it their home since they left North Carolina. Other family members who had made similar moves lived nearby. Most all were abolitionists and active in the Underground Railroad. The laws in Indiana made it difficult for slave catchers to operate. Accordingly, they were reluctant to even try. The Littlefields were now reasonably safe. Their next route would take them north through Indiana to Michigan and the city of Detroit. From there, they would travel to Canada.

Wilbur, Marie, and Celia lived free the rest of their lives on their own farm near Toronto, Canada.

When the Civil War broke out, Leroy returned to Michigan and joined the Union Army. By the time the war ended, he was highly decorated and returned to Georgia during Reconstruction. It was there, in the Deep South, he met a pretty young girl named Lena. They married in a Methodist Church in Athens. Leroy and Lena had several children, their last being a girl they named Hattie.

Chapter Thirty-Eight

As the year pressed forward, the "date which will live in infamy" grew ever nearer. On December 7, 1941, the United States was shocked by a surprise Japanese attack at Pearl Harbor, Hawaii. Japanese Admiral Isoroku Yamamoto, their naval marshal general, intended the strike to neutralize the United States Pacific Fleet as Japan invaded British and American territories for natural resources of oil and rubber. It was a strategic success for the enemy. Four US battleships were sunk, along with three cruisers and three destroyers; and out of 402 airplanes, 188 were destroyed and159 damaged. Over 2,400 men were killed and 1,282 wounded. Due to the nature and timing of the attack, enemy losses were light.

Some have alleged that Roosevelt had advanced knowledge of the attack, but ignored it in order to gain Congressional support for America to enter the war. It was later learned that several sources had followed the six Japanese aircraft carriers once they left port and alerted the United States. Whatever the case, the United States was now at war.

As a result, everyone's plans were put on hold. Nearly eleven million men were inducted into the armed services. Wartime need for additional materiel forced more women into the workforce, making up for the men called to duty. Our lives were changed forever. Rationing made us sacrifice those things we had previously taken for granted. We practiced mock invasions and pulled the shades for blackouts. Stomping on tin cans to be saved for the war effort became a common exercise. Families with members in active service hung a service flag with a blue star in the center in their window. The star was changed to gold if the member died in action. Before the war ended, over 400,000 such stars could have been displayed. It was a solemn time that changed the lives of everyone.

* * * * *

No one knows exactly when Ed Reno accepted the fact they would never go back on the road. His father had admonished him for not considering that possibility when the opportunity arose for Pauline and Dutch to acquire a house of their own. Nevertheless, such a time had to occur, and the resulting pain was well hidden behind a more optimistic disguise.

* * * * *

One night in a dream, Ebenezer Scrooge lived in the past, the present, and the future. When he woke up, he pledged to live in each of those times and not shut out the lessons they taught. We all live in multiple worlds. One is real, and the others are dreams or fantasies. We must have them all or we would lose all capacity for expectation and hope. The cast of Reno's Funmakers gave up the life they loved to live in a world that was real.

Our lives start out slow and time seems to never pass; but then, when we reach a certain age, it speeds like a cheetah with a zephyr at its back. Conversely, our memories last somewhat longer. They slip away slowly, like the smoke from burning leaves.

I've chosen to relate the story of Reno's Funmakers, its hardships, good times, hopes and fears, as I remember them told by my parents, relatives, and friends. These events took place a long time ago, and no doubt I've forgotten more than I recall. The flood of 1957 washed away the photographs and evidence of their past life. Time is erasing what little memory is left of the traveling tent show. I guess what remains will have to do, until we all hear Roy sing "Happy Trails" again—this time for real and in person.

Epilogue

The saga of Reno's Funmakers was brought to an end when America entered WWII. The lives of all those involved naturally continued, but without the determination to return to the road. Living a restricted and complex existence was a stark reality, and perhaps the only relief came in the form of a sweet dream reliving the past. Major events occurred around the world on a daily basis. Their significance would be better learned in the years to come.

Dutch continued working at Manco Manufacturing, and earned recognition and several promotions. His last title was superintendent of operations, a job with more salary and commensurate responsibilities, along with the associated stress.

Pauline enrolled in a correspondence course in accounting and graduated with high honors. She also put her talent for storytelling to good use; some of her stories were bought and published. The money wasn't great, but every little bit counted. After she received her degree, she spent a few weeks searching for a bookkeeping job. Her search ended with a positive result.

Ed also remained at Manco, but stayed on the lookout for a day job.

Gladys practiced the piano. Ed, finding it difficult to get any sleep at home during the day, tried harder to find a day job.

The children played school, played dress up, played house, played quietly, and played outside.

Because of the war, food and gasoline were rationed. Like most people, Pauline and Gladys found the program difficult to accept. Everyone received a dated War Ration Book. The books contained stamps with point values that allowed the purchase of the rationed food, such as meat, fish, poultry, eggs, and cheese. Ed and Dutch found the restriction on coffee to be the most draconian. Only one pound every five weeks was tough on those referred to as coffee hounds. When not working, the Funmaker family seemed to always have a cup in their hands.

Gasoline was rationed in a similar manner. Since he worked for the war effort, Dutch received a B sticker. That allowed him to purchase eight gallons per week. Those in the general population could purchase only four gallons. Recreational driving was frowned upon. In reality, with little to no gasoline, it became impossible.

Planning a meal put women to the test. Just because they had the proper ration coupon didn't mean they always got the food. Along with being rationed, foodstuffs were scarce. Stores were often out of popular items. Cereal became a standard food, not only for breakfast. It was occasionally eaten as a bedtime snack. General Mills introduced Cheerios, an O-shaped cereal. It became instantly popular with adults, as well as children.

Because food was limited, it became a standing rule to "clean your plate" at every meal.

Dutch, ever resourceful, fenced in a portion of the side yard and raised chickens. He made friends with a co-worker who owned a farm; he provided the starter chicks. Eventually, Pauline bartered the extra eggs for other items. Dutch also came up with another novel idea. Butter had yet to be rationed, but it was in short supply. Dutch would buy fresh milk from his farmer friend and let it set until the cream rose to the surface. He poured the cream into a quart fruit jar, tightened the lid, and fastened the jar to the washer blades of their top-loading washing machine. Once he started the machine, it acted like a churn, and a short time later they had butter. When margarine became available, the homemade butter process was discontinued.

For the more serious minded, living during a world war created a great deal of nervous tension and mental strain. Few happenings are appreciated as well as when the world is at peace. The tragedies of war even haunt people in their dreams. There were some events, however, that were so bizarre, they were almost humorous.

* * * * *

Adolph Hitler's deputy, Rudolph Hess, flew solo over the English Channel and Scotland and parachuted to the ground, breaking his ankle. Ostensibly, he wanted to negotiate a separate peace with the United Kingdom. He was placed under arrest by a farmhand with a pitchfork. While many conflicting stories arose as to why he'd committed such an unusual act, the real reason probably was mental illness and stress. Hess would spend the rest of his life in prison, dying at the age of ninety-three, in 1987, at Spandau Prison in West Berlin.

The enemy did make serious assaults on the United States mainland. The Atlantic Ocean offered German U-boats easy access to the US east coast. It was like shooting fish in a barrel for the *Wolf pack*. The Germans sank 348 American ships during the first four months of 1942. We only destroyed two enemy subs. City lights on the east coast had to be dimmed at night, because they illuminated the images of our vessels, making them easier for the U-boats to spot.

Relief came when England and Canada reassigned warships to the United States. We now were able to provide warship escorts for trans-Atlantic shipping, along with air cover. Losses were greatly reduced.

Japan also had submarines operating on America's west coast. While not as effective as the German U-boats, they sank several allied vessels.

Prior to the attack on Pearl Harbor, the *Chicago Tribune* editorialized that Japan would never go to war against the United States. When America was attacked on December 7, the nation was in a state of shock. Over the years, people on the west coast had started to fear and resent the growing Japanese community. Farm jobs went to the Asian immigrants, and many felt that the Japanese were responsible for the high Depression-era unemployment rate. Like the Europeans before them, the Japanese tended to remain in their own communities. Isolation fostered rumor and innuendo. The truth of the matter was, we just didn't know them.

What we did know was the United States had been attacked by Japan. President Roosevelt, also unsure as to who the Japanese immigrants were, ordered all Japanese on the west coast interned in War Relocation Camps—a total of over 100,000 people, most of which were American citizens. Since 90 percent of Japanese in America lived on the west coast, it made sense to FDR. Later, the US Supreme Court upheld the constitutionality of his exclusion order. Those who were interred, or their family members, were eventually granted nearly two billion dollars in reparations by President Ronald Reagan.

Hugh Mulcahy, the Phillies pitcher, became the first major league ballplayer to be drafted into the army during the peacetime draft. He was honorably discharged after serving ten months. Two days later, when the Japanese bombed Pearl Harbor, Mulcahy was back in for four more years. Ted Williams enlisted as a Navy aviator and served in two wars, WWII and the Korean War. Williams, perhaps the greatest baseball player that ever lived, sacrificed several years, while in his prime, to serve his country.

In other events, Americans raised their spirits by going to the movies and playing phonograph records. Duke Ellington recorded "Take the A Train"; Count Basie "One O'clock Jump"; and Bing Crosby sang "White Christmas."

Walt Disney introduced *Bambi*. *Citizen Kane* premiered in New York, as well as *Casablanca*.

Elsewhere, Mount Rushmore was completed and Anne Frank began to keep a diary.

* * * * *

As 1943 rolled around, Ed found a daytime job with American Marietta, a paint manufacturing company. Dutch continued with Manco and designed improved hydraulics systems that gained the company more government contracts. All patents were considered property of Manco. Dutch did receive a little more pay—and a lot more stress and even longer hours. President Roosevelt ordered a minimum forty-eight hour workweek for the war industry. Dutch was putting in nearly seventy hours each week. At the same time, he was building kitchen cabinets for Pauline. Finally, while cutting a piece of wood paneling, he felt pain behind his neck and down his left arm. He called for George Edward to get his mother, and then collapsed. The doctor arrived in short order to find Dutch unconscious. Pauline was beside herself with shock and worry.

"He's beginning to come around," the doctor said.

"Is he going to be okay?" Pauline asked.

"Okay for now," the doctor replied, after administering a hypodermic injection and listening to Dutch's heart. "I want to see him tomorrow in my office."

The next day Dutch was diagnosed as having had a stress-related heart attack. The doctor's prescription for treatment was complete rest.

"Yes, I know you have a very important war industry job," he said when Dutch protested. "But in all likelihood, it's that job that caused your heart attack. If you want to live to see your son grow up, you need to do what I tell you."

Dutch took a medical leave. The first few days he lived in his bathrobe. Pauline watched over him like a hawk, making sure he didn't overexert himself.

It was like a bomb being dropped on the family. Ed found it hard to understand how a man in his late thirties could have a heart attack and pass out like that. Gladys only considered worst case scenarios. That kept Pauline in a perpetual panic and wishing Hattie were there for her. Meanwhile, Dutch was feeling better and began to increase his activity. His most recent doctor's visit pleased Dr. Hamilton. The doctor hadn't seen a recovery so complete in such a short time.

"Things look pretty good, Dutch. You ask me, when can you go back to work? Well, let's give it another month and we'll see," the good doctor said.

Eventually, Dutch got a release from Dr. Hamilton, brightening the outlook of the Funmaker family.

* * * * *

The war also began to brighten everybody's outlook. The RAF bombing raids were taking their toll on Germany. The bombing of the Ruhr area crippled German steel works and synthetic oil production. In addition, cities were bombed deep in Germany, with devastating results on enemy morale.

Elsewhere, James H. Doolittle bombed Tokyo, and Russia proved the victor in the greatest tank battle in history. At Kursk, over 6,000 tanks took part in a battle in which the German offensive was thwarted. Enemy losses were huge; Germany lost 2,900 tanks. And it marked the first time a major enemy offensive was stopped without a breakthrough. FDR, Churchill, and Stalin agreed on Operation Overlord—D-Day

In another important victory, Italy surrendered to the Allies.

Here on the home front, and for the duration of the War, frankfurters were replaced with victory sausages. Due to the shortage of meat, a portion was substituted with an unspecified amount of soybean meal. The sale of sliced bread was banned, in order to reduce bakery demand for metal parts. Sugar, butter, and cheese were rationed, and meat was restricted to less than two pounds per week.

As we entered 1944, Dutch was back at Manco Manufacturing. His doctor had released him to work part-time. No one worked part-time in the war effort, and soon Dutch was working as he had before his attack. Things went well for three months, until, while sitting at the kitchen table, Dutch experienced the familiar pain, this time in his chest. George Edward ran for his mother. When Pauline rushed in the room, her husband was on the floor, insentient. Dr. Hamilton was out making house calls, so his office called the ambulance. Pauline applied a cold washcloth to Dutch's forehead and nervously waited for the ambulance to arrive.

Dutch had regained consciousness by the time it showed up. At the hospital, he was admitted and taken to a room. He spent the night resting comfortably. The next morning Dr. Hamilton reviewed his chart.

"I'm afraid it's going to take more than a few months rest," the doctor said firmly. "Your job gives you too much stress. Dutch, you're going to have to find a different line of work. This is the second heart-related episode in less than a year. The next one will probably kill you. I've known your family for over twenty years. I also know you're resourceful enough to do something else. You're going to be okay this time, so you and Pauline think it over."

While Dutch recuperated, his mind was in a fog. The only real line of work he knew was on-the-road entertaining. In the meantime, Gladys had spread the word about Dutch's condition. Her sister, Leota, came up with an idea. She and her husband Joe knew of a small farm near theirs that could be purchased at the right price. To them, farm life was very restful, and Dutch wouldn't need to work the land. He could raise chickens and sell the eggs. In fact, that was what the previous owners had done for many years. Everything was set up for a chicken ranch.

The idea was wild, but nothing better came to mind. Dutch's decision to give it a try was inexplicable. Yet the house on Croswell Street was put on the market, and in a short period of time, Dutch, Pauline, and George Edward were on their way to Hurdland, Missouri.

The small farm was rather picturesque. In addition to the house, a smokehouse stood near to it. Farther down a slight decline in the yard was the barn. It was in excellent condition, its loft packed with hay. George Edward spent many a day up in the loft, dreaming about owning a horse. To the left of the barn were three brooder houses designed to house and hatch chickens. A winding, free-flowing brook worked its way through the farm and disappeared into a forest of hardwood trees.

During the summer months, George Edward chose to sleep in the smokehouse. Many nights he listened to the wolves and coyotes howl, and wondered how far away they were. Both animals were freely hunted for bounty.

Several large rocks lined a portion of the creek. He used them to fashion a dam, making the water three or four feet deep in the backed up area—great for swimming on those hot Missouri summer days and nights.

Some of the drawbacks the family had to get used to were no electric power and a dirt road. It would be three years before electric power wires were strung to the area. Dutch purchased a kerosene-operated generator and used it for the house. Even so, oil lamps burned in the evenings. The lamp of choice was the kind that used fiberglass-like mantels. George Edward was cautioned never to touch them, but he had to try it, just once. He found they crumbled like powder and never did it again.

School gave the youngest Moon a new experience. The schoolhouse in the neighboring community had only one room. Grades consisted of rows; i.e., first grade in row one, second in the next, and so forth. George Edward was scheduled to enter fifth grade. That row was empty.

The teacher decided it would be best for him to sit with fourth graders. A teacher's chore in a one-room schoolhouse was prodigious. She had to be competent in teaching subject matter up to the eighth grade, yet have the ability to shift into different maturity levels.

George Edward was fascinated by it all. By sitting in the fourth grade row, he learned about agriculture and farm animals. Those subjects weren't taught in Kankakee. Having previously learned most of the other subjects, he had time to concentrate on special assignments the teacher provided.

He became friends with a boy named Melvin Kaufman. Melvin greeted him the first day by asking George Edward's mother what grade he was in.

Pauline politely answered, "He's going into fifth grade."

"He's kinda small, ain't he?" Melvin said.

"He's only nine years old," Pauline said.

"Oh, well, that accounts for it. I'm fourteen," Melvin said.

Melvin was going into sixth grade … again.

* * * * *

The farm by itself was idyllic. Restarting it as a chicken ranch proved to be another matter. That winter was one of the coldest in years. The heating systems in the brooder houses were undependable and often malfunctioned. Chickens tend to huddle close together when disturbed or cold. After a bitter winter night, it wasn't unusual to find two or three hundred smothered to death the next morning. Any hopes for profit were dashed by Mother Nature. Replacing the cash reserve required Dutch to accept carpenter work in the general community. Eventually, several homes displayed built-in kitchen cabinets, custom-made by the ersatz chicken farmer.

* * * * *

On the other side of the world, the bombing of Germany was relentless, and now the United States joined the attack. General Eisenhower set D-Day for June 6, 1944. Perhaps the luckiest soldier in England was RAF Sergeant Nickolas Aldemade. While returning from a bombing raid over Berlin, the tail gunner's plane was attacked by Luftwaffe fighters. Out of control and on fire, the Avro Lancaster bomber spiraled toward earth. Finding his parachute burnt and unusable, Aldemade was faced with two choices: die in the imminent crash or leap to his death. Choosing the later, he jumped from the plane and fell 18,000 feet (about three and a half miles).

Apparently, Aldemade was holding hands with fate, because the fall was broken by pine trees and a deep snow drift. He suffered only a sprained leg.

His Gestapo captives wouldn't accept his story about jumping from a plane. Later, they found the wreckage and acknowledged the fact.

At home, President Roosevelt announced that he will run for a fourth term and the Republican governor of New York, Thomas E. Dewey, entered the presidential race.

Meat was no longer rationed, and Bing Crosby sang "Swinging on a Star."

In Hartford, Connecticut, a fire occurred during the afternoon performance of Ringling Brothers and Barnum & Bailey Circus. With the performance attended by 7,000 people, it became one of the country's worst disasters. The fire began as a small flame about twenty minutes into the show. The audience was urged not to panic, but ushers couldn't maintain all those people in an orderly fashion, and the terrified crowd stampeded. Nearly 170 people were killed, either burned or trampled, and another 700 injured.

The tragedy resulted in the circus having to pay five million dollars in damages to the victims.

* * * * *

In the fall of 1945, Pauline learned that George Edward qualified to attend the school in Hurdland. The grade school and upper levels were both included in one building. It made the auditorium and gymnasium available to all students. It certainly was an upgrade from the one-room schoolhouse in Novelty.

The passing summer had been restful and enjoyed by all. On Labor Day, Pauline and Dutch held a picnic at the farm. In addition to Pauline's aunts and uncles, neighbors came from miles around. Each family brought a covered dish. They ended up with enough food to fill four picnic tables. One table was assigned to only desserts, and there wasn't enough room to hold them all.

Leota and Joe brought the tables in Frank's pickup truck. They were borrowed from the Baptist Church, and, naturally, the minister and his family attended. Of course, the main meat was chicken. With over a thousand of the cluckers on the premises, it was rather easy to predict big platters full of chicken would be found on every table. The neighbors also brought ham and beef. The Moon family was delighted. It had reached the point where Pauline couldn't look another chicken in the eye. A different kind of meat was like ambrosia.

The afternoon was quite hot. The temperature was well into the nineties, and George Edward's homemade swimming lake turned out to be a popular place for young and old alike. After the main lunch, three ice cream makers couldn't keep up. The day didn't come to a close until lightning bugs dotted the air with blinking illumination.

The festive event was happily talked about for several days. Then most conversations reverted back to the war. President Roosevelt defeated Dewey and began his fourth term, only to succumb to a cerebral hemorrhage on April 12. Vice President Harry Truman was sworn in and became our thirty-third president.

WWII was coming to an end. The relentless bombing of German cities, Russian victories, and the success of D-Day culminated in Germany's surrender May 8, 1945. It took atomic bombs on Hiroshima and Nagasaki for Japan to finally capitulate on August 15.

The winter of 1945 was worse than the previous year. Dutch lost a thousand chickens. They were mostly smothered due to inadequate heating in the brooder houses. The following spring, he decided to give up the idea of a chicken ranch. His closest neighbor raised cattle and wanted to expand. With meat no longer rationed and the war over, beef offered a very good return. The chicken ranch would give him added pasture, plus a better resource of water than his existing pond. He made Dutch a good proposal, and Dutch sold the land at a small profit.

Pauline yearned to see her parents. When school was dismissed in May, it was back to Kankakee for the Moon family.

* * * * *

They found themselves living in the Wildwood house once again, but only temporarily, until Dutch found work. While on the job hunt, he played piano in the evening at the 880 Club, a popular watering hole on the west side. The attention the ladies gave him made Pauline green-eyed. The job offer came none too soon for her.

Dutch took a job as an engineer with the Weather Seal Company. Weather Seal manufactured attractive storm windows made from redwood and handled difficult applications, such as large church windows. Each job was an engineering task and required custom design. Dutch was well suited for the position.

Once their income became steady, the Moons moved to an apartment, and then another, and finally found a house rental in what was called White City, the neighborhood on the northwest side of Kankakee.

Pauline belonged to a women's circle that met every Tuesday. She became close friends with two ladies in particular, and the three devised a scheme to open a delicatessen. Since all three were talented cooks, it seemed like a natural. They called it the Cozy Cupboard Delicatessen. They were the only deli in town and business was good. Conflict arose when it came to disclosing their family recipes. All three were reluctant. The issue could only be resolved by each preparing her own guarded recipes. That also created a problem, because Pauline had the most. Accordingly, she had to do the most cooking. When one of the partners moved out of the state, the workload increased for the two remaining. When they only broke even the first month, the other partner wanted out. Pauline found herself doing all the cooking. The delicatessen grew in popularity, and Pauline found herself cooking all night. Meat loaf, potato salad, coleslaw, baked ham, and an assortment of pies were all sold out before noon. Dutch wanted to hire more help. Though the workload was getting to her, Pauline still refused to release her recipes. The only solution left was to close the store. Years afterward, people still remembered how good the potato salad tasted.

Some other of the events for the year included:

The Franklin Roosevelt dime was issued.

Major league baseball players began jumping to the "outlaw" Mexican League. Ted Williams refused an offer of $500,000 to do the same. Major League baseball granted a $5,000 minimum salary.

The first bikini bathing suit was displayed ... in France.

George Orwell published *Animal Farm,* and President Truman officially proclaimed WWII was over.

* * * * *

On a warm summer day, people stood on the sidewalk by the Kankakee Public Library and watched Departmental School burn down. Children cheered the occasion, believing they no longer would have to attend grades seven and eight. Much to their chagrin, they later learned the adjoining building was assigned that task that fall.

Pauline found employment at the Fair Store, working in the shipping department. Her responsibilities included keeping track of received inventories. It was an interesting and important job, without the stress she suffered with the delicatessen.

There are those who felt Kankakee was at its best then. For such a small community, activities abounded. While some were a little on the edge, such as gambling parlors, slot machines, nightclubs, and houses of ill repute, more wholesome entertainments were easily found. The former businesses gave the city a noted reputation. In fact, the army declared the less noble establishments off-limits to soldiers. That alone guaranteed packed houses nearly every night, with many of the customers in uniform. The latter entertainments included three movie theaters, a drive-in theater, numerous good restaurants, a state park, and the Kankakee River.

It was a good time in America. It was a time when the stores stayed open until 9:00 p.m. on Mondays and closed on Sunday. It was also the time Congress enacted the Taft-Hartley Act. Prior to the act, unfair labor practices were only prohibited by employers. Unions were frowned upon for striking while America was at war. Once the war ended, over five million workers were involved in strikes. The strikes were so extensive, Congress believed they imperiled the national health and safety. The Taft-Hartley Act evened the playing field, so to speak, and gave the president power to obtain legal strike-breaking injunctions.

The United States had returned to peacetime production. Demand was high for just about anything we produced. This was especially true in Europe, where most manufacturing facilities had been flattened by enemy bombs.

The Marshall Plan, designed to help rebuild European countries, gave billions of dollars for that endeavor. Many cities lay in ruin, along with their manufacturing structure, agriculture, transportation, and docks. The plan provided the aid desperately needed for reconstruction.

America also benefited. Much of the money we gave was repatriated when European countries purchased American manufactured goods and raw materials. The Marshall Plan was a success, and by 1952 every participant had surpassed pre-war levels.

The Royal Navy stopped the ship *Exodus1947* from reaching Palestine, and drew worldwide criticism. The fact that the ship contained 4,515 Jewish passengers, most Holocaust survivors, made matters worse. Britain controlled Palestine by a mandate received from the League of Nations after the First World War. The government limited Jewish immigration, but illegal immigration continued in spite of these regulations. Passengers aboard *Exodus 1947* were removed, temporarily held in Cyprus, and then returned to Germany and held in the sector under British control. A forced return of Jews to Germany created a whirlwind of denunciation by the media. The British Mandate for Palestine ended in 1948.

The Soviet Union blocked the Western Allies' railway and road access to the sector of Berlin under Allied control. They wanted to be the ones to supply Berlin with food and fuel from the Soviet zone, thereby giving the Soviets control of the city. In response, the Allies countered with the Berlin Airlift, and carried supplies to West Berlin via air transport. It lasted for one year. The embarrassed Soviets saw their blockade was unsuccessful and ended it. Two separate German States were then created.

Elsewhere, the USSR sentenced Cardinal Mindszenty to life in prison. He remained there until the Hungarian revolution in 1956. And the Soviets raised the concern of the free world when they tested their own atomic bomb.

Other events over a two-year period were less dramatic and included:

Jackie Robinson was named rookie of the year.

The first Little League World Series was held.

Howard Hughes flew his "Spruce Goose."

The first TV soap opera, *A Woman to Remember,* appeared.

RCA introduces the first 45 rpm single record. Because of its size, it opened the way for the jukebox.

Children's TV shows, *Kukla, Fran and Ollie* and *Howdy Doody,* premiered.

Polaroid offered the new Land Camera for $89.95.

Sugar was no longer rationed.

* * * * *

Dutch continued working for Weather Seal; however, aluminum storm windows began to hit the market. They were mass produced, driving down the prices. The need for custom-made windows declined, and the current US recession made their niche product, custom-designed windows, less popular. Weather Seal was forced to join the competition. Dutch's role changed. He now supervised the installations and became more active in sales.

The Fair Store changed ownership. Pauline, recovering from a short hospital stay for a ruptured ulcer, was presented with a raise in salary and more responsibilities. At the same time, a woman's hosiery store offered her a position for basically the same amount of pay. The small shop was more appealing than the large department store, with its tier of layered management, so she took the job.

George Edward began high school in the fall, making his class the last freshman group. From that point forward, Kankakee Senior High taught grades ten through twelve. Sylvia Gladys (Dodo) entered the new Kankakee Junior High School.

The new junior high offered a benefit the senior high school didn't have—a hot lunch program. Students from both schools were able to take part. A cafeteria pass could be purchased for the upcoming week. Single tickets were also available. For George Edward, money was in short supply. Many weeks he used his lunch money for other activities, making lunch a catch-as-catch-can situation. Secret admirers were ready to give him tickets, but he often refused for fear of being obligated.

There are those who claim life after high school is only an aftermath. Not so for George Edward. While in high school, he was an integral part of the Moon household and worked part-time, both evenings and weekends. Summer provided an opportunity to work longer hours. The money he earned helped the family and allowed him to save for college.

Perhaps his boldest move came during his senior year. A local factory advertised for their second shift. George Edward applied for the job, declaring he was eighteen. After the interview, he was hired, but he needed to provide proof of age. He was told his selective service registration card was acceptable. The problem was, he didn't have one. As he saw it, the solution was to go downtown, lie about his age, and register for the draft. After executing his plan, the secretary for the draft board handed him his registration card, making him a year older.

A week or so later, he began to worry about being drafted early, maybe while he was still in high school. So, back to the draft board to question the secretary how old he needed to be in order to register. She told him he needed to be eighteen. Well, apparently he had been confused about it, he confessed, since he was only seventeen. The secretary gave him the fish eye, but took him off their records. George Edward apologized for any inconvenience he might have caused and told her to expect to see him again in a year.

Since his last class of the day was study hall, he would leave school early, run down the street to the factory, and punch the time clock before 3:00. Then when the shift was over at 11:00 p.m., he walked the mile and a half home. He did that five days a week until the school year ended.

In June, 1953, George Edward graduated from Kankakee Senior High School. His life from that point was never an aftermath.

The Funmaker children both attended college. Sylvia Gladys (now called Dode by her friends) enrolled in a school for nursing. After graduating, she passed the state board exam and became a registered nurse.

George Edward worked his way through school, fell in love with a singular beauty, and married before his junior year of college.

In the meantime, Ed's sister Ruth and her husband, Harvey Connell, owned and operated a small resort at Kasoag Lakes in Williamstown, New York. Harvey was twenty years her senior, and when he passed away, Ruth was faced with running the hotel and bar alone. Her daughter, Glenna, moved from San Diego to help her, but for Ruth, it just wasn't the same without Harvey. She lost interest in the business and wanted to be with her sister Auline. She explained her feelings to her brother Ed and beseeched his help.

Gladys would have no part in it. She would rather visit her family in California, Minnesota, and Missouri. An agreement was reached. Ed would travel east and help his sister, and Gladys would travel west and visit her brothers and sisters. After six months or so, they'd have to agree on a permanent location. Most likely, it would be in New York.

They met with Pauline and Dutch and explained their plans. In addition, they offered to sell them the Wildwood house in order to keep it in the family.

Gladys lived in a small apartment near the Wildwood house. She demanded her independence and refused to stay with Pauline. Ed had agreed to maintain the apartment for a short period of time, after which she had to come to New York. It just wasn't in God's plan, though. They found her, lying on her bed, with the evening newspaper across her waist. The doctor said she left this world peacefully, perhaps in her sleep.

Gladys, defiant to the end, didn't go to New York. Instead, Ed came back to Kankakee. This time, however, he came to bury his wife.

Ed returned to New York, where he had been elected a councilman for the city of Williamstown. His efforts had turned the resort profitable, primarily from the sale of lakeside real estate. A newly erected dance pavilion served as home for a Saturday night TV show. Many of the TV personalities built vacation homes around the lakes.

Ed took a one-month vacation each year. It coincided with the opening of the Fairgrounds race track in New Orleans. Spending each day at the track was his main enjoyment. His friendship with the owners, plus the ability to pick winners, nearly always paid his vacation expenses. The annual routine came to an end when he was diagnosed with colon cancer. His surgery was successful, but the condition remained. His daughter, Sylvia Gladys, was able to be with him through the illness. The son of Edward Munn Reno passed away two days before a new year began in 1963.

Pauline and her sister had lost both their mother and father. Sylvia Gladys met her husband and continued to live in New York. Pauline and Dutch moved back into the Wildwood house. Eventually, Dutch retired from Weather Seal and devoted a portion of the week to contracting carpentry work, mainly building kitchen cabinets. Between jobs, he redesigned the house. He built a new bathroom and an addition for Pauline's new kitchen.

While living their alternate life, Pauline and Dutch took more interest in the daily spate of other events. The pressure of rehearsals and evening performances were long gone, replaced by listening to the radio and watching television. Theatrical participation was exchanged with being a sedentary observer. Instead of entertaining, they were entertained.

The singing evangelist was now hardened from carpentry labor. Hands that at one time had entertained by tickling the ivories had become stiff and calloused. But his blue eyes had not dimmed. Oh, those beautiful blue eyes still reflected the enchantment of the previous life. On a cold and rainy day in December, 1971, the Lord called home the kindest man the family had ever known. Pauline, who had suffered for years from emphysema, was reunited with her husband five years later.

The Funmaker family is now down to only two. The writer and his faux sister, Sylvia Gladys, are the only ones left of those who once stood under the big top tent and sang and danced upon its stage.

Today, not many can remember that far into the past. Fewer yet understand what it was like to be part of it.

Like the saying goes, you had to be there to appreciate it.

It's been said that the days of our lives are like tokens filling a bucket. Each token represents a day. We flip them as if the supply is endless. Only when we get near the bottom do we realize that not many tokens remain. Today we live in a very active and complex world. Our lives are filled with fast-moving activity. Never has it been more important to examine that token carefully, before it gets tossed away.